TALK

Center Point
Large Print

**This Large Print Book carries the
Seal of Approval of N.A.V.H.**

TALK

MICHAEL SMERCONISH

CENTER POINT LARGE PRINT
THORNDIKE, MAINE

This Center Point Large Print edition is published
in the year 2014 by arrangement with
Cider Mill Press Book Publishers LLC.

The text of this Large Print edition is unabridged.
In other aspects, this book may vary
from the original edition.
Printed in the United States of America
on permanent paper.
Set in 16-point Times New Roman type.

ISBN: 978-1-62899-208-3

Library of Congress Cataloging-in-Publication Data

Smerconish, Michael A.
  Talk / Michael Smerconish. — Center Point Large Print Edition.
    pages cm.
  Summary: "A political thriller about an influential radio talk show host
who could control the outcome of the next presidential election by what
he chooses to reveal"—Provided by publisher.
  ISBN 978-1-62899-208-3 (library binding : alk. paper)
  1. Radio talk show hosts—Fiction. 2. Political fiction.
    3. Large type books. I. Title.
  PS3619.M45T35 2014
  813′.6—dc23
                                                          2014015945

TALK

CHAPTER 1

"Fire, tits, and sharks are TV gold. But on radio you need to make 'em hot the harder way. Through the ears."

Welcome to the media world according to Phil Dean. The new year had just begun, we'd only been connected for five minutes, and already he was on a roll.

I'd called him on my iPhone just as soon as I'd cleared the shitty mobile reception of the underground lot at Whiting and Ashley beneath the radio station where I work in downtown Tampa. It was our first skull session since before Christmas break, but there was no holiday rust apparent in his rapid-fire delivery. So far his advice for the coming year sounded pretty much the same as ever. My hunch was that he was about to hit me with his 3C mantra, and sure enough, it came in his next sentence.

"Remember, Stan, the three C's are still king. . . ."

I finished the sentence for him, pulling his chain.

"Compelling, compelling, compelling."

"*Conservative,* consistent, and compelling," he

quickly corrected, stressing c-o-n-s-e-r-v-a-t-i-v-e, just as he had in virtually every conversation we'd had in the several years prior.

There was a certain routine to these chats which were always scheduled for weekday mornings after my air shift. As usual, I'd pulled out of the parking lot and given my customary nod to the tall, 60-something, short-sleeved black guy fishing in MacDill Park on the Riverwalk with ear buds, beneath an enormous piece of red modern art that I could never figure out. (Just what were those intersecting pieces of metal? They reminded me of the game of pick up sticks.) He was there every day, probably looking for snook or red fish. We didn't know one another and we'd never chatted, but we crossed paths here each day.

He could be a listener for all I know. I've got tens of thousands of them, but even if he was, I doubt he'd know who I am by sight. Then again, with some of my recent cable TV appearances, he just might.

Northbound on Ashley, I headed for 275 South, passing the big beer-can better known as the Sykes building and spying a billboard that said, "Retire Worry Free." Not me. Not yet. But maybe someday if Phil's advice paid off. With his three C's still echoing in my head, I steered my car down my familiar path toward Clearwater Beach and home.

Phil believed that compelling radio conversation should primarily come from conservative politics. And there were many successful talk radio personalities across the country who were practitioners of his advice. He'd always held the names of his star pupils close to the vest, but I could recognize his weapons in the arsenals of the biggest names in the business. This morning's call was one of his standard tutorials.

"Remember, Stan, you need red meat for the troops."

That was another of his staples.

"And add an occasional slice-of-life segment. Sprinkle in some *Seinfeld* shit."

For the latter, he was forever imploring me to look outside the normal mix of newspapers and cable TV shows for my program content. He believed that too many talk radio hosts didn't balance the hard news of the day with whatever might command attention at workplace water coolers and coffee machines across the nation. Phil paused, maybe needing to catch his breath in the thin desert air of New Mexico. "If listeners aren't using your stuff for stupid talk with people they barely know, then you didn't nail it on air, Powers."

What he said made professional sense to me and I usually followed his advice, but I'd heard some of it more times than I could stomach. The thing with Phil was this: about 90 percent of his advice was repetitive or irrelevant bullshit, but the other 10 percent was radio gold. Sifting through all the crap could make a career, and right now, I was counting on him to make mine. Of course, finding talk radio gold wasn't always easy.

Like the time when in the middle of some abstract history lesson about the marketing failure of New Coke, Phil told me that a good talk show host should be able to go the length of an entire program without taking a single call from a listener. He actually challenged me to do it on my next program. That tutorial was a keeper.

"But isn't that the purpose of a talk radio program—for the host and the listeners to talk?" I'd naively asked.

"Don't be ridiculous, Powers. The purpose of a talk program is the same as the guy talkin' on a fucking CB—to get people to listen. It's all entertainment."

And then he said something I've never forgotten.

"Nobody is listening to your show, or any other talk radio show, because of the callers. They listen for the host. You will never meet a listener who tunes into your program because of your callers. They are listening to hear you, Stan. And if you don't entertain them, they won't listen at all. No matter who your callers are, or what horseshit they have to say."

Until then, it hadn't occurred to me, but he was right. Not once had anyone ever emailed my web site or spoken to me directly about something a caller said on the air. For better or worse, all the feedback was about me.

These mid-morning chats were never "conversations," because truth-be-told, Phil did most of the talking. Which is kind of funny given that between the two of us, I was the one who got paid to speak for a living. Now, however, I was getting paid by the suits in management to listen. Which was fine, when I was decompressing on the drive home after my show.

I'm usually spent and in need of a nap by the time I reach the end of a morning shift, especially if I've been out carousing the night before. I get up in the middle of the night and arrive to work before most breakfast cooks are out of bed. The program is four hours long, with four six-minute breaks per hour for commercials, news and PSAs. During those commercial breaks I am usually obligated to read live spots, which leaves little time to even take a piss. So there is really no stopping once the "on air" light goes on, and by the time it turns off at 9 a.m., I've got very little to say. Which is why on this, my first work day of the new year, I was content to listen and drive.

Twenty minutes after I pulled away from WRGT, Phil was fully cranked as my Lexus IS convertible crossed the scenic 14-mile stretch of the Courtney Campbell Causeway: two lanes headed each way with majestic water on both sides. High up above were military jets from nearby MacDill Air Force Base, flying to far-off places in support of the war on terror. And by the time I passed the sign saying "Welcome to Clearwater, spring home of the Phillies" and the original Hooters ("Since 1983, delightfully tacky, yet unrefined"), I could almost smell suntan lotion as I neared the beach.

All along my drive on 60 West were the types of businesses that paid my salary. Car dealers, pawn shops, pizza joints and assorted honky-tonks—these were my lifeblood, the sort of entrepreneurs who were advertisers on my station. I tried not to lose sight of the fact that the people who walked through their doors were the ones who allowed me to live a pretty damn comfortable life. By the time I could see the Fort Harrison Hotel on my right shoulder, better known as the HQ of Scientology, I was about to cross over the Clearwater Memorial Bridge from which I could see the outline of the beachfront high-rises in Sand Key off in the distance. The distinctive, sleek shapes of the Glanoe, the Meridian and the Ultimar formed the skyline of Tampa/St. Petersburg's most expensive addresses, including mine. Not bad for a former slacker.

On this particular day the sun was shining but my car roof was closed because I wanted to hear every word Phil had to say. If I had been the type to make New Year's resolutions, I would definitely have set national radio syndication as my number-one goal for the coming year. I could already taste that next level of radio, but to get there, I had to keep trusting Phil Dean. Yes, he'd been a pain in my ass for the last several years, but professionally speaking, he hadn't led me astray. Even though following his advice made me increasingly uncomfortable, there was no question that it worked. The ratings didn't lie. And for a year now, we'd been specifically strategizing as to how to take advantage of the political calendar that was about to unfold. My listeners were concentrated in the I-4 corridor, the stretch between Tampa and Orlando, and they had been known to tip the scales in more than one presidential race. As the top-rated talk host in a mid-sized but hotly contested market, I could very well find myself at the political epicenter of the upcoming election. The stage was set for my career to really pop, and I didn't want to blow my shot. My only concern was whether I'd be able to reach my goal with some shred of dignity intact. That wasn't looking likely.

"Did you ever hear of David Ogilvy, Powers?"

I had a vague awareness of the legendary adman to whom Phil was now referring.

"He's the genius who came up with the slogan, 'At 60 miles an hour, the loudest noise in the Rolls Royce comes from the clock,' " he went on.

As was often the case, I didn't get the connection to talk radio. Phil proceeded to explain that the advertising guru had solved a concern about an old-style clock in what was then the fanciest car of its time.

"The sweeping hand-style clock didn't seem to fit the swanky new car. But instead of running from it, Ogilvy made it the focus. What was a subject of concern now became the chief attribute. Talk about shit from shinola, Powers, this guy took a complaint about a product and turned it into an asset."

Good story, but I still didn't understand the relevance. Nor did I interrupt. This, I quickly decided, was part of the 90 percent bullshit.

I'd worked with a handful of media consultants over the years, and Phil was easily the best of the lot. Hell, he was legendary. I'm naturally suspect of the entire group of them. I mean, if these guys knew how to do my job, I'd always wondered, why weren't they *doing* it? True, some didn't have the requisite melodious voice, or as we say in radio, "the pipes." But many of them did have great pitch, far better than mine, which only fueled my suspicion about their advice. Usually, if any of these clowns had ever actually worked in a radio station, it was on the other side of the glass—the production side, doing technical work with the other folks who at one time ran their high school's filmstrip projector.

"A good talk host hangs up on at least two callers per air shift," was typical of the shitty advice you got from Phil's competitors. I'd actually heard that pearl of wisdom during a panel discussion at a convention sponsored by *Yakkers Magazine*, the print bible of our industry. In front of a room full of blowhards like me, three consultants sat on their asses and traded wit like that. I never understood the thinking. Exactly which callers was I supposed to hang up on, and why? But I could see the rest of the room rapt with attention, taking notes, and eager to get back to some daytimer in Bumblefuck and hang up on some poor sap who took the time to call.

I once heard a caller say to a host, "If you really think that, you should run for office yourself."

To which the host said, for no apparent reason, "You're a crumb bum."

And then—click. He cut him off.

Listening somewhere, I'll bet some B-level consultant got a chubby.

But Phil was different. He didn't throw out lines just to be provocative. He meant everything he said, even the crazy shit. And I was inclined to listen to him because unlike the rest, he *had* been there and done that. Not as a talk host, but in the format where I'd started, as a classic rock DJ. He'd earned his stripes as one of the true progressive rock pioneers, a young guy back in the early 1970s breaking bands like Genesis (before Phil Collins took over for Peter Gabriel), or Emerson, Lake and Palmer (in the era of *Brain Salad Surgery*). When it came to the future of rock music, they used to say that Phil could see around corners.

"Phil Dean gave good ear," was the way my agent, Jules DelGado, put it. I love that expression. High praise.

Phil Dean had been the top DJ in a big market, Los Angeles, and he'd had it all before flaming out on a combination of drugs and booze. He had been a small step from superstardom—one level below Sterndom—when it all came crashing down. The end came from a missed morning shift after a bender at a strip joint the night before, which not only got him fired in LA but also blacklisted by program directors coast to coast. There's no such thing as being late for work when you are the namesake of a radio program. And in his case, not even a string of more rehab stays than Lindsay Lohan could convince program directors, or PDs, to take a chance on giving him back his own slot.

The story would have ended there for most, but in his case, it really was the best thing that could have happened to him. While no PD was willing to hire him for shift work, they all still wanted his expertise. He became the guy who programmers would solicit before determining their talent and playlists, calling upon the intuitive talents that he'd employed for years. Eventually that work expanded beyond classic rock to other formats, including talk. Which explains why now, at the crack of dawn from a home studio somewhere near Taos, New Mexico, a 65ish Phil was wired to a headset, philosophizing to me about the world of talk radio. He was being paid big bucks to sit on his ass and critique snippets of radio for a select number of jerkoffs across the country, including me. The word on the street was that he had developed a new addiction—food—and tipped the scales at 400 lbs. I couldn't say for sure because I'd never set eyes on him; my vision of him was based on a 20-year-old promotional shot from when he was still on top and wearing some fucking Hawaiian shirt. Which kinda fits our business, one where apart from the names, the audience never sees the talent and is left to conjure up an image of what the host looks like. In my experience, that's in everyone's best interest because based on the personalities I've met over the years, their physical appearance rarely matches their pipes. There's a reason why people talk about a "face for radio."

When I'd first arrived in Tampa to do mornings,

Phil had come with the territory. Ours was a shotgun marriage if there ever was one. I'd agreed to spend time on the phone with him on a weekly basis as a concession to my new employer, a Christian conglomerate that had just bought the radio station where I worked. I'd been hired to host a music show and had no experience in the talk format, but after my role was recast, I'd been told that Phil would show me the ropes. Coincidentally, Jules had once repped Phil pre-crash.

"You're a perfect match," he'd told me. "He's fuckin' nuts, like you, but he has flashes of brilliance." Then he'd hurried off the phone to speak to another client.

Jules was a big mahoff based in New York City who often wound up on Page Six when movie deals got made. He represented all sorts of entertainers in Hollywood and New York, and a few he hoped were up-and-comers like me, a radio guy in Tampa who was probably his smallest client. I was forever fighting for his attention, but I stuck with him because he was wired like no one else, and it had not surprised me to learn that he had once been Phil's agent.

These days there was so much mystique about Phil's client list that I was proud just to be on it, even if I didn't positively know who else was. Although his clients were all said to be in radio, his opinions extended to all forms of communication—print, TV, and Internet. And I frequently received more than a few of those opinions myself.

What I'd never admit to the suits was that I'd actually come to look forward to these calls. They were a bit cathartic, high on entertainment value, and better than any of the 40 or so stations of crap on the terrestrial radio band, especially talk radio. I may be a radio host, but it doesn't mean I want to listen, especially to the format for which my station is known. For the past three years, WRGT had been offering four different hosts during daylight hours, including me, each kicking the shit out of President Summers on account of what we called his "radical socialism." The only thing that ever changed was the voices and the guests; the message was always the same. Boring? Monotonous? Well, it worked. And it was pretty much the same at every other talk radio station across the country that had the usual mouthpieces. And if the stations didn't feature the biggest names in talk, they employed a B-team of even worse imitators. You'd think it would wear thin, but our P1s— that's radiospeak for our most ardent listeners— couldn't get enough. They may comprise a relatively small segment of society, but there are no more faithful radio listeners than fans of conservative talk. Which is another reason why I needed Phil Dean whispering in my ear. Because

19

the sort of thing they wanted to hear from a guy like me was not exactly the message I was naturally inclined to offer. I suspected that Phil knew my personal politics were not those that he had me spouting, but he didn't seem to care, so long as I towed a consistently conservative line on air.

"It's not what you want to say, Stan, it's what they want to hear. Always remember that."

Years ago, Phil had seen the whole right-wing thing coming. And I'm talking even before Rush Limbaugh capitalized on the outbreak of the first Gulf War in 1991 and went on to dominate the medium. See, prior to Limbaugh, there weren't really national talk players, and the stations that carried talk had more diversity of hosts and political viewpoints than you would find anywhere today. It didn't matter if you were left or right. All that mattered was whether you could sustain a good conversation. Personality was king, not ideology. Guys like Irv Homer in Philly. You know what he did before he was a talk host? He was a bartender. Perfect training for that era. Because any good bartender knows both how to initiate a conversation and how to cut off a barfly who, like a caller, stays too long.

Phil was just getting back on his feet as a consultant after another round of detox when a station out in San Diego called and said it was contemplating a flip from talk to classic rock.

Phil's job was to recommend some jocks and then establish the playlist. Pretty standard stuff. But before the switchover, he found himself listening to talk, the format he would be abandoning. He tuned in to the station 24/7 for a few weeks' time while driving around in a rental car before finally advising the owner to keep the format and let him change the lineup.

"Fire the food and wine guy, can the real estate show, and replace both of them and your two liberals with some angry white conservative guys," he told them.

Naturally the station resisted, in part because it was fearful of losing the revenue from the week-end specialty programming—always a ratings loser but a money generator. Also because the two liberals were old timers and they feared a discrimination lawsuit. But when Phil outlined his reasoning, it made such perfect sense that the brass decided the downside of any litigation was outweighed by the financial upside.

"Talk radio is a clubhouse for conservatives," Phil had explained. "It's an intimate place where people on the right can go and be with like-minded folk while having their opinions reinforced. Without talk, they are homeless in the media."

Remember, this was pre-Internet and before the explosion of cable TV channels, including the advent of Fox News in 1996. The media landscape back then was Rush-free, Hannity-free and Beck-free, and consisted mainly of the *New York Times*, the *Washington Post* and the big three networks: NBC, ABC, and CBS. Americans got their news from the likes of Sam Donaldson and *60 Minutes*, and in the post-Watergate era, the slant was decidedly liberal. A whole generation of reporters had cut their teeth trying to be the next Woodward or Bernstein by bagging an elephant, and this had created a void. Talk radio, Phil recognized, could be a place where conservatives got the red-carpet treatment. But first the welcome mat had to be extended. Well, he rolled it out. The rest is history. And after his advice created big business on the right, a similar model took hold on the left, albeit with less success.

Phil's motives were strictly financial, not political. I figured he could just as easily have programmed the opposite end of the ideological spectrum; in fact, my hunch was that he was personally more into ganja than government. Never in our hundreds of conversations had we ever discussed his personal view of the world. And I could sometimes sense that he was humored by his ability to create a political groundswell. He enjoyed guiding the puppeteers who manipulated the marionettes, and drew perverse pleasure from the way the audience reacted to every movement of a limb.

Now he reiterated one more time, "This could

be your year, Stan, so long as you remember to always be . . ."

"Yeah, I know," I told him. "Conservative, consistent, and compelling."

That was Phil's blueprint, and it had certainly worked for me so far. But as he monitored me from the New Mexico desert, he was quick to pick up on any deviance from this media menu, or any intonation in my voice that suggested my heart wasn't in it.

Like when the whole illegal immigration debate had kicked in after Arizona passed a law to get tough on those crossing the border. Naturally that was big on my program.

"Our Mexican border is wide open because the feds have been derelict in their duty," I'd said.

So far, so good.

But Phil didn't like what came out of my mouth next.

"Arizona had to act, but by drafting their law so broadly, I think they have left their police vulnerable to claims of unconstitutional traffic stops."

When he heard that, he pounced.

"You're not teaching law school, Powers. Stop confusing the audience with your nuanced bullshit. Praise Arizona; condemn the fucking feds. Like everything else, make it the failure of the federal government."

When it came to colorful opinions, Phil had no interest in shades of gray. Just black and white.

"The audience will think you're a pussy, Powers. And pussies don't get nationally syndicated."

That statement was usually enough to right my way of thinking. Especially where there was no mistake about whether his counsel worked. The ratings for my program, *Morning Power*, proved it did. The more I followed his advice, the more I saw a spike in the numbers.

"Stan, let me repeat for you a lesson from 'Talk Radio and Cable TV 101'," Phil often told me. "There is no political middle. It doesn't exist on radio. You will never get anywhere saying anything moderate or mushy. Either you offer a consistent conservative view, or you're not getting traction."

My idiotic response: "Well, isn't democracy based on an exchange of ideas, not just one point of view?"

"Fuck democracy, Stan. You're not a Founding Father, you're a talk show host. This business is all about ratings, not governing. And here is the secret. Ratings are driven by passion, not population. They are not controlled by general acceptance."

"Three extremists are worth more than ten moderates," was yet another favorite Phil-ism on this point.

Now, as I drove past Sand Key Park, he ranted, "When it comes to cable TV, Powers, you show America a woman in Borneo who is topless, getting eaten by a shark with her house on fire, and they could never turn it off!"

Oh boy. I was almost home and Phil was finally circling back to "fire, tits, and sharks." So far, in this, our first conversation of the new year, I hadn't heard any of his aforementioned brilliance. All he had for me was an idea for a TV show where some naked chick was getting eaten by a shark in her pool while the roof burned. And I'm not even sure her radio was playing.

The call had now run longer than a half hour. I was finally turning onto my street when my iPhone hummed and alerted me to another incoming call, one from the "212" area code, which I hoped was a cable TV booker. Either that, or it was Jules, which would be unusual because most often I had to call him, not vice versa. I gave Phil the hook and answered the phone just as I pulled up to the gate outside my building.

Was I willing to go on TV that night and debate the construction of a 2,000-mile-long moat along the Mexican border as a means of stemming the tide of illegal immigration?

Hell yes.

"The bastards are breaking into our country!"

I barked to the twentysomething TV producer using a paint-by-numbers kit to arrange the evening broadcast.

"Good. We will see you tonight."

CHAPTER 2

"Me? I'm a dentist."

Standing next to me at the bar, I heard my buddy Carl—a real estate developer—laying that rap on a fortysomething floozy who claimed to be 35, wearing a tube top that looked like she'd pulled it from a 1970s costume shop.

"Good," she purred. "Cause I got a cavity that needs filling."

That may or may not have been her reply. I may have been imagining. What I know for sure was that he was prepared to order her another round of Novocaine, just before all hell broke loose.

I was leaning against one of the 50 or so stools around the oval bar inside Delrios, my favorite dive. It was about a week after my long call with Phil, but talk radio and politics were the furthest thing from my mind, just when both of those worlds were about to get turned upside down.

The first sign that anything was unusual at Delrios was when somebody suddenly pulled the plug on the jukebox. What had been the thumping beat of the Dropkick Murphys' "I'm

Shipping up to Boston" was replaced by the murmurs of conversation and somebody yelling "Quiet!" In the front corner of the bar four guys paused their game of pool. Near the entrance to the men's room, toward the back, two other dudes clutched their feathered darts and stopped a game of baseball on an old wooden board. It took me a moment to realize all eyes were now on a giant flat screen that hung about 20 feet from where we were standing. The TV that was usually tuned to ESPN now showed President Parker T. Summers, looking very serious, sitting behind his desk in the Oval Office.

The sound was too low on the set for me to hear a damn thing he was saying, and then, all of a sudden the people closest to the TV erupted in cheers. It immediately reminded me of when people had first heard we'd killed bin Laden.

"What'd he say?" I shouted at no one in particular.

No one close to me had any idea. Then a guy who'd been closer to the set broke the news.

"He said the economy sucks and there's no way he can do what it takes to fix it and run for re-election at the same time."

"Holy shit."

Every American knows where they were and what they were doing when President Summers made the announcement. For me, that night had started out like any other Tuesday, meaning that I was busy getting fucked up with my two drinking buddies, Clay Troutman and Carl Verazano. Clay was a chiropractor who I met after I threw out my back playing a pick-up game of basketball outside a local high school. Carl was a real estate developer who'd once owned the building where I now lived in Sand Key. None of us was married although we each had a sometimes-significant other. But on Tuesday nights, we had a standing pass to get together.

I'd met them both at around the same time and introduced them to one another. Clay's a bright guy who has built a pretty incredible practice in a strip center where he sees a combination of Medicare retirees and middle-aged chicks for back manipulations and so forth. He's also supported by at least one hollow leg; the man can really put away his booze. Carl's a fairly imposing guy who's taken more than his share of knocks in the topsy-turvy world of Florida real estate. I met him at the height of one of his cycles, and judging by the Bentley he's driving, I think he's still on the upswing—but I don't ask. With Florida developers, it's always feast or famine and it's not my place to inquire which. That's just bad taste. Besides, one of the best things about Tuesdays was that none of us talked any shop when we were together. And unlike Debbie, neither Clay nor Carl would ever dream of giving me a raft of shit about something I said or stood for on the radio.

Debbie M. Cross was my oftentimes significant other. She was a lawyer who practiced with the white-shoed law firm of Dilworth & Beasley, not far from my studio in downtown Tampa. I'd seen her around town before I met her; she's a stunning brunet who wears her hair in a bun while sporting expensive Oliver Peoples frames that give her the look of some lab technician you'd love to bang. We met a few years ago at a cocktail party after *Tampa Bay Magazine* named her one of the area's "40 under 40", meaning 40 people to keep an eye on who were under 40 years old, in the same issue where they profiled my program under the headline: "Tea Partier."

Debbie's father was a hardcore air force colonel stationed at MacDill, and he looked like he could kill me with nothing more than his car keys. He also made no secret of his approval of the sort of bullshit that Stan Powers spewed on a daily basis. In fact, he was effusive with his praise, not only on his own behalf, but also on behalf of those with whom he served.

"Stan, me and the boys are grateful of your understanding of the need to keep Gitmo," he'd once said.

"Stan, you have no idea how correct you are about our use of enhanced interrogation techniques."

"Thanks, Stan, for your continued support of the surge in Afghanistan."

Each time he'd say something like this in Debbie's presence she'd roll her eyes at me in disgust. Not so much because she disagreed with her dad, but because she saw through a lot of my on-air bullshit. How do I know? Mainly because she told me.

Which wasn't entirely fair, because some of the stuff her dad liked I actually meant.

For example, I was in full support of kicking the shit out of the al Qaeda motherfuckers who took down the Twin Towers. I just wasn't as enthusiastic about using 9/11 to justify building bases around the globe in places where we had no right to be. I figured each time we built a new base we were stirring up a hornet's nest and increasing the odds of another 9/11—but that's not the sort of thing Stan Powers would ever say on his show.

With her Hermes bag and the Blahniks on her feet, Debbie was too classy for Delrios. "The booze is cheap and the grub gets no fancier than hot wings," Carl had told me the first time he brought me here. And he was right. If somebody ever ordered a cosmopolitan in this place, they'd get thrown out. Plus, there was a pretty substantial part of me that didn't want Debbie to see just how comfortable I was in a scene like this. Besides, Delrios is a lecture-free zone.

Delrios is well located but discreet. It's just two blocks down from the Fort Harrison Hotel which is the giant place on North Fort Harrison Avenue that the Scientologists call a "religious retreat." I'll say one thing for the Scientologists, they're good neighbors. The hotel is immaculate and their other holdings are nicely maintained, but the neighboring blocks quickly change and most of the storefronts are abandoned. That's where, set among the vacancies, you'll find a nondescript maroon door with a big "D" on it without any more clues as to what lies beyond the entrance. I'm not sure it's by design, but the quiet exterior and rundown location seem to deter the tourists. Not even during spring break do you normally see anybody in here who doesn't live nearby, which is pretty remarkable given how overrun Clearwater gets at certain times of year. And those that do wander in mostly wish they hadn't.

"Check out the guy with the Irish tan wearing Tommy Bahama," Clay would say, using what he called his "tourgar"—or gaydar for tourists. "Just arrived on the Jet Blue flight from Newark."

Then we'd sit around and watch Ralph, the primary bartender, deliberately ignore the poor guy. He'd keep 'em waiting ten minutes for his first drink and even longer between rounds. And if the guy ordered food, he'd be told, "Sorry bud, we just ran out." Only a place like Delrios, with a loyal local following, could get away with such rudeness.

That kind of camaraderie was also why it had become one of my regular stops. The last thing I wanted after hours was to be hassled by a listener when I was looking to unwind. It used to be that I could go anywhere and fly under the radar. But with an increasing number of cable TV news appearances under my belt, I was starting to think those days were numbered. I had no idea if the Tuesday crowd at Delrios knew me, nor did it really matter, because there was a cone of silence that seemed to protect the patrons. Probably because I wasn't the only one looking for a little anonymity; some of the women looked like pros, and a couple of the guys looked like they made a living helping others fill their nasal canals. But I appreciated the clientele because I sure as hell could not afford to have one of my family values-driven P1s present if I was trying to get fucked up on a Tuesday night.

One reason we picked Tuesdays to hang out was that it was kamikaze night. If you ordered a beer, it came with a shot of tequila, triple sec and lime juice. If you ordered a kamikaze shot, they brought you two. Clay, Carl and I would typically arrive at about 8 o'clock, and each pony up for one round.

"Just one round, that's all I'm going for," we'd

tell our respective ladies. "We're just going out for one round of drinks."

But that was actually six shots per guy, and within 30 minutes, my knees were ready to buckle. Which was pretty much my condition at the moment when President Summers announced that he was not running for re-election.

There were probably about 100 people in the bar that night and the immediate reaction touched off a miniature version of the wave you see fans do in football stadiums. It began right in front of the TV with the people who'd actually heard what the president said, and then spread toward the back. Once everybody heard the news, Delrios went absolutely batshit. The sort of crazy you'd probably see if the Bucs ever won another Super Bowl, which kinda surprised me. It was the start of a 48-hour grown-up version of "ding-dong-the-witch-is-dead" in much of the country, particularly in the so-called Red states. But Florida isn't decidedly Red or Blue, it's more Purple, although certain parts fall decidedly into one camp or the other. I had never stopped to think about the politics of the locals who hung out at my favorite taproom before that moment. To this day, I'm not sure whether they were really anti-Summers or just happy to have an added excuse to tie one on.

The news that night temporarily sobered me like the site of a flashing light in your rearview mirror. While I kept sipping beer and Carl worked on Miss Tubetop, inside I was feeling pretty shitty—and it wasn't just from too much booze. I felt sorry for the guy. I really did. I had a vague recollection of Summers once telling one of the talking heads, maybe Diane Sawyer, that he'd rather be a really good one-term president than a mediocre two-termer. I figured he meant it. Which only made me feel worse. The former senator from Wisconsin had inherited a disastrous economy and was forever trying to sell a stimulus agenda in an era of austerity. That made it easy for many of us to peg him as a big-spending liberal, just the sort of thing that kept our P1s glued to their radios and ready to buy survival gear.

Then Carl lined up yet another round of kamikazes, sharing one of his with the dental patient, so I quickly decided I'd drown my guilt. This, I later decided, was the equivalent of getting wasted in Times Square on VJ Day while secretly wishing the Japs had not surrendered.

The next morning I was an even bigger shit. I could've still blown a 2.0 on a Breathalyzer when I went on the air and rejoiced in the death of "American socialism." I'm sure listeners misread my drunkenness for exuberance. Or maybe they knew I was shitfaced and chalked it up to celebration, which they also would have approved. Still, I delivered all the talking points, even after having read the transcript of the president's eight-minute speech from the night before and concluding that Summers was sincere. On the program, I even went so far as to play his words over a music bed of the Soviet anthem with an enormous crowd cheer at the end.

"I can think of nothing more selfish than for me, in the midst of this economic morass, to now spend the next year fundraising and traveling the nation campaigning," he'd said.

I wondered whether Summers would have regrets. He was a young guy, only 56. It seemed a bit impulsive. And clearly, it would completely destabilize his own party, the Democrats, in the upcoming presidential race. But even though the president's words cut me to the quick, they didn't stop Stan Powers from celebrating his political demise with callers.

"Hello, caller, you've got *Morning Power* on WRGT."

"Stan, good morning, you are a real American."

"Thank you, *you* are a real American."

This was our usual circle jerk, only this time, we congratulated one another and acted like we were Founding Fathers who'd just toppled King George III.

Rod Chinkles, my technical producer, was absolutely euphoric. If I didn't know he was a holy roller, I'd have sworn he'd smoked or ingested something that morning to give him the buzz that showed in his face. Standing there in his tortoiseshell glasses and pressed white shirt, he would awkwardly fist pump whenever a caller made reference to the news. I felt like he was staring at me while I worked the call-board, weighing whether my enthusiasm for the bloodless coup was legit. Fuck him.

Rod was never my guy. Not even my hire. He was a technical producer, or "board op," a job usually reserved for the just-out-of-junior-college geeks who've majored in radio and TV and see themselves on my side of the glass someday. Not Rod. He's a fortysomething guy still fighting acne whose father was on the board of directors at MML&J, the Bible thumpers who owned WRGT. Rod liked to tell people that he had "applied" to work in Tampa. My ass. I'd had no choice but to take him when the new ownership took control. As if I would ever have hired a guy who shows up for the early shift wearing a fucking bow tie. But like father like son, I am told—his old man was known to strut around the Atlanta headquarters in three-piece suits. The buzz was that he was light in the loafers, so to speak. Not that I give a shit. But don't hit me with the self-righteousness if you're hiding more than a few skeletons in your own closet.

Typical of many I'd met in radio, Rod was both

the consummate professional and more than a bit off. He was never late, never absent and rarely fucked up the board. He never played the wrong cart, or let dead air be broadcast. For all this, I was grateful. But he also had more idiosyncrasies than I could count, like the clockwork schedule with which he'd use the bathroom every shift. I could set my watch by him needing to piss when I went to break at 6:30, 7:15, and 8:30 a.m. He was also a true believer in the conservative talk brand, who (correctly) suspected I was not really down with the program. But he was hardcore. He drove some late model American-made car to work each morning (way over the pay grade for a board op) sporting a tricorn hat on the rear window dash that symbolized his support for the Tea Party. He once asked me why I didn't have likewise in my Lexus.

"I have one in my other car," I'd deadpanned. "The Volvo."

He had zero sense of humor and whereas I could always push the intercom button and joke with Alex, my executive producer, about the topics and guests during commercial breaks, Rod would have none of it. He would sit there, stonefaced, and take to heart his responsibility of riding the "dump button," which would mute anything inappropriate for the air as long as it got pushed within seven seconds of the utterance. Sometimes callers would get worked into a lather and let fly with a "shit" or "pussy" and Rod would spring into action. One expletive drowned out by the "dumper" and he'd glare for the rest of the morning like somebody had farted in church.

But Alex was an entirely different story.

Alex Hausen had proven herself to be the best surprise at WRGT. When Steve Bernson, the VP from MML&J who brought me to Tampa, first told me they planned to hire a proven talk producer because all they had in the a.m. was a woman who was a "wannabe classic rock DJ," I'd asked to meet her before he made a move. I knew a little something about wannabe classic rock DJs. Not surprisingly, we clicked immediately.

"Look, I know more about AC/DC than Afghanistan," I told her when I began, which made her laugh.

I also told her that I did not expect to last, that I was trying talk on a flier, so she could look at the next 30 days as a paying experiment while searching for a more suitable job. As far as I know, she never did. Since then, no shortage of politicians have arrived at WRGT for interviews and prejudged her based on the color of her hair (that day) or her multiple piercings, not to mention the ink and the way she swings (assuming they can tell). But if they spend any time with her, they quickly realize that she is an extraordinarily able radio producer. Several of our competitors have even tried to hire her away. She is a type A, organizational freak and news junkie who has a knack for knowing exactly when it's appropriate to speak without interrupting my flow. She quickly learned how to play the role of an on-air foil in a way that was both challenging and respectful of our audience. Privately, though, during a commercial break, she'd come into the studio, on the other side of the sound-proof glass from Rod, and blast the conventional conservative wisdom.

"Stan, you don't really believe that shit?" I'd simply roll my eyes.

On air, in limited doses, I'd call upon her to provide a feminist response to my boorish banter. Frankly, she had the easier job because she got to say what she really thought.

Me: "The Gov-er-na-tor's relationship with his maid is none of anybody's business. All that matters is that he acted with propriety while running the affairs of California."

Alex: "Stan, you really disappoint me. He was a man in a position of power who took advantage of a female employee. Next you'll be telling me hookers cannot be raped."

Me: "Hookers can be raped, but anyone applying for that job needs to know it's a recognized employment hazard."

And so it went. The audience really seemed to

enjoy the interplay, without any clue as to what either of us was really all about. That would have been too much for most of them to handle.

But above all, her most important quality was pure and unadulterated competence. She had a knack for getting shit done. And in radio, as is the case in any other workplace, that skill was always in short supply.

Straightlaced Rod had a difficult time dealing with Alex, whom he sat next to in a confined area for four hours a day. For the most part, he kept his opinions and any discomfort to himself, save for one time a few election cycles ago when his coping skills became particularly problematic. As we got close to that November election, we had a daily onslaught of surrogates in the studio and on this particular day, we were expecting Mary Cheney, the daughter of former Vice-President Cheney, who was now a pundit. For once in her life, Alex was legitimately excited about one of my Republican political guests.

"Stan, I'd like to bring Becky in tomorrow to watch some of the program if that's ok," she said, referring to her roommate with whom I was already acquainted.

"Sure thing," I responded.

It didn't occur to me until the interview began why both Alex and Becky revered Mary Cheney. Becky sat between Alex and Rod while I was conducting the interview, and when the segment was over, the two women had a photo taken with Mary as I looked through the glass and took note of Rod's disapproving scowl. Well, the following day, Alex called me after I'd just gotten home.

"Some freak leafleted my car."

"Huh?"

"When I came out to my car, Stan, someone had left a printed card on it that said: 'Even if you were born gay, you still need to be born again.' "

"So what. That shit happens. I don't think it's a big deal."

But the following day it happened again. Only this time Alex had the presence of mind to look at the other cars in the WRGT lot, and none of them had anything similar on their windshields.

"I know it's the Chinkster," she said that day, meaning Rod. "I don't think he got me until he met Becky."

"Do you want me to speak to him?"

"I don't want you to get involved. I know his old man is important. I just want you to be aware of it because he scares me sometimes. This is Westboro Baptist sort of shit, Stan."

I debated whether to discuss it with my boss, Steve Bernson, but pussied-out. If I said something to him, I feared he'd say something to Atlanta which might get back to Vernon Chinkles, and I couldn't afford that. Plus, I didn't want Alex to take any heat. Thankfully nothing further came of it, but it was a wake-up call regarding Rod. We continued to exist, our odd little trio, held together by the one thing we had in common: our dedication to the program, and the goal of producing the finest four hours of conservative talk in the country. And many days, we did.

The day after the Summers shocker, Alex was her usual, stoic, competent self. Her mannerisms, as usual, gave no hint as to what she was really thinking, although she may have been sporting more black in her attire than usual, I couldn't tell for sure.

And good old WRGT never missed an opportunity to turn news into a promotional/sales event, so programming immediately created a new station jingle that was put in rotation every hour. Set to a fife-and-drum music bed, it said:

"WRGT, where freedom-loving Americans assemble and lay claim to the rights that make America great. We're already praying for our *next* president!"

It was over the top. I mean, you'd think they could spare a few prayers for our current president given the state of the country. But the listeners were loving the tumult and you'd think they had wintered at Valley Forge instead of on the Gulf of Mexico. Don Fortini, our head of sales, always anxious to turn a national crisis into coin, quickly expanded the ad campaign to include a list of sponsors who were willing to pay just to be tied to Summers' downfall.

"WRGT, where freedom loving Americans assemble and lay claim to the rights that make America great. Among those already praying for our next president are Fred Pork's family of auto dealerships, Dr. Horace Furston, the man you call when it doesn't last four hours, The Survivalist Shops, and Gary's Gold Emporium." The one person who wasn't caught up in the euphoria was Phil, who called me the minute I signed off the air the morning after the announcement. He'd been on the phone non-stop with his talk radio host clients across the country and by the time he got to me, he was spitting blood.

"This is really bad, Stan. We just killed the golden goose."

"Huh?"

"All you guys have been getting a free ride. Summers was a gift from the talk radio gods, better even than Clinton after his blow job or Obama post-healthcare, but it went too far. I had a feeling he'd bit off more than he could chew with the spending requests, but I never figured he'd pull a Palin on us."

Through what was left of my kamikaze haze, I reminded Phil that Sarah Palin had quit half-way into her term whereas Summers was saying

44

he would fulfill his, just not run for another so he could focus on the economy instead of campaigning.

"Today's not a day for your persnickety bullshit, Powers. Better you instead spend your time putting on your game face. Our whole business is in fuckin' free fall."

In the world of talk radio, Phil was worried that this was the day the music—well, talk—died. So much of the nation's talk material, my material, was based on kicking the crap out of Summers' presidency. He wasn't sure there'd ever be another Summers. He also predicted trouble for cable TV.

"Fox is fucked," he railed into his phone. "No amount of leg shots of those lipsticked blond bimbos can make up for what they had going with Summers. And those commie bastards at MSNBC aren't much better. Time for them to find a new butt boy."

I took that as pretty much an admission from Phil that the whole media world had become a circus, even though he'd never admit it. For some time now, the media outlets on the left— having seen the big business generated by conservative perspectives on the right—had been employing a similar model. I could almost stake my career on the fact that there was some lefty Phil clone who had whispered in Keith Olbermann's ear when he was kicking the shit

45

out of George W. Bush with all of his "special comments" in the last few years of W's term. Hey, the guy might have fucked up by taking us into Iraq, but since when do we say that a president should be prosecuted as a war criminal? In the same way the right was now lockstep and predictable, so too was the left. Each had their own media outlets and pundits who in turn had a stranglehold over politicians. In fact, not only did I suspect there was a leftwing Phil out there, it wouldn't have surprised me if it was Phil himself. He was all business, and in our many conversations he had never once pretended to have any real concern for the country, much less for its chief executive. Now, however, he was intently focused on the implications of the president's decision on the talk radio world. For me, he had a plan.

"Stan . . ." he was breathless now. I thought I heard him gasp for air. "You're the only one in the country for whom there could be a silver lining."

That line would be my hair of the dog. Phil Dean now had my undivided attention.

"My advice is that you immediately go on the warpath against Bob Tobias. He's got a real shot to win the Democratic nomination with Summers out. He's perfectly positioned to jump in quickly and grab the mantle. And you're perfectly positioned too—to be his chief nemesis. Own that turf."

My head was still spinning so much from Summers' LBJ move that I hadn't even had a chance to think about who would replace him as his party's nominee. On the Republican side, the race had already been going on for months, with the five candidates sparring in a flurry of early debates. But Phil Dean had just changed my focus. Bob Tobias had just been re-elected as governor of Florida, despite the unpopularity of his party nationally. He was a moderate guy who had survived due to a combination of constituent service and avoidance of the political extremes. Responding quickly to coastal storms and an oil spill in the Gulf of Mexico had really earned him stripes with residents along the coast. It didn't hurt that he was a football hero in a state where pigskin was king.

"Think about it, Stan. He's the young, handsome governor of a swing state who defied the odds in a GOP year. When this hangover ends, both parties are gonna figure out that he's the man."

Fuckin' Phil was right. Sitting in that adobe shack in Taos, probably stuffing his 400-lb frame with Tex-Mex between calls, he had a more keen insight into the politics that were about to unfold than I did, and according to him, I was sitting at ground zero.

"Focus on that wife of his," he frothed.

"Susan Miller? Floridians love her, Phil."

Susan Miller was Bob Tobias' other half. She was a homegrown beauty he'd met in college who'd proven to be his greatest political asset. She was smart and assertive, but not in a way that was threatening to men. She had previously been one of the state's top-notch lobbyists. Often I'd heard people say they'd rather have her running Florida than him. But to Phil, she was a talk radio prop.

"She's a suntanned Hillary for Chrissakes! Get to it, Stan."

Phil clicked off, no doubt to go give marching orders in some other radio market. There was no way he could have known it, but he'd finally hit a wall with me. I could spout off all the conservative bluster he'd want, but there were personal reasons why attacking Susan Miller, Florida's first lady, was out of the question. I drove home to get sick and grab a nap.

CHAPTER 3

President Summers' late withdrawal rendered the Iowa Caucus and New Hampshire primary meaningless for the Democrats. If South Carolina could print new ballots in time to accommodate the quickly emerging Democratic field, it would be the first real contest. But it was more likely that Florida would have that distinction.

It was a different story on the GOP side of the aisle. The Republican field had been set for nearly two years, but now the calculus was about to change. Previously it had been about who was best suited to defeat a liberal, sitting president. Now it was about who would be the strongest against whoever ultimately emerged from the sudden chaos among the Democrats where the outcome of that contest was unpredictable.

Vying for the Republican nod were two governors, one senator, one businessman and one retired military man. Margaret "Molly" Haskel, the conservative, stunning-looking, silver-tongued governor of Texas, had been the frontrunner for nearly 18 months. Of course, nobody ever used her surname. To her hardcore fans, she was "Molly Hatchet," on account of the fact that there was no state program in Texas that she had not hacked away at or cut entirely during her two terms in office. That record had helped Haskel placate the base in more than a dozen debates during the last several months, and she was benefiting from an intra-party skirmish amongst three conservative candidates who were running even further to the right and splitting the fringe vote.

The other state CEO competing for the job was Wynne James from Colorado. Governor James was my kind of Republican. He'd balanced Colorado's books without needing a hatchet. And he'd overseen the state's implementation of the legalization of marijuana in a businesslike fashion without theatrics. James not only embraced same-sex marriage, he'd actually officiated the union of one of his cabinet members to a longterm partner. He was both a fiscal conservative and a social libertarian, which caused him to be viewed with suspicion and some derision by the evangelical forces within the party. His open support for abortion and gay rights—two positions that, I believed, actually reflected true conservatism since they meant less government involvement in people's personal lives—made him a pariah in many quarters. But he didn't seem to care and had refused to bend to the political winds of a very conservative primary process. Thus far he'd refused to court crazy, and it had cost him amongst the party's most passionate. If Governors Haskel and James had squared off in the GOP that presided after Reagan first took office, James would have cleaned her clock. But instead he was trailing in the polls and many doubted he'd get out of single digits in any state but his own. He was the last vestige of a party that had once had as its standard bearers the likes of Nelson Rockefeller, George H. W. Bush, and Bob Dole. But this was not his father's GOP.

The remaining three Republican candidates used James for cannon fodder as they tried to out-gun Haskel from the right, a feat not easily accomplished. Senator Laurent Redfield of Georgia was a Tea Party purist. He professed to never having voted for a tax increase during a career that spanned 10 years in the Georgia legislature and two terms in the U.S. Senate. He opposed abortion in all instances, including rape and incest, and had called evolution "lies from the pit of hell" during a debate, which was typical of the way he courted conservatives. That sort of thing played well in primary season but was a death knell in a general election.

Colonel George Figuera was a Marine who had distinguished himself in Iraq and received the Navy Cross, the nation's second highest award behind the Medal of Honor. Figuera was a one-issue candidate, running on a platform of strengthening national defense. He talked non-stop about the U.S. withdrawal from Iraq and Afghanistan—both of which he had opposed. Figuera argued that the U.S. should have maintained control of both countries, and Iraq's oil, a position that might have garnered him more support had fracking not begun to convince Americans that the days of energy dependence on Muslims were coming to a close. When Governor James quipped in an early debate that "Colonel Figuera never saw a U.S. base he didn't want to expand," he was hissed at by the audience, and Figuera took it as a compliment. Handsome and charismatic, Figuera showed no signs of generating broad support, but the reaction he was drawing from military-minded Republicans was strong. As James had learned the hard way, any whiff of criticism of Figuera ran the risk of being branded un-American. Ever since then, the other candidates had been loath to criticize the Colonel. They left him alone on debate stages like an island unto himself.

The final Republican candidate was no less a character than the other four: William Lewis had never run for any office before seeking the presidency. He was a billionaire who'd made his money in private equity and who enjoyed 100 percent name ID across the nation. Sadly for him *that* nation was the United Kingdom, where he owned one of the English Premier League's football clubs, and not the United States. While American kids were taking to soccer, I couldn't see any evidence that American voters were ready to elect a WASPy team owner, much less of a foreign franchise. Lewis was a free-market purist who was quick to drop Karl Marx's name when rhapsodizing about a "Washington out of control." The base loved that line. But he never volunteered any thoughts outside of this comfort zone. The debates had been the only times when Lewis said a peep about foreign policy, or Figuera was forced to comment on domestic policy matters.

But then Figuera stunned observers by narrowly winning the Iowa Caucus, although few thought he'd sustain the momentum. Iowa had a history of picking losers who were ideologues. The morning after the Iowa Caucus, I commented on air that it reminded me of Rick Santorum winning in 2012. If the GOP were smart, they'd reconfigure the primary process to dilute the influence of its fringe, because they kept nominating candidates who didn't have a prayer in a general election. Before Iowa, everyone in the party had pretty much assumed Figuera was headed nowhere. Now, post Iowa, others were rethinking his prospects, but it hadn't changed my view. Shy of a Muskie breakdown in New

Hampshire, I figured Margaret Haskel was it. As I predicted, she rebounded by winning there.

The Democratic race wasn't as linear, to say the least. The only opposition President Summers had faced in the Iowa Caucus had come from Mississippi Congressman Ezekiel Evers. A civil rights leader and Baptist preacher, he had opposed a sitting president in his own party for what he said was an abandonment of the civil rights agenda. How and where Summers had done that, I wasn't exactly clear. Neither, apparently, were Iowa Caucus voters, because Evers didn't get out of single digits. Now, Summers said that he would release all of his delegates from Iowa and New Hampshire without making an endorsement. In keeping with Granite State tradition, there were two-dozen candidates on the New Hampshire ballot, but only President Summers and Congressman Evers were established politicians. Moving forward, South Carolina's ballot still had only Summers and Evers printed on it. But by Florida, it looked like the field would be crowded.

Against a backdrop of candidate announcements and hurried fundraising, the DNC immediately set about negotiating a system of standards by which the states next in line to vote would amend their filing procedures and deadlines to accommodate a field that was not yet established. Despite the fact that some states had had early filing deadlines in November and December of the previous year, the state legislatures were working in concert to pass emergency measures to change this. In a few cases, governors and state election commissions were able to make changes without direct legislative action. But in states where reducing the number of signatures was deemed necessary to facilitate the timely printing of emergency ballots, there was no way to prevent a plethora of unknowns from gaining access to the ballots and getting their names in the mix. The free-for-all that ensued was good for the party insofar as it generated non-stop interest in the election— but it ran the risk of making the abbreviated nomination process a bit like *American Idol*. The situation also promised a bit more than the usual election day chaos where campaign supporters flanked the polling stations and used signs and stickers to try and ensure that their candidates' names stood out on suddenly crowded ballots.

The fact that the Florida primary, just weeks away, would be the first real contest amongst a newly constituted Democratic field was obviously to the advantage of Governor Bob Tobias. The question was how he would fare in the primaries *after* the Sunshine State. Nevada, Colorado, Minnesota, Missouri, Maine, Arizona and Michigan would all hold their primary elections within 30 days. And then would come Super Tuesday.

Amidst the confusion, there quickly emerged seven seemingly serious Democratic candidates. Besides Governor Tobias and Congressman Evers (who had been billing himself as "the frontrunner" ever since Summers had dropped out), the field included another governor, a former ambassador, two other congressmen, and a senator.

I figured Governor Vic Baron was Tobias' biggest threat. A former trial lawyer in New York City, he now governed the Empire State as its chief executive and was formidable on many fronts, not the least of which was that his state offered a rich number of delegates. That the state was New York cut both ways. In many parts of the country, namely the South, there persisted a distrust of Northeastern liberals even within the Democratic ranks. But smart money said Baron and Tobias would be the last two standing.

Ambassador Bill Brusso had been the U.S. representative in Luxemborg two decades ago. Brusso, the scion of a family fortune made in Canadian cadmium, had gotten the post the old fashioned way: he bought it with campaign contributions. Along the way, he'd mistaken his plum position for an earned career in foreign service and had begun to think of himself as a modern day James Baker or George Mitchell. He had no discernable base, but like William Lewis on the other side of the aisle, he appeared willing to spend vast sums from his personal fortune to continue his quixotic bid.

Congressman Coleman Foley was the second member of Congress to get into the race. Foley represented that portion of Western Pennsylvania that had often elected Jack Murtha before his passing. Foley was a Blue Dog Democrat elected to office by constituents whose parents had twice swung to Reagan because of the appeal of his plain speak. I doubted whether he had appeal outside the Keystone state and suspected his bid was a no-risk way to raise his national profile. Roy Yih was the third and final member of Congress seeking the Democratic nod. Asian-American Yih lived in Silicon Valley where he had been a software inventor. Asian Americans had become a reliable Democratic constituency in recent years although not yet at the level of Hispanics. Yih had zero national recognition and I gave him less than a zero-percent chance of winning. Same for the final candidate, Laura Wrigley, the female senator from Vermont. I don't know what it is with New England, but Wrigley was Bernie Sanders in pant suit. Had she served with George McGovern, she'd have made *him* look conservative.

What had already been a long vetting process for Republicans was about to be compressed into six months for the Democrats. Less, really, if someone put together a string of victories. Come Super Tuesday, 10 states would be casting ballots on a single day in April. New York and Pennsylvania would not vote until later the next month, which was too bad for Governor Baron. If New York and Florida had swapped primary dates, Baron would have the edge now enjoyed by Tobias. It was impossible to guess what was going to happen. Even California, usually of little national consequence when its primary occurred in June, could this time be relevant for both parties.

"The only guaranteed winner in this thing is you, Powers, so long as you don't fuck it up," Phil told me. "Florida will again be key and to win Florida, you need to control the I-4 corridor, you lucky bastard."

Lucky for me, because when it came to talking politics in the I-4 corridor, WRGT was the only game in town. That meant I had reach where the key votes were up for grabs. While the northern part of the state reflected the conservative politics of the Deep South, and urban centers like Miami were heavy Democratic areas, the middle of the state—especially Tampa, its political hub—was home to a beehive of swing voters. And who could reach those voters better than anyone? Stan Powers. Florida realtors like to talk about location, location, location, and as a talk host in the I-4 corridor during a heated election season, I had it.

The Republican candidates had already figured this out, and I'd had all the candidates, save William Lewis, as my guests in recent months. That Lewis had not done my program was testament to the unconventional nature of his campaign. Margaret Haskel had done the program twice, Governor Wynne James twice, Senator Redfield once, and Colonel Figuera once. Each had been phoners and I hadn't played favorites. I couldn't say it on air, but I'd found Governor James the most impressive. Senator Redfield was stone cold crazy. I admired Colonel Figuera's service, but his comments reminded me that there's a reason we have civilian control over our military. Still, I always toed the line.

"Well, somebody needs to take a hatchet to the federal budget, Governor Haskel."

"I applaud the level of your conviction, Senator Redfield."

"Thank you for your service, Colonel Figuera."

I'd kissed each of their asses, except, of course, for Governor James. I played it straight with him, and asked basic questions, never putting through the listeners who telephoned the program while he was on. That was to his benefit.

"James is a RINO, Stan, a Republican In Name Only. We don't need another Arlen Specter," said the first caller I took after cutting James loose.

The listeners were merciless in condemning the one candidate who I thought had the broadest appeal. But of course, this was primary season where there are no words dirtier than "moderate" or "compromise."

None of the interviews I did with the Republican candidates made any real news, but each was important in reinforcing my bona fides with both the candidates and the audience. I knew they'd all be looking for more airtime as the Florida primary drew near which would be good for everyone, including me. If I wanted to achieve syndication, it was important for me to cement *Morning Power* as the hub of political discourse in the Tampa/St. Petersburg area leading up to the election. Which is why, despite the fact that I spent most of my time trashing all things Democrat, I said I'd be happy to speak with Governor Vic Baron when one of his people asked Alex for some airtime.

"You better rip his fucking head off," was Phil's angry advice when I told him about the booking.

"But then he'll never come back."

"You don't want him back. You will ruin your credibility if you kiss his nuts, Stan."

But I didn't follow that advice, much to Phil's fury. I pretty much treated the Democratic governor of New York with dignity and respect, and in Tallahassee they'd taken note. Now Governor Bob Tobias was asking for equal airtime.

CHAPTER 4

Like me, Governor Bob Tobias was a Florida native. But that wasn't all we had in common. A shrink might even say he was partly responsible for my coming to Tampa to do morning drive. *Yakkers Magazine* once wrote about me: "Such were Stan Powers' political convictions that he was willing to risk an established persona in classic rock just to make his imprint on the dialogue of the day." My ass. If they only knew that instead it was a story as old as time: Another guy looking for fame and fortune, and hoping to catch the eye of a woman.

If they'd taken a vote at Fort Myers High School back in the 1980s, I would have been voted least likely to end up as a talk radio host, or least likely to do anything productive for that matter. Truth is, I was a bit of a stoner and played soccer before the sport got cool. I was into three things: trying to get laid, music, and trying harder to get laid. I had a few close buddies and not much of a career plan. My grades were average, which only deepened the mystery as to how I finished in the 85th percentile on the SATs.

"Stan, you have either been purposely shitting the bed throughout your school years, or you just got damn lucky," my father said at the time. I'm sure my Mom knew which it was; Dad, however, was content to wonder if the stars had aligned for just one Saturday morning.

I'd taken the test only because I told my parents I would. I never promised them I'd go to college, and I never did. The idea of compounding my lack of a plan by sitting in two or four more years of classrooms was just not something Stanislaw Pawlowski was prepared to do. Stan Powers probably would have taken a different path. But that go-getter wouldn't be born for another quarter century. This I can tell you: Powers would have had little regard for Pawlowski. Probably would have called him a "pothead liberal destined to suck on the social tit of America."

Stan Pawlowski got a tattoo of a pirate on his left butt cheek on a road trip to New Orleans with his high school buddies, and later, one of a tiny cannabis leaf on his left forearm. Nowadays, the first stays hidden under Brooks Brothers boxer shorts, the other behind a long-sleeved blue or white Oxford, at least when I am working. Even in Florida, long sleeves are a must for me unless I'm truly among friends because of that indiscretion of my youth. The country has become far more accepting of smoking pot, but there is still no way my P1s could handle the sight of a drug reference unless they were convinced it was a Ron Paul–style libertarian protest in the name of God's green earth.

Needless to say, I didn't grow up wishing or intending to be a talk radio host. The people who do are the board ops who end up on the other side of the glass. Seems we hosts all get here after lots of twists and turns in the career path. But if my career was a roadway, then it had taken a hairpin curve to put me here.

The short version is that I graduated from high school without ambition or a clue. For a while I did nothing, until my dad had finally had enough of me sleeping late on his dime. What started as a weekend job clearing tables became a full-time gig bartending at a joint called Shooter's, located in a strip center along a commercial stretch of I-41. The place was totally no frills, and the décor consisted of a Confederate flag behind the bar and a sawdust dance floor. The most notable feature, however, was the trough-style urinal in the men's room where guys stood and took a piss next to each other. The thing was about eight feet long and inevitably had a couple of beer mugs in it left by guys who had walked into the head carrying their brew, then drained the glasses and themselves. Of course, guys being pigs, the empty mugs didn't stay that way for long. It was the ultimate dissociative experience: somehow when you were standing there tying a load on, playing target practice with a partially empty mug, you didn't get spooked by the idea that you might see that mug again the next time you came to Shooter's, sitting on a coaster, filled with the latest draft.

The crowd was strictly local and all cracker. They were mostly blue-collar types and a rough class of women. Lots of ink and ankle bracelets. But no matter the gender, they all came to drink beers and do shots and listen to music, much of it live. The live stuff was supplied by local cover bands with names like Image or Dionysus that played Bob Seger–style rock and roll, interspersed with a Kid Rock–type of rebel country.

My hours were long and ended late but there were some perks. For starters, there was no shortage of easy ass from chicks who were sauced. And the pay was decent, mostly from tips. But they came with a catch: Every time somebody tipped, I was supposed to put the loot into a bigger-than-life holster over the bar, and fire a starter's pistol to signify that somebody had ponied up at Shooter's. I felt ridiculous, but every once in a while we'd get some newbie who didn't know the drill and, upon hearing a gunshot in redneck bar, would hit the deck. That was funny.

Shooter's was owned by Willy Blake, a retired

local cop who had gone out on a disability. Local legend had it that Willy had taken a couple of druggies out during a bust in Sarasota where he shot first and asked questions later, but not before one of the bad guys managed to get off a shot of his own which hit Willy in his left leg. That incident was the origin of both his limp and the name of the bar. Willy had a son who was a year ahead of me in high school and a fellow stoner, which is the only reason I got hired. Today, whenever reporters for the radio trades ask me about mentors who have been instrumental in my success, Willy Blake is always the first person I mention. ("What station did he program?" is usually some shithead's reply.)

The live music was Wednesday through Saturday nights, and after I'd worked there a few months, Willy asked me to cover the house sound. In other words, on those nights, I would not only serve 'em up, but also supply the piped-in music whenever the bands took a break.

"Play some music, Stanley," he'd said, misstating my given name but addressing me more like a son than an employer. "I don't so much as care what you play, so long as you play something. The one thing you can never permit is silence. Silence is death in my business."

Willy, the ex-cop didn't miss much whether it was the way he profiled his clientele or how much was in the till at the end of the night. He quickly figured out that there was a bump in his gross whenever I covered the house sound. I didn't have a microphone, I just played music. But spinning the tunes in between the live sets was something that gave me a rush, and it definitely beat bartending. I was good at it. Having spent way too much time reading liner notes in my bedroom, I knew music and I loved playing it. I started to map out in advance how I would fill the 20-minute intermissions and I paid close attention to the crowd reaction to my choices. I don't mean that I watched the dance floor or judged faces. My barometer was the cash register.

What I figured out is that some songs are more suited to drinking than others. I learned that "Dream On" by Aerosmith was a solid song, but it's not a chug-your-beer-and-order-a-shot number. Bad Company's "Shooting Star" or Queen's "Bohemian Rhapsody" might get somebody laid, but it was not a bottom's-up kind of crowd pleaser.

The winners, I determined from my unique style of focus grouping, were the hard-thumping, guitar-featuring classics of rock: "Dancing Days" by Led Zeppelin, "Ain't Talkin' Bout Love" by Van Halen, and "Hell's Bells" by AC/DC. Those were songs you didn't dare play until you had a few cases of ice-cold longnecks and a fifth of Jack at the ready. The working class crowd at Shooter's couldn't get enough of them. It didn't take long for Willy to notice.

"Stanley, I've decided to increase the band breaks from 20 minutes to 30 minutes."

And that wasn't all.

"I have also decided to give you a raise."

I was ecstatic. For the first time in my life, I was steadily employed, making decent money, and having fun at the same time. The musicians were pissed that their intermissions were now 10 minutes longer, but they had no choice. The decision was strictly business. Strictly bar business.

It never occurred to me that there was a career path in what I was doing. That observation was first offered by a waitress Willy hired during the second summer of my employment. She was between her sophomore and junior years at Florida State University. And unlike her colleagues, her wages were not entirely dependent on the bump in tips that I could make happen by spinning some classic vinyl. With her looks, customers were already tripping over themselves to have her take their drink order, and they had no problem leaving generous tips. And who could blame them? She was an original hardbody, before the age of Pilates, with a strong slender frame, thin waist and breasts that were full enough to get noticed but not so large as to become a distraction. So long as she was clothed, the first thing that would strike you about her would be her eyes: sparkling and green, set against a permanent tan, and framed by blondish brown hair, naturally lightened by time in the sun. You just never knew what she was thinking behind those eyes. Of course, if she were naked, you'd never even notice them.

I was taken with her from the moment Willy introduced us. Damn good looking. And she had real presence. There was an air about her that suggested she was too smart and sophisticated to be waiting tables at Shooter's. I figured she needed the money for tuition.

"Keep your eye on this one, Stanley," Willy said.

At first I figured he meant on account of all the rednecks getting hammered and pawing all over her. Over time, I convinced myself that he'd brought her on board to keep me happy spinning tunes that were making his place jump. Either way, there was no use trying to hide my attraction to her because she had street smarts that matched her looks. It was pointless trying to lay a rap on her. You'd just as soon tell her you were hoping to end up in the sack, because anything shy of that was going to come off as pure bullshit.

I did look out for her though, and I think she appreciated it. On the nights when I was both bartending and doing the sound, I was pretty much running the joint so I got to make the waitress assignments. The fullest tables were always those closest to the makeshift stage, so I'd hook her up. She'd flash me a smile from time to time letting me know that she knew I was helping her out.

Willy made all the girls wear short suede skirts with fringe at the bottom, and cowboy boots to match. She wore both well. Several times I'd be admiring her frame only to have her turn and confront me with those piercing eyes. Nothing was said, nor did it need to be. In fact, I closed that deal just one week after she started with probably less than 30 minutes of spoken word between us.

Partly that was due to the nature of the work. We busted our asses at Shooter's, particularly on those nights when there were drink specials, and a kind of camaraderie developed among the staff due to the thumping music, the smell of suds, the sound of the pistol firing, and the general vibe of lots of people in close quarters getting sweaty and having a good time. We were all getting paid a decent buck, most of it under the table. All in all, it was a pretty good place to be for a guy who was barely 20 and didn't have anything figured out.

One night we were both working and as usual I was doing my best to keep an eye on her, partly because I wanted to make sure nobody else was hitting on her, and partly because like Willy, I didn't want some Nascar nutjob crossing a line. By now the regulars had nicknamed her "Envy" on account of those piercing green eyes, and believe me, they very much wanted what she had. I temporarily lost track of her, and I guess my head on a swivel got a bit obvious because while I was pouring a draft, she came up behind me and popped her knees into the back of mine, causing me to buckle and spill what I was pouring. Two guys in front of me hooted and I caught my balance just in time to see the back of the suede skirt and boots headed through the wooden gate that separated the bar from the dance floor.

The next time she came back for a tray, she said something like, "I guess I make you weak in the knees." To which I responded, "It's not just my knees." Like I said, with her, there was no use hiding anything.

And that was about the extent of the foreplay.

Willy had a keg freezer out back where I would head to make a beer run several times on a busy night, or whenever I needed to cool down when the bar just got too stinking hot. One night in mid June, some garage band was belting out a cover of Journey's "Faithfully" when I decided to head in that direction on account of the heat.

I heard the sound of the pistol firing just before the rear door to the bar closed behind me.

Then I opened the freezer without noticing that she was right on my heels. But once we'd both cleared the threshold and were amidst the stacked cases of beer and kegs, there was nothing in doubt. Hiking up the suede skirt while seeing each of our breaths, I mentally calculated that there were 10 minutes left in the set—which was about five more than I needed.

"Unless they're playing 'Free Bird' next, you better hustle back," she laughed afterwards as we both stood there, flushed, breathing heavily and readjusting our clothes.

"Free Bird"? I could only hope to equal the 15 minutes it took Lynyrd Skynyrd to perform that song live. But on that night, I was more in the range of the radio play version of "Sweet Home Alabama," and feeling embarrassed about it. Performance had never been a problem in high school, or with the usual hook-ups I'd pull out of Shooter's. But this was different.

For starters, anyone who looked at the two of us would have thought we were an obvious mismatch. She had a sense of maturity about her and a refined, well-coiffed look, even in that goofy uniform. I, on the other hand, usually sported a beat-up pair of jeans, a faded concert t-shirt, and unkempt hair that hung almost to my shoulders. At just a tad over six feet, with a 32-inch waist, I could probably be best described as lanky. I didn't work out and paid no attention to my diet, but was still at an age where I could get away with that. Mine was a deliberately sleepy, disheveled look that had always worked well for me with chicks. I had lots of friends who were girls, and the jocks at school had let me get close to their women because they viewed me as unthreatening. The girls found me to be a sympathetic ear for their guy troubles, never suspecting that I was willing to listen to their bullshit in large part because it often meant I could nail them. I played the role of the sensitive guy and it worked.

But Envy was tougher to manipulate than someone in homeroom. She was far more confident and in control than anyone with whom I'd gone to high school. You could see it in the way she so easily dismissed the Dale Earnhardts who hit on her at the bar night after night. They'd undress her with their eyes and say all sorts of inappropriate shit, and she'd just tune them out and scoop up their $1s, $5s, $10s and $20s. Her appearance on the whole exuded class. It was the self-assured way she walked, even while juggling a tray of longnecks. Her makeup, much lighter than that of the typical female crowd at Shooter's, was always perfectly applied, and gave her a natural, effortless beauty. And even in a beer shed, she smelled special. While I never remembered to wear cologne, she had a scent that reminded me of the feminine bars of soaps my mother used to stick in my underwear drawer no matter how often I told her to stop. The only thing we seemed to have in common was where we worked, and even that separated us. For me, Shooter's was a real job. For her, it was a way to make money for college at FSU. The thought entered my mind that maybe for the first time in my life, I was somebody else's sympathy fuck. Which wouldn't have been so bad, if only I'd delivered. Not having done so only made me want her again.

Stepping out of the freezer and back into the bar, we went back to work without another word spoken between us, and for the rest of the night, I kept looking at her, watching for some sign or signal about what it meant. But there was nothing. Every time she walked up to the bar carrying her tray, she gave me a drink order just as she always did, with absolutely no hint of emotion or recognition in her voice about what had just taken place.

"I need three drafts of Bud and two shots of Turkey."

On any other night, I'd have gone home with some sense of conquest. Instead, by the time I shut down the sound system and walked out to my car, I was feeling pretty miserable, and partly convinced I'd dreamt the whole thing.

Over the next few nights, she remained all business, acting like it had never happened. I, of course, could think of nothing but those few moments in the freezer. All day long and behind the bar at night, I replayed the scene over and over in my mind. Her scent. That skirt. The haste. And every time I went out back to retrieve a case of beer, I'd survey the space like it was a crime scene around which I was about to hang yellow tape. Then I'd wonder if it had really happened at all.

Finally I decided that I needed to say something but couldn't decide what it should be.

"My knees are weak again."

"It's hot as hell in here, but I know a place where we could cool down."

"Feel like giving me a hand with some kegs?"

Everything I came up with sounded too damned juvenile. She had me in a funk, totally intimidated, and from that sense of vulnerability, feeling even more attracted to her. The lines continued to run through my mind. What I really wanted to say was, "Give me another shot." I wondered what college fraternity guys said when they were laying their rap on a coed, but I was clueless. Nothing I came up with sounded right. So that's what I said: nothing. And fortunately in the end, I didn't need to.

"How long is 'Stairway to Heaven'?" she asked me on a slow Wednesday night after I'd spent about five days in purgatory. I was so caught off guard that I was about to give her a serious answer—about eight minutes—when she suddenly turned and walked away.

Now I personally loved that song, but knew it was a barroom loser. Nobody chugged (or tipped) until the final Jimmy Page guitar riff, so I never played it. This night, however, I made an exception. Hell, I'd have played Barry Manilow singing "Mandy" if I thought it'd do the trick.

So just as soon as the house band signaled for a break, I cranked the system.

Two minutes later, Envy was on top of me in the freezer. I looked into those green eyes up close, then buried my face in her neck, and as we embraced our lips met, providing a sense of intimacy that had been missing in our first encounter. I could hear the faint sounds of the music although I couldn't make out any of the words being sung. I doubt I lasted until the point where John Bonham kicked in with the drums, but it wasn't as bad as the first night. Which in itself was quite an achievement given that I'd been thinking of little else all week. Again, there was nothing said when it ended, but I wasn't about to push my luck by acting like a chick. If this is the way she wanted to play it, that was alright with me.

And that paid off, because very quickly, the freezer runs became a nightly event, something I'd look forward to during a shift—and in every other waking minute of my life. I convinced myself that there was a chemistry between us and that the rest of the staff had it figured out, but probably no one did. At least nobody said anything. Then one night while we were in the freezer a few weeks later, the music set wasn't the only thing that ended prematurely. I was using a stack of St. Pauli Girl cases as a beanbag when I suddenly saw Willy standing in the open doorway.

"Stanley, you are needed in the booth," was all he said, even though he clearly saw that I'd been defiling his stock.

I wasn't sure where I stood with him until the following afternoon when we were unloading a delivery of cases and kegs into the freezer, and he asked wryly, "Is there any particular way you'd like your apartment arranged?"

The answer to that question, actually, was yes. I'd figured out that five cases of beer was my perfect couch. Four cases meant my knees would have to bend. Six cases meant I'd have to stand tippy-toed. And the best part was that the 40-degree temp gave me a ready-made excuse for making short work of the beer stage I'd created.

He gave me a look that told me I didn't need to answer, and we never spoke about it again. The truth was that we were both too valuable to Willy that summer for him to get in our way. Me for the sound system, her for the local following of guys who showed up every night hoping to drink her bathwater but would accept Willy's booze as a lesser alternative.

Once when we were putting ourselves back together before returning to the bar, she smiled suggestively and said, "I'd like to see you function in warmth." But whenever I'd try to make that happen, she was elusive. I asked her out multiple times to no avail.

"I don't know if that's a good idea," she'd say anytime I suggested we go somewhere besides the ice box. She offered no further explanation, so of course, the more she begged off, the more I wanted the chance to try to expand her perception of me, which I figured was pretty limited. I had no idea what she thought of me. Summer fuck buddy? Local stoner? Easy, albeit fast, lay? Clearly she didn't want me to be her boyfriend, and I started to obsess over why. The most obvious reason was that she was smart and beautiful and clearly going places, while I was bartender in a strip mall. Then finally one night, we had a real conversation.

Last call at Shooter's was 2 a.m. and I'd gotten into the habit of trying to time my walk to my car with hers. We'd make small talk and always end up going our separate ways but I'd usually linger in my car, smoke a bone, and wait until I saw her rear tail lights leaving the lot. Sometimes I was tempted to follow, wondering where she lived and if there was a boyfriend waiting, but I never did. One night, I watched as she walked to her car, but after ten minutes, her headlights still hadn't come on. I turned off my car radio and then heard the faint sound of her engine turning over but not starting.

I got out and went over to her car. "Do you need me to jump you?"

"Again?"

We both laughed. I pulled the cables from my trunk and had her running in no time. This time, when I asked her if she wanted to hang out, she told me to hop in. Within minutes we were parking near the beach.

I had a doobie in my shirt pocket and asked her if she wanted to get high.

"No, but you go ahead."

We sat there with the windows down on a steamy summer night with her engine off and an accessory cassette deck playing the Rolling Stones' *Goat's Head Soup*. Soon after I fired up, I felt her hand reaching for a hit. Thus began our first real dialogue. We mostly talked about the bar. She wanted to know how long I'd been there, why the guys called her Envy, and whether Willy had ever said anything about walking in on us.

"Never a word," I told her.

We goofed on some of the regulars, and continued to get high.

"You ought to be playing songs for more than a barroom, Stan," she said.

"You mean like a club DJ?"

"No, I was thinking radio DJ."

The thought had never occurred to me. She said that she thought I had a real talent for knowing what people liked to hear.

"You make them happy."

"I think watching you in a suede skirt while getting shitfaced makes them happy," I said.

"Don't let yourself get stuck at Shooter's. You're too talented for that."

Her comment was both an endorsement of my skill and an affirmation of what separated us. She wasn't getting stuck at Shooter's. In another month, she would be heading back to college, a few grand richer for having spent a summer waitressing, and I'd still be spinning classic rock for a bunch of rednecks. It was a more effective wakeup call about my situation in life than any speech I'd ever heard from my parents or a guidance counselor.

As the summer wore on, I dreaded September. I knew that once she went back to FSU I was doomed. I kept trying to come up with ideas that would keep me relevant when her semester began, but nothing seemed plausible. And then just like that, we were done. One night as we were closing up, she mentioned that it was her last night at Shooter's, and before I could pull her aside to say goodbye, she disappeared. She returned to FSU and I never saw her again. Nor did I stop thinking about her. The one the locals called Envy.

Susan Miller.

I certainly knew what had become of her—the entire state of Florida knew her bio, and soon, so would the entire nation. She had met Bob Tobias during her junior year at FSU and, as the press releases and magazine profiles told it, fallen head over heels in love. In those days, Tobias was the antithesis of me. A total stud, he was a football phenom with a 4.0 who had the world by the balls. While I was still clutching a bong in my bedroom upstairs in my parents' place or pouring drafts at Shooter's, he was throwing touchdowns on national TV. They married soon after graduation in a wedding that was featured in all the Florida papers. She became a lobbyist in Tallahassee, bore him three daughters, and as his political career ascended, became a poster girl for everything right about the Sunshine State. Now, she was possibly poised to become the nation's first lady.

As the years went by, it was almost impossible for me to avoid hearing about her. Even after I'd left Florida, I would spot her and her husband in the local press whenever I returned home to visit my parents. I charted her path as best I could and wondered if she'd ever taken an interest in mine. I had come a long way since she'd known me at Shooter's. Stanislaw Pawlowski hadn't been in a position to influence much of anything, let alone her husband's presidential aspirations. But Stan Powers could throw up a roadblock or two if he followed Phil Dean's advice. That seemed unfair given that Susan Miller had done more than just about anyone else to put me on the career path to where I was today.

After Susan returned to college, I'd realized I had to get out of Shooter's. For one thing, going to work was pure agony. I couldn't unload a beer truck without thinking about her. It seemed that every song I played would conjure up some memory of what had apparently been only a summer fling. Everything in the bar reminded me of her. Of us. It was time for me to get my shit together and find the next thing, and the only idea I had was the one she'd given me.

My mission was to find a job that paid me to do what I'd done for Willy only without having to serve beers and put money into a huge holster. That opportunity came when I pestered a 5,000-watt daytimer outside of town to hire me for minimum wage as a weekend morning guy. The station was one step removed from a boom box. It broadcast from beneath its own transmitter in a building surrounded by livestock, and could only be heard during sunlit hours, which meant that my first hour on the air at 5 a.m. was for a crowd of one—but I didn't care. I was being paid a couple of bucks to do something I enjoyed, and I was no longer trapped in a bar where I kept obsessing over a girl who got away. A sense of ambition I never knew I had began to kindle.

Twenty years, five stations, and 1100 miles away later, I was broadcasting live from a classic rock station in Pittsburgh. It was called WBXM and was owned by radio giant Star Channel Radio. It was also where Stanislaw Pawlowski, now known as just Stan or Stan the Man, did afternoon drive every weekday from 4 p.m. to 7 p.m.

"You're tuned to Buxom FM, WBXM, now let's get *Stanned*."

I wish I had a nickel for every time that line came out of my mouth in the Steel City. But the catchphrase worked. And I could rightfully take the credit because at a time when consultants and company playlists were becoming the norm, I had minimal interference from the suits and basically relied on the instincts I'd developed at Shooter's. When my fingers thumbed the carts on which the station library was stored, I asked myself one thing: is anybody ordering a shot over at Shooter's when they hear this, and will that fucking fake pistol fire? If the answer was no, I looked for something else.

Pittsburgh was the perfect training ground. It

was the nation's 25th radio market and a town with a working-class mentality that I really dug. These people worked hard, loved their Steelers, and liked to unwind by drinking shitloads of Iron City beer while listening to rock music. And there was something else: a major concert venue in the Mellon Arena, or as the locals still called it, the old Civic Arena. It was home not only to the Pittsburgh Penguins, but also to every touring act from the Rolling Stones to Radiohead. Our station was on the call list of every major record and concert promoter, many of whom would offer interviews with bands releasing albums or touring. If they were touring, they were coming to Pittsburgh. And if they were coming to Pittsburgh, they were going to want to sell tickets on Buxom FM.

The interviews were usually run by a service out of California that would book a particular band member in eight-minute increments, so one second a rock god would be talking to me in Pittsburgh, and the next he'd be talking to a guy in Dallas. Or Phoenix. Or Philly. This didn't allow me to develop a rapport with any of the artists, not in the span of a few minutes, and more often than not, the singer or bass player was confused as to what market he was reaching. "Hello, Cleveland!" Still, I loved it, and allowed the suspension of belief to set in like we were old buddies. These were the guys I had grown up idolizing. They were the musicians whose lyrics I had once spent hours reading on album jackets because I thought they had all the answers. And if one of them so much as answered a question by including my first name, it gave me a woody.

When tours came to town, I could sometimes finagle tickets and a backstage pass from the promoters and attend a meet and greet with the bands. That was great too, and I'd often take not only a date, but also my tape recorder, partly so that people knew I was in the biz, and partly to grab some audio for the afternoon show.

Some of the stuff that happened backstage you couldn't make up. Jon Anderson from Yes was always one of my favorite singers. Well, he came to town on a solo tour at a 500-seat club and I was given a pair of tickets and a pass. I jumped at the opportunity to hear the man who sang "Roundabout" and "All Good People" in a setting of just a few hundred. After the show, I flashed my laminate and expected to be one of 30 or so who would get to shake his hand and maybe grab some audio. Only this time, there was no meet and greet. There was just me, Jon, and his beautiful wife, Jane. So we sat and talked, and somehow the conversation turned to politics and the c-word. Yes. *That* c-word. It's probably the only word even I will not say, much less put in print. He launched into a dialogue about how the word was beautiful, and how it had been defiled by men around the world and how I needed to play a role in bringing it back.

Oddly enough what set him off was a controversy over whether American politicians should hold the hand of the Saudi King. Of all things, a photograph of President George W. Bush holding the king's hand had really riled up the usually sedate singer. The Saudis, Anderson said, had a "serious damn problem on women. They don't treat women with any respect at all, for God's sake. No, they don't treat women well. And woman is the earth mother, for God's sake. Come on, we've got to wake up!"

I tried to change the subject. But before I could, Anderson blurted out:

"There's a great book called *C-nt*. Everybody's got to buy it."

Thank God this was taped. I didn't need George Carlin to tell me that word should not be broadcast.

"You know, 'c-nt' was a beautiful African word for the divine, the flower of the woman, the vagina. C-nt!" he continued. "It's an African word and it's a beautiful word. But you know, men fucked it up. They changed it into something misogynistic and derogative."

Well, the following day that aired on Buxom FM—all beeped, of course. Even so, it was huge. In fact, I think the beeps added to the rebellious nature of the conversation. My interview even got a brief mention in *Rolling Stone*! And even after all this time, I found myself wondering whether Susan might have read or heard about it. Sober, I was not.

Another night, Ted Nugent came to town and I was offered the opportunity to go to his hotel room and interview him before he left to do a local show. I took a buddy of mine with me who couldn't believe that we were about to encounter the Motor City Madman in his suite. He thought I was pranking him right up until the minute that Uncle Ted greeted us in his doorway in stocking feet and welcomed us in.

Now I've never been too good with electronics—I have a clock/DVD player at home that still blinks "12:00" 24/7—and that night, I had some crappy old tape recorder that actually recorded on cassettes.

We were all sitting around a dining table in Nuge's suite and he was on a roll talking both politics and rock. The man was both insane and an interviewer's dream, sounding off on everything from music to hunting to politics. We seemed to hit it off and I remember him telling me that I was his "blood brother" and so forth.

Then all of a sudden I felt something on my foot and looked down to see that the cassette tape had spooled out of the machine and was now running onto the floor. Nugent didn't notice.

Now I had a real dilemma. Should I tell him and acknowledge that the 15 minutes he'd given me was for nothing, or just try to finish up the interview and scoop up the tape without him noticing? I grew worried. They didn't call him the Motor City "Madman" for nothing.

I sat there deliberating and ultimately figured it was in my best interest to fess up. When I did, he had a surprise for me. He reached into an ankle holster and pulled out a cannon the size of the one Dirty Harry wielded. Nuge pointed it at the cassette recorder and asked my permission to "blow it the fuck up." Then he smiled and said to come to the show and catch him backstage and we'd try again. I hustled out the door with Memorex tape between my fingers. Later that night he made good on the offer. When I told the story on the radio, complete with Nuge wanting to nuke my recorder, some liberal prosecutor in city hall heard me and issued a warrant for his arrest because he hadn't had a carry permit in Pittsburgh!

These interviews became a signature of my program. Now "Getting Stanned" meant hearing music that would make you chug and interviews that would make you listen.

I had just turned 40 and I had money in my pocket, some local fame and more ass than a toilet seat, and I was doing something for a living that I was good at and truly enjoyed. Even my parents were proud, although my father couldn't understand why Stanislaw Pawlowski wouldn't fly as my on-air moniker.

"Why are you so embarrassed about your heritage?" he'd say. "If your grandfather Stanislaw hadn't got on a boat, you wouldn't have the ability to sit and play records and get paid."

Dad figured it was some anti-Pole conspiracy, no matter how many times I told him that last names were out, no matter what they were.

"You're selling us out like FDR did at Potsdam," he'd say. I didn't understand the historical reference then, nor have I taken the time since to figure out what the hell he was talking about.

"And another thing. Why do you say '*Stanned*. Getting *Stanned*'? It sounds like you have a speech impediment like your cousin Vodge."

I figured he wasn't ready for an answer to that. I felt guilty enough about what I'd put him and my mother through during high school, and I wanted them to enjoy my success. Strangely enough, their pride made me miss Florida in a way I never would have expected when I first packed up to leave.

Which was one reason why I was willing to listen when I received a call from Jules DelGado informing me that he'd been contacted by Steve Bernson, VP of programming for all of Star

Channel Radio which owned Buxom FM, asking if I would ever consider moving to Tampa. Pittsburgh and Tampa were comparable markets in terms of size; I couldn't claim to be taking a giant step up the radio ladder by moving from one to the other. But this call was for prime time—morning drive—on a 50,000-watt flame-thrower called "The Rock." Star Channel also owned The Rock (and, so it seemed, every other station in America) so Bernson could call my agent and sound me out while I was still under contract in Pittsburgh. Doing afternoon drive at Buxom FM, I was making $100k per year. For mornings in Tampa, I was being offered $300k plus incentives with an ironclad three-year deal. I wouldn't exactly be going home, but it was close: One market removed from where I'd grown up and where my parents were still living in the house where I was raised. Not to mention the warmer weather. And just maybe, spinning vinyl for an audience that included an ex-flame.

So was I interested in morning drive in Tampa? Hell yes.

And just like that, I was packing and heading south.

I arrived in Tampa/St. Pete about ten days before my start date, moved into a one-bedroom rental, and had yet to even see the new studio when a second surprising call came from Jules.

"This is one of those radio good news, bad news calls," was how he put it, before blowing his nose into the phone and making me wait another minute or so to hear what he had to say because he was juggling two calls at once.

"Star Channel has just sold ten of its stations to MML&J Media, which is a bunch of holy rollers based in Atlanta," he said. "They publish Bibles, but have decided to branch out into radio with an eye toward owning an imprint in talk."

One of the stations they'd acquired was The Rock in Tampa. In other words, they were my new employers and they were flipping the format. I was now working for a bunch of fundamentalist Christians from Georgia.

"I'm still waiting for the good news," I told Jules.

"Your new deal guarantees that MML&J will assume Star Channel's contract and pay you three bills for three years," he told me. "And if the format is gone, they have to pay you to sit on the beach. You don't have to work, Stan." He went on to explain that I was under no obligation to provide any other services. They'd have to pay me $900,000 over three years and all I would lose would be the opportunity to make bonus money that would have come from hitting the top five in the ratings among men 25-54. It was the kind of news I would have welcomed a decade earlier, sort of like I'd hit the lottery. Funny thing was, now I wasn't so psyched. In fact, I was immediately concerned about becoming irrelevant.

Jules said Steve Bernson wished to speak to me directly to "explain some other developments and ideas." Jules usually found a way to make himself a part of any conversation that might result in a deal, but in this case said he had no problem with me speaking to Bernson directly, so I called him at Star Channel headquarters in New York City, where he immediately took my call. Bernson was the classic corporate media guy, more TV than radio in his appearance. Nice tan even in winter. A perfectly styled, expensively cut head of dark hair. Nattily dressed in a suit. French cuffs. Tasteful tie. He always seemed to me like he could deliver the weather for a TV network affiliate in a top 10 TV market.

He said, "Buxom FM was not one of the stations that was sold, Stan. But they've already hired your replacement in Pittsburgh."

I told him I didn't understand.

"Well, if you are dead set on returning to Pittsburgh and WBXM, I suspect we can find you another time slot. You're well regarded within Star Channel, so there's also the chance we can find a suitable shift for you on one of our other stations."

If, however, I worked for the "old company,"

as he put it, I would not get the guaranteed money. And he repeated what Jules said, that I could sit and do nothing for the next three years and collect a fat check.

But he had an alternative. I was all ears.

"Stan, I'm part of the Star Channel/MML&J deal myself. I'm leaving Star Channel and joining MML&J Media as their VP of Programming, and I would like you to consider coming with me. I, too, will be based in Tampa."

I still didn't understand.

"As Jules probably told you, The Rock is flipping formats but it's all happened so suddenly that I don't have the talent assembled yet. Will you consider doing mornings for a few weeks until I can field my team?"

He told me he'd already recruited both a midday guy and someone for afternoon drive. He said he'd picked up an old-timer with some talk experience in the market to cover overnights. But the morning man with whom he was negotiating had not yet come to terms, and in a best case, could not arrive until 30 days after the change in format.

I couldn't believe my ears. He was both confirming that I was about to get paid nearly a million dollars for sitting on my ass, and asking me to come try my hand as a talk radio host for a month.

So I asked the obvious.

"What the fuck do I know about talk?"

Followed by the essential.

"What's in it for me if I don't have to work?"

He answered by first asking if I'd ever heard of Phil Dean.

"Of course, I have. In the same way that any kid pitcher has heard of Nolan Ryan," I said.

"Well, he's heard of you," Bernson said. "In fact, more than hearing *of* you, he has actually *heard* you. And he was very impressed with your delivery."

I still didn't understand.

Bernson told me that Phil Dean was about to come aboard with MML&J to advise them on their acquisitions from Star Channel. He said it was Phil who suggested that I try my hand at talk when he heard that I'd just signed a contract for which I would not have to perform.

"Phil says that your formatics are great, and he can school you on what you need to develop for content. He also likes your interview style and that's a key part of doing good talk."

Bernson went on, "He said that you know how to play the hits and that is all talk will require of you. You'll still be playing the hits, but instead of playing the usual songs, you'll be offering the tried and tested sound bytes. Same formula, just different material. And he will personally guide you once he's on board."

It was intriguing, but I still wasn't convinced. "Why would I take that gamble?"

"Because it's a 'no risk' experiment. If you suck, then Stan Powers gets retired and you sit back and collect your pay anyway."

"Who the hell is Stan Powers?"

"You are. And your new program is called *Morning Power* on WRGT."

"WRGT?"

"That's the new name for The Rock. I told you. The plan is for the station, all the MML&J stations, to become right-wing, conservative talk."

I didn't reply. While I wasn't entirely sure what a conservative was, I was pretty certain I wasn't one.

"Chances are you will only do this for 30 days. But if it works, you can be bigger than any DJ could ever be. Look at what Limbaugh is making."

The prospect of making that kind of dough might make my decision easier to swallow. Pittsburgh was great, but if I couldn't have my old time slot, I wasn't going back to my old employer for one-third the money of what I was about to make in Florida. I felt that I'd already peaked in that market and wanted a new challenge. I knew and liked Tampa. Plus, the idea of returning to my home state and earning big bucks for a career that began there in a dive bar gave me a sense of accomplishment, a feeling of closure and self-worth that I very much wanted to experience. Still, the new format was intimidating, and I wasn't sure I could—or wanted to—make such a drastic transition.

Mulling over the decision while hanging in my new, tiny apartment, I decided to pour myself a cold one. Then I grabbed a "welcome to the neighborhood" package left by my rental agent, and moved out onto the deck, which had a view of the water only if I craned my neck. Inside the envelope was an assortment of coupons for free car washes, pizza discounts and maid service, as well as the latest issue of *Tampa Bay Magazine*. On the cover, smiling and looking radiant, was Susan Miller. It was then that I called Jules and told him I'd give it a shot.

After hanging up, I sipped my beer and said out loud, "This is Stan Powers and you're tuned to WRGT." Funny, it didn't feel right from the first time.

CHAPTER 5

Governor Bob Tobias, former football hero, husband to Susan Miller, and rising Democratic star, had been my radio guest on two prior occasions. Both were short phoners about local Florida politics. This time, Phil was insistent that I bring him into the studio for a face-to-face interview so that cameras would capture the two of us together. He wanted the interview to lead the cable TV news and said that audio alone would not suffice for what we needed. It was essential that we both be in the same video frame.

"Preferably with him leaving pissed," was how he put it.

This was easier said than done. First off, I didn't often have many radio guests who were Democrats. Tobias had previously been a big exception because it had suited both our interests. Like every other politician running statewide in Florida, he needed to remain in good stead in the I-4 corridor, and while he was never going to win over my P1s, it enhanced his appeal with independent types if he could tame the otherwise irascible Stan Powers. Meanwhile, I'd had my own reasons for wanting to keep the prior exchanges civil. First, there was a certain prestige that came with having a rapport with the state's sitting governor, even if he was from the other side of the aisle. That's because while the mainstays of talk radio are usually heated national issues like illegal immigration, terrorism or federal spending, the state stuff is important for what it means to people's daily lives. School vouchers, auto insurance, and fishing rights are but a few of the things that come up routinely where the governor gets a major say. Being able to present Tobias to my audience, particularly where he had taken listener phone calls, was important to the brand of the program which billed itself as a news format based on talk. Having him on from time to time made me credible and relevant.

Secondly—never to be uttered on air—I personally liked the guy's politics. Tobias was a moderate Democrat not tied to the Northeastern, liberal establishment. He hadn't raised taxes, had opposed giving driver's licenses to illegal immigrants, and had signed a bill that legalized marijuana for medicinal purposes—three things that made sense to me. And finally, I didn't want him going home to the governor's mansion in Tallahassee and complaining to Susan Miller about some asshole on the radio named Stan

Powers, even if the name didn't mean anything to her.

But now, with President Summers suddenly packing it in, things had just gotten a bit more complicated. Preserving the status quo was no longer the aim. Tobias wanted to be president. I wanted a bigger platform. And whether we could serve one another's goals as we had in the past was now considerably less likely. Nothing would further my career more than thwarting his, or so said Phil.

When Alex had initially invited Tobias onto the program more than three years prior, she'd had to swear a blood oath that I would not be a douche bag. His staff was so concerned about how the appearance would go that they'd wanted to know my questions in advance. I refused to submit a list, but did participate in a call with one of his staffers where I shared the broad strokes of what we would cover. Like I said, things had gone well, but that was before his national star took off like a rocket. This time, as Alex tried to work her magic to make it an in-studio interview, Phil was breathing down my neck and ranting about how I needed to lead the insurgency against Tobias' budding presidential campaign from within his own state.

"The guy is a pothead. He's waved the white flag on drugs, Stan."

"No he hasn't. He's made it easier for people

with debilitating illnesses to get access for medicinal purposes."

"There you go again. Getting all wordy and defensive. Just say he's given kids their gateway to heroin."

Phil was driving me batshit. He was simultaneously demanding that I begin my attack on Tobias before his people had even committed to a face-to-face interview, and requesting twice-daily reports on Alex's efforts to lure him into my studio. He pretended not to hear but backed down somewhat after I reminded him that Tobias would never cement the invitation if I was already on air saying the things Phil was recommending. Meanwhile, I was kind of hoping that Tobias couldn't manage to come into the studio now that he was running for president. While I recognized the PR value and knew that the attention could be just the kind of circus that boosts the career of a guy like me, I didn't relish the idea of confronting him in the way that Phil had in mind. The upside for him would be to show that he could appeal to centrists who would play a pivotal role should he receive his party's nomination. After all, if Governor Bob Tobias could hold his own on *Morning Power*, maybe he was the type of fusion candidate who could get the left and right to coexist? Still, I figured the odds of him consenting to an in-studio interview were slim, even after I had been hospitable to his main rival—but then Alex delivered the thunderclap.

"I got him," was all she said, handing me a printout of an email she received at the end of the day's program. "They heard your interview with Vic Baron and now they want in. And he's willing to come to the studio." The fact that she offered no further words told me she shared my dread of what might unfold when he walked through the door. Alex was intuitive like that. I never let her into my thinking, but then again, I didn't have to. I took the paper out of her hand.

"The governor looks forward to continuing his civil dialogue with Stan Powers," wrote some media flack in the email. Oh shit.

For a few seconds I contemplated not sharing the news with Phil and scuttling the interview with a fake scheduling conflict. He'd have no way of knowing if I didn't tell him. Then my ego got the best of me. This was a potential coup on the road to syndication. Phil's instincts were, as usual, correct in sensing opportunity. Tobias was the newly anointed Democratic frontrunner coming from an electorally rich swing state, and the fact that he was sitting down with a regionally important, conservative talk host guaranteed that this would make news. This could be the start of a six-month run that would culminate when the GOP convention came to town and all the print, blogosphere and cable television news outlets wanted interviews with someone on the ground who knew the Florida political scene—and I could be that guy. A major interview now, with a Democrat, would cement that role.

"He's coming in next Tuesday," I said on my cell while driving home.

"Perfect," was Phil's response.

"You've been handed a golden opportunity, Stan. Don't fuck it up," he warned before proceeding to assure me that he'd come up with some talking points. My stomach turned as I listened to his plan.

"In a word, religion! You've got to expose this heathen."

I knew instantly what he was thinking.

Bob Tobias had never been one to "Tebow" in order to get elected. Throughout his political life, he'd consistently refused to detail his religious convictions, saying that he believed all faith was "a private matter that has no place in American politics." That earned him praise from the likes of Bill Maher and Richard Dawkins, both of whom interpreted his unwillingness to play the usual game as a sign of a lack of faith, something Tobias never confirmed. But he'd created a YouTube sensation when someone with a cell phone had captured part of a speech he delivered to a reform Jewish group in Miami where he said that "America was founded on the notion of freedom of religion, and freedom from religion," emphasizing the latter part of the sentence. The blogosphere went bonkers with speculation that Tobias was an atheist or an agnostic. Ever since, many a Florida barroom conversation had included someone asking: "Tobias, what kind of name is that?"

Fucking Phil was right, of course, in sensing that Tobias' past proclamations about religion, while they might be sustainable in a swing state election where voters were familiar with the entire package the man presented, could seriously hamper his ability to emerge on a national stage. Being labeled as an atheist before the public knows anything else about you is a nonstarter.

"No religion, no morals. Remember that Stan. He can't be president without embracing the Judeo-Christian roots of America."

That was another perennial trope in my line of work. "The Judeo-Christian roots of America." A great sound byte offered by me and repeated by many but with no real meaning. I don't think any of the Pilgrims were Jews, and Thomas Jefferson said nothing about Christianity in the Declaration of Independence. But, of course, I said none of this to Phil.

Sensing reluctance from the silence at my end of the phone, Phil followed up by saying, "Do you want to play on the national stage or not?"

That always shut me up. I did, and he knew the strength of my desire. I wanted the attention. I wanted the power. And I wanted the money that would come from reaching a few hundred affiliates. I was already doing a program that I believed surpassed that of many national players, and it would require no more effort on my part to reach millions more people. I just needed a bigger soap box. I had wanted a bigger platform ever since I got my bearings on air in Tampa. I thought of myself as a musician who had built a good set list and had sold out clubs in medium-sized cities. What additional professional effort was required to go sing those same songs in front of a stadium crowd? None. But taking that larger stage was about to come with an escalating personal price.

Part of my angst about the interview was that I was expected to play political hitman. But I confess that I was also feeling more than a little unsettled about meeting the man who was married to Susan Miller. The fact that she and I had never crossed paths in the years since I had established myself as a radio host was testament to the political and ideological divide within my industry. I often thought about whether she'd heard my radio program (probably not) or had seen me on television (probably had) and whether she'd recognized that Stanislaw Pawlowski was now Stan Powers (wasn't sure). But the odds were about to increase that all three questions would be affirmative if her husband came back home Tuesday night and complained at dinner about how some right-wing asshole had set him up on religion.

In the end, South Carolina was unable to turn around a new ballot in time for the Democratic primary, so Florida now would be the first state to go to the polls with the new candidate roster— a big advantage for Tobias. Already, all seven of the candidates were swarming the state and the presumed frontrunner was now coming into my studio.

"Good morning Tampa Bay, it's 7:35, 35 minutes after the hour, and you're tuned to *Morning Power.*"

On the day of the interview, the program began as it always did without any on-air hint of the spectacle that was to unfold. Inside WRGT was a different story. Governor Bob Tobias was about to make his third appearance on my program, only this time he'd be in studio, and with a hoard of media in tow. From the time I'd first gone on air at 5 a.m., there had been a slew of technicians laying cable in and around my studio and a satellite truck parked out front. One of the network morning shows was going to do a live cut-in and simulcast at least a part of the interview. And we'd been told that several members of the national press corps were now traveling with Tobias and would be in tow.

That morning I went through my usual ritual

right before the "on air" light went on. After I'd completed my prep, I went to the can down the hall from the studio and splashed some cold water on my face. I usually paused for a moment and stared into the mirror while wiping myself dry, studying the likeness in front of me. Maybe I was looking for some final assurance that the listeners won't see the image of the person about to say the things that earn my keep. But I was careful to never allow too much time for second-guessing. Within seconds I'd turn off the light switch, walk ten paces back to the studio and illuminate the "on air" light that tells a passerby the show is hot.

During the preceding commercial break, Alex had told me that the governor was running 3-5 minutes late, which wouldn't seriously curtail the interview time, but meant there'd be no private words spoken between us off-air. We didn't have a green room, and the control area where Rod and Alex sat was too cramped to hold guests for any significant amount of time. In the rare instances when I had an in-studio guest, I'd usually walk out into the adjacent hallway and say hello before we went on air. I'd try to be courteous while keeping the pre-air conversation to a few simple pleasantries, lest they say something interesting and then leave it in the locker room. But there'd be none of that today. With Tobias behind schedule, it meant whatever was spoken between us would all be in front of live microphones.

On my side of the studio glass things were mostly business as usual. I was wearing my standard uniform: an Oxford cloth button down shirt, conservative sport coat, pair of Lucky jeans, and Bruno Magli shoes (no socks). (I stopped wearing them for a few years after OJ, that cocksucker, gave them a bad name. But they're so damn comfortable that my protest ended after a couple of months and a lot of experimentation.) Normally I sat alone in front of the big electronic bank of blinking lights, knobs and switches illuminated in front of me, but today I had the cameraman from the network morning show to keep me company. Notes and newspapers spilled out around me, and on my left were two computer screens, one connected to the Internet and logged on to the *Morning Power* web site or my Twitter feed, and the other showing me the information that Alex gleaned from callers. "Joe . . . on a mobile . . . from St. Pete . . . thinks you're a jerkoff." Across from me sat two chairs for guests, each with its own mic stand and pair of Sony headphones. I'd recommend you get a tetanus shot before you wear 'em. When I was working in Pittsburgh, we had an old-timer who used to do a weekend Beatles show and he'd come into the studio with his own cleaning supplies and hose the place down, spraying Lysol on the microphone and headphones before he'd start. I used to laugh at him, but no more. The one thing I can't afford to be in my business is sick.

I sat with my back to a wall, looking at a landscape that consisted of the console, guest positions and finally, 15 feet away, the glass separating the broadcast studio from the control room, with Alex and Rod seated on the other side in close quarters. Alex was on the right, dressed in drab with a t-shirt that said, "There Is No Plan B." A small looped earring protruded from her left eyebrow, and she wore a sleek headset with a mouthpiece that made her look like she was working in a call center in Mumbai. Rod sat a few feet away, wearing his bow tie, while his outstretched arms and hands ran "the board" as we call it. His job was to maintain audio purity, keep close track of time and play the commercials. It's a job that demands attentiveness and organization, and although I personally found him to be a major ass pain, I had to admit that he was damn good at it. The obsessive nature of his personality was one of the reasons that I never wanted to see him outside the studio, and the same reason I wanted to make sure he *was* there when I was working. Rod looked suitably dour, no doubt at the prospect of a prominent Democrat having been invited onto our show.

But today, Alex and Rod also had company.

Jammed into the already narrow confines of the control room alongside them were three cameramen from the local Tampa network affiliates, plus two guys I assumed were print reporters more on account of their scruffy looks than their tablets. Funny how the media world is evolving at a rapid clip, but the newspaper guys always look the same.

"We're awaiting the arrival of Governor Bob Tobias here in the WRGT studios," I began. "He'll give us the latest in his thinking about his run for president, and I'll try to include your calls."

I killed some time by recapping what had been going on in the race, namely how the Democratic Party was more unsettled in its nomination process during this election cycle than any other in recent memory. With seven serious candidates, including the governors of two big states—Florida and New York—readying to do battle, the primary process for the Dems still had all the makings of a cluster-fuck. President Summers' announcement had caught everyone by surprise, and there hadn't even been time for the candidates to use that old canard about how "people have asked me to consider it" when in fact they were dying to run. Tobias was garnering support from some party elders who believed the Democrats were behind the eight ball and needed to quickly coalesce around a candidate who could appeal to centrists. Proving that appeal was no doubt one major reason that Tobias was about to walk through my studio door.

As I jabbered more or less on autopilot, sharing tidbits about the bios of the more serious candidates, I kept the right-wing rhetoric to a minimum and kept my eyes fixed on the other side of the glass, looking for a sign of Tobias' arrival. The harbinger came when the three cameramen all turned on the lights atop their cameras, and then swung their gear in the direction of the corridor that led to my studio. I couldn't see what they were focusing on but I knew it had to be Tobias. Rod looked like he'd just seen Janet Jackson's nipple. That was to be expected. But Alex's expression was more unusual. She looked surprised. As the cameramen got their shot of something not yet visible to me, I watched as her eyes widened. Then her head swiveled to look squarely at me, still with that quizzical facial expression, while the heavy soundproof door to my studio swung open. Something was coming and it wasn't good.

I was trying to process all of this while carrying on a coherent conversation with my listeners, an ability I'd honed from years on air, which has also served me well atop plenty of barstools.

"And here he is right now. Joining us for *Morning Power* at WRGT is the Governor of the great state of Florida, Bob Tobias," I intoned, as the governor strode toward me with his arm outstretched. With my headphones tied to the console, I could only half-rise and shake his hand, lest I'd be disconnected. The headphones also muted my ability to actually hear him because he was not yet close enough to the microphone.

". . . surprise . . . the First Lady . . ."

His words were muddled. But then I saw who he was referencing.

My eyes moved quickly from the governor to Alex's frozen expression, to someone else who'd entered the studio behind him. I think I inhaled her scent before I actually saw her. It had been many years, but I thought I recognized that smell. Funny how the olfactory sense can jog the memory. It immediately took me back in time. And then there was her hemline, revealing those toned, tanned calves as they walked toward me. I raised my eyes and they locked on the pair of green ones directly in front of me. It was her, alright. Susan Miller was now standing three feet away, with her own right hand reaching toward me while the governor, now getting settled in front of a microphone, continued to speak words that I could now hear.

". . . which is why I thought it'd be great for your listeners to hear from Susan, too. . . ."

I stood there like some fucking Cirque du Soleil contortionist trying to shake her hand while not traveling too far from either my headphone connection or my microphone, and simultaneously trying to digest the enormous knot that had just formed in my stomach. I thought I had planned for every eventuality concerning this interview, but it had never occurred to me that she would come with him.

"I've always appreciated our frank conversations, Stan, and so I was glad to accept your invitation," the governor said as he settled into his seat.

Thank God he was in wind-up mode, requiring little or no prodding from me because I couldn't think straight. Did he know that I knew Susan? She now sat cross-legged in front of me, as sexy as ever, with a Nancy Reagan–like focus on what her husband was saying. It would have been easier for me to concentrate if a truck had hit her in the intervening years. But instead she looked amazing. Did she even know it was me? She gave no hint. The governor continued to talk about who the fuck knows what while I did some mental calculus. I figured there were three possibilities. Number one was that she had no idea who I really was. It had been many years since Susan Miller had banged a guy named Stan Pawlowski, a stoner in a redneck bar whose only knowledge of illegal immigration was Led Zeppelin's "Immigrant Song." It was entirely possible that she did not make the connection. What reason was there to think she'd ever thought of me after she left Shooter's? None.

Possibility No. 2 was that she absolutely knew it was me and had shared with Tobias some sanitized version of our prior relationship, which is why he wanted her to come along and help him curry favor with this conservative nutbag (me) who he now needed to behave. The third option was that she knew it was me, but had not told him, in consideration of which, I got instant wood. Dammit she was beautiful.

"Assuming you run, will you feel obliged to offer national voters a greater insight into your personal life than you have afforded Florida voters?" I said, trying to regain some of my footing.

"Stan, I'm confident that voters will view my long career as a legislator and chief executive for one of our largest states as appropriate preparation."

He didn't answer my question, but I didn't give a shit. This was all preliminary, passing time until I could go for the jugular. My attention was now evenly divided between Susan Miller's legs and the legal tablet in front of me. Phil had been so precise about what I was to ask that I'd written out his edict:

DO YOU PERSONALLY EMBRACE THE JUDEO-CHRISTIAN PRINCIPLES ON WHICH THIS NATION WAS FOUNDED?

Those were some important buzzwords in my trade. I might just as well have asked, "Please convince us that you are one of us and not one of them." I'm convinced that most of my listeners could not even define the Judeo-Christian principles to which I was referring, even though they demanded that presidential candidates swear allegiance to them. But Tobias would know the intention of the question. It was a shot across the bow with network cameras watching. And it was a set-up, given his prior unwillingness to play this game. Of course, lost on my colleagues and those listeners who denounced anything but strict adherence to the Constitution was the fact that there were 55 delegates to the Constitutional Convention in Philadelphia who never wanted a religious test of any kind, Judeo-Christian or otherwise. Article 6 of the Constitution expressly forbids a religious test as a qualification for office, but Phil knew that in the minds of our listeners that didn't apply to a presidential candidate. The test they wished imposed was a blood oath to some amorphous Judeo-Christian principles that no Muslim or atheist could agree to. Funny thing—they loved to cite Thomas Jefferson or Abe Lincoln, but overlooked the fact that the first was a deist and the second refused to join any church.

I also wondered what Susan's reaction would

be. She had now redirected her gaze from her husband and was watching me. Or so I thought. I didn't dare return the look. Was she studying my face? Did I detect a hint of recognition? I felt like a spotlight was shining on me. Maybe this was an opportunity to let her know I'd expanded my horizons since Shooter's.

"But Governor, we've already tried spending our way out of this economic morass."

"Well, that's exactly right, Stan, which is why I favor a balanced approach between spending cuts and improvement of our infrastructure."

Damn, this guy was good. He made even our points of disagreement sound like consensus. I could see why the combination of his bio, home state and charisma were vaulting him to the front of the donkey pack. But my desire to impress Susan with my ability to host a substantive conversation was interrupted by the realization that somewhere in a mud shack in Taos, listening by Internet feed, fat fucking Phil was having a conniption over the chummy nature of an exchange that was supposed to be my golden opportunity for candidate assassination.

I glanced again at my notepad, but still didn't say it aloud.

DO YOU PERSONALLY EMBRACE THE JUDEO-CHRISTIAN PRINCIPLES ON WHICH THIS NATION WAS FOUNDED?

Tobias kept talking while I tried to refocus. I looked around. One of the local network cameramen had turned off his light. That was a bad sign. And the two print guys were not writing anything. Even the cameraman inside my studio looked bored as hell. I felt the moment slipping away and grabbed my balls.

"Governor, there are many across the country getting their first look at Bob Tobias. So let's not assume they know your background."

I was trying to get closer to religion, but he took my poorly phrased, open-ended question and used it to his advantage.

"Thank you, Stan. Like you, I am a native Floridian. . . ."

Like me? How did he know that? Was it because Susan had given him a briefing? So she did know it was me! Or not. Maybe he had just read my bio from the *Morning Power* web site. My head spun. Suddenly I wished I was playing "Toys in the Attic" back in Pittsburgh.

It was true that Tobias and I were both natives of the Sunshine State, although we had been raised in opposite corners. For him it was St. Augustine where his family history ran deep. His father was a blue-collar guy who was a local fire chief and coached Pop Warner on the side. Daddy knew he had a ringer in Bobby and so did the rest of the state by the time he was in his freshman year. He went on to set so many passing records that I knew his name clear across the state when we were both in high school because he was a stellar quarterback for a team that reached state finals. High school football was so big then that the championship game was televised on cable statewide. Tobias' team didn't win but he ended up with a free ride to Florida State University where his All-American play cemented his status as a Florida god. I don't know of too many things you could do in this state to make yourself more of a household name than play quarterback for FSU. Maybe drive NASCAR or take off for the moon from the Kennedy Space Center, but I doubt it. Football is king. When he entered political life by running for the state legislature not too long after college graduation, it was a lock that he wouldn't leave Tallahassee without first being governor.

". . . where I played quarterback, although many in the Sunshine State will never forget how I came up short in the final game. . . ."

I'd tuned out again, lost in a peripheral view of the glow of Susan's lip gloss, perfectly manicured nails and bronze skin. I told myself to stop looking at her and concentrate on him.

". . . and wanted to serve my state in the legislature. . . ."

I felt too guilty to make eye contact, so I stared at the repeated H's on his bright red Hermes tie. Then I lost my concentration again wondering if Susan had picked it out for him. It didn't matter. He was spinning.

". . . and while I haven't made a final decision, I am listening to an increasing chorus of people who are telling me that the type of solution-oriented governance I brought to Florida is what the nation craves."

Tobias was cruising on autopilot and sure sounded like a man running for president. After all, everyone knew he was going to formally announce in St. Augustine the following weekend. I knew this was getting away from me. My audience would be disappointed. And Phil would be furious. So I finally interrupted, trying to get back to the narrative Phil had prescribed.

"Let me ask you about your family. . . ."

He took that as an invitation to talk about his parents, their work ethic and deep Florida roots. I swallowed. He rattled off the names and ages of their three daughters, before walking into the militarized zone.

"For them, my greatest gift, I can thank their mother, my wife Susan. . . ."

The mention of her name from *his* lips gave me a temporary bout of courage, and I looked again at my notes. Phil had said that it was important that at this moment I be looking right at him so that our face-to-face would appear direct. I looked back at the tie, hoping that on camera, it would look like we were mano-a-mano.

"Right or wrong, Governor, when you step onto the national stage you must do so knowing that the media spotlight will shine brightly on your personal life."

It was like he didn't hear me. Like a sprinter who was now in an open field, arms and legs pumping, all motion synchronized, Governor Tobias kept talking. He had yet to comprehend what was unfolding around him. Instead he offered his understanding of how a national campaign would change his life forever while simultaneously wishing for the ability to raise their daughters with some continued sense of normalcy.

"Should you run, you surely know you will be exposing your personal life and that of your family to a level of scrutiny never seen in any Florida election."

"Well, I'm confident that my family can withstand any reasonable scrutiny that respects our privacy."

I glanced at the digital on my console. Time was running short. We had a hard out at 7:58 for network news and so the interview, which I fully recognized had been a bust up until now, would soon end. It was now or never.

"Do you believe that matters of faith are fair game in a presidential contest?"

Tobias paused before speaking, something he

had not done when responding to my prior questions. Time seemed to stand still for a moment. Through the glass, I saw the print guys pick up their notepads. The third camera light suddenly flashed back on. Rod Chinkles' eyes were so focused they looked like an ad for x-ray vision goggles. I could see Alex suddenly put a caller on hold. I sensed that her initial concern for my well-being was now being replaced with a sense of disgust.

I didn't wait for him to reply. I rephrased.

"Governor, my fellow Tea Partiers would be right in wanting to know whether you, like the signers of the Declaration of Independence, believe we are endowed by our CREATOR with certain unalienable rights?"

It wasn't exactly Phil's line, but it was as close as I was comfortable in going right then.

"As I have often said Stan, my faith is something deeply personal to me. I believe this country was founded in support of both freedom of religion and freedom from religion."

Music began to play which signaled we were headed into a commercial break. That cue told me I had only 30 seconds to wrap up. It was pointless to probe any further on a matter of substance. I was a total pussy and Phil was going to be pissed.

"Governor please come back, we thank you for appearing on *Morning Power*."

"I look forward to that Stan; I wish all of your listeners a good day."

The volume of the music increased and the segment ended. Again, Tobias and Susan both stood up and extended their hands, but I remained anchored to the console because I now needed to read a live spot for a home medical supply firm. Tobias shook my hand first and was headed toward the door. Then Susan reached for me and our eyes locked. With her not on microphone and me still wearing headphones, the best I could do was lip read.

"Nice to see you again, Stan."

Maybe it was, "Nice to meet you, Stan." Or was it, "We should do this again, Stan"?

I had no idea. And I would have paid a thousand dollars to not have to sit there, read a commercial about incontinence, and then do another hour of talk after that disaster. It only magnified the angst I felt about having to face Phil, at least over the phone. I had turned his idea of a searing cross-examination about religion into a softball which simply enabled Tobias to repeat one of his well-worn lines from previous campaigns. It was a missed opportunity, even though I knew the national media would still make a big deal out of Tobias reaffirming his belief that the Constitution protected those of faith, and those of no faith equally. He might have been sent by Floridians to Tallahassee without spelling out his personal faith, but no way was he getting to Washington without some affirmation of a belief in a divine being. The line that always won him plaudits on the Florida left simply wasn't going to be sufficient in a national campaign. But his more detailed reply on faith, whenever it came, would now make somebody else a star, not me.

The culmination of Phil's script was supposed to have been my asking: "Will you today, on this radio program, at least assure the American people that you are a person of a mainstream faith?" Maybe without Susan sitting there I'd have said it. But with those eyes only three feet from mine, I just couldn't.

When the program finally ended an hour later, I couldn't wait to get the fuck out of there so I sprinted for the door but was intercepted by Alex. She handed me the day's stack from the WRGT mail bin. There was the usual assortment of letters addressed in crayon, and a return address or two with long numbers in it meaning that it had come from the slammer. And, within the stack, two phone messages—one from Phil, which was unusual because he never called the station switchboard, although that was probably because he knew I wasn't anxious to pick up my iPhone—and another that stopped me in my tracks:

TO: Stan Powers
FROM: Wilma Blake
SUBJECT: Shooter's
And then a phone number with an "850" area code.

Poor old Willy Blake had passed away five years prior. There was only one person who would call using that as an alias. It had taken many years, but Susan Miller finally knew that I'd taken the advice she'd given me long ago. It was a phone message I had long wanted to receive, but suddenly one I was not anxious to return.

CHAPTER 6

There was only one person who was pleased with my Tobias interview: Debbie.

"I was really proud of you today, Stan," she said that night over dinner at Villa Gallace, a terrific Italian spot in Indian Rocks Beach about a 20-minute drive from my condo. I like to go there for a good, quiet meal. When I'd made the reservation a night or two earlier, I figured I'd be celebrating my being trumpeted on all the right-wing blogs for having stuck a knife in the political heart of the leading Democratic presidential candidate. So sure was I that this would be a big night for my ego that I'd deliberately planned to skip the anonymity of a Tuesday night booze-fest with Clay and Carl at Delrios in favor of a night on the town at a see-and-be-seen place with the lovely Ms. Cross. Now, as it turned out, I was dining with the only person I knew who was pleased with my weak-kneed performance.

"You let the man talk, Stan. You showed him some respect. And your listeners got to hear some dialogue for a change. I was really proud as I listened."

She'd never said that before. She meant her words as a compliment, but each assertion was its own indictment for a guy in my profession. In talk radio, letting the other side speak, showing respect and facilitating civil conversation = death. That'll get you overnights in Poughkeepsie.

"Debbie, nobody wants to hear that shit. Maybe on headphones tuned to NPR while doing Zumba, but not where I work."

"You're wrong. Maybe not the people who listen to your brand of talk, but people I know and those I work with are sick of the circus our political system has become. They want less of a shout fest. You're good at what you do. You have a skill set that transcends talk radio. Otherwise you would never have been a success as a DJ before you turned to talk. You're better than this. And you underestimate the power you have to make real change."

Normally I cut short her lectures or at least put up a fight. But I didn't tonight. I was too frustrated to push back while I drowned myself in a vat of Kettle One, and besides, she was making a certain amount of sense. Debbie was convinced that politicians were the tail of a dog that was talk radio and cable TV news. She thought that people like me had debased the level of dialogue in the country because those who got elected to office took their marching orders from pundits and personalities instead of the broad electorate, and that the whole process therefore became a self-fulfilling prophecy.

"The country's not run by lawyers, like me, Stan. It's run by people with microphones, like you."

I'd heard this pitch from her countless times before. And while I gorged on a calamari appetizer I settled in to hear it again.

"You guys spout opinion for entertainment value in order to get ratings. You succeed not by moving the masses, but by winning the support of a relatively small, but exceedingly loyal group of listeners or watchers who are ideologues in their political thinking. They are the ones who turn out religiously in primary elections where nobody else is paying close attention. They vote for fringe candidates who are often ultimately elected because we have so many hyper-partisan districts across the country where one party dominates. So when those candidates take office, they are beholden to the same talking heads who spread the talking points."

Pretty insightful for a military brat with no political experience of her own.

Debbie paused long enough to sip her chardonnay.

"You're supposed to end with 'I rest my case,' " I offered.

"No trier of fact could find otherwise."

As I looked at her across the table, I reflected that Debbie was the total package. She was smart. She was a looker. And she was fun to be with. I think the only reason that I hadn't worked harder at this relationship was that being with her forced me to take a hard look at my own choices and career path, which lately was not a pleasant task. Many nights I had wondered what she was doing with me. On an impulse I decided to ask.

"I know the real Stan, or at least I think I do. And I really like him. I believe he is a critical thinker who if he were himself and not behind a microphone, would never for a minute be a part of that conversation. The guy I know sees through the bullshit and could count on one hand the number of politicians that he thinks are worthy. Beyond the professional, I think he's good looking. I think he's engaging. I think he's funny as hell. And I am convinced that others would like him too if he ever gave them a real glimpse."

This third-person schtick was wearing thin with me even if I liked what she had to say. Kinda like when Bob Dole used to talk about "Bob Dole." I figured we were finally past the Tobias interview and what it said about me, when she blindsided me.

"So what's she like?"

"Who?" I replied lamely, knowing full well that she wanted the skinny on Susan Miller.

"His wife. Don't tell me you weren't sweet on having her in your studio, Stan, I know you too well."

"I didn't really have a chance to check her out. They were late and nothing was said between us that didn't air," which was about the only accurate thing I could have said without opening a can of worms.

My iPhone hummed throughout dinner as it had all afternoon but I didn't even look down. I knew it was Phil and there was no way I was prepared for his review. In fact, I waited until Thursday before I returned his emails, texts and old-fashioned phone calls. I knew he would be pissed about how I went easy on Tobias, and I probably would have waited even longer except that Jules called me and said that Steve Bernson had telephoned him because word had reached the suits at MML&J that I wasn't responding to "their consultant." Give me a fucking break. I had reliably utilized Phil's advice ever since I arrived in Tampa, and they'd made a boatload of money from *Morning Power*.

When we finally spoke, Phil was so worked up that he sounded like he was about to pass out and I could catch only every other word. It was an alliteration of P's. Those that I could discern sounded like:

". . . pussy . . . Powers . . . back in Pittsburgh. . . ."

I remained silent and after spewing for several minutes, he calmed down and demanded an explanation as to why I'd gone soft.

"Well, see Phil, I used to bang his wife and I've carried a torch for her ever since, and the minute she walked into the studio I lost my fucking mind."

Of course I didn't say that.

Instead I fed him some line about the dual distraction of Tobias' tardiness and the presence of the local network affiliate cameras taking me off my game. I don't think he bought it, but he let me off the hook and went from being adversarial to advisory.

"Lightning strikes only so many times, Powers," he said. "You are finally on the radar screen of the big three syndicators, but the way you treated Tobias doesn't fit any of their business models. Milquetoast doesn't cut it. Nuanced is for nobodies. They need to know you're going to be conservative, consistent, and compelling."

I thought of Debbie and suddenly wished that she was on the line with Phil and me. She'd be more of a match for him than I ever was. But the two had never met (even I had never met Phil!) nor spoken, and Debbie only knew the dribs and drabs I had told her about him.

I assured him that the interview was an

aberration, and knowing that he'd be monitoring me the following day, I went on the attack against Bob Tobias on Friday morning.

"Carl in Dunedin, welcome to *Morning Power*. Go ahead."

"Yeah, Stan, Tobias is a secularist without regard for the basis on which this country was founded."

The caller spit out the word s-e-c-u-l-a-r-i-s-t as if it were a loathsome disease. So I forced myself to buy in.

"Well, I agree with you. This country was founded on Judeo-Christian principles and it's right there in the Declaration of Independence, 'All men . . . are endowed by their CREATOR with certain inalienable Rights, and among these are Life, Liberty, and the pursuit of Happiness.' Now, when he was in this studio, he would not embrace that view of our history. And it makes you wonder what hymnal he's following."

"Stan, do you think he's an atheist?"

"Well, why else would he refuse to answer my questions?"

That had been Phil's latest recommendation ("openly question on air whether he is an atheist") and it worked. That afternoon, Drudge ran with a squib that said "Florida talker questions whether Tobias is an atheist" and linked to a piece of my audio commentary. Nobody at WRGT had supplied the mp3; only Alex gets access to our air checks, and there was no way she'd have distributed something like that without checking with me first, so I figured Phil had made it happen. I knew he had the ability to monitor all of his clients' broadcasts and pull air checks, so the idea of him sending it to Drudge wasn't farfetched.

The national reaction was instantaneous. By that night, I was doing a TV satellite interview with a blond whose name I can't recall and whose heavily lipsticked lips said "blow me." There was a monitor in the Tampa studio where I did the interview that allowed me to look at her while we spoke. It showed her seated at a desk made out of glass or clear plastic, lest anyone should be denied a good leg shot. And here she was questioning me on matters of faith and family values. Go figure.

It's funny how TV bookers work. An appearance on one cable news show is always a guarantee that other invitations will follow. It's like if Bloomingdales has it in the window, Saks has got to be selling it too. The most essential piece of furniture in the office of a TV booker—sorry, "segment producer"—is a power cord and bank of television screens on which he or she keeps tabs on the competition. So long as I did not completely shit the bed on one station, I was guaranteed a phone call from another. By the time the Friday night interview ended, I already had two texts inviting me to do others with cable competitors. The first was with Wolf Blitzer (a name that was a gift from the TV gods) and then with Chris Matthews. My pitch was the same all over.

"Look, Chris, I'm not saying the guy worships Lucifer. I'm just saying we have a right to know."

The cable stations ate it up. After all, this is what they're wired for, both the left and the right. No need to allow a little substance to get in the way of a good liberal-conservative argument. So long as the issue allows itself to be presented in black/white terms, cable television news and talk radio can sell it, however contrived. They might not reach a majority of people, but those they do reach will walk through fire for their right to engage in a pissing contest that they think is based on principle.

The more cable TV news I did, the more I began to think that it was even worse than talk radio in terms of its staged nature. Radio usually delivers one guy with an extreme point of view taking calls from likeminded listeners. On TV, you often get some horseshit debate that may as well have been staged by Central Casting with two actors reciting talking points. It reminded me of the Saturday morning wrestling I used to watch as a kid, when Vince McMahon really was a pencil-necked geek. There was a bad guy (usually with a spooky manager like the Grand Wizard of Wrestling or Captain Lou Albano) and a good guy. One was a black hat, the other a white hat, and you knew which was which. (If there was ever any doubt, the bad guy was the one who carried a "foreign object.") There was no in-between—and this is the way that talk radio and cable TV news are today.

The professional advantage for me in appearing on cable TV was being able to reach a lot more people in a shorter period of time, and hopefully building my platform. The personal advantage was that cable TV will get you laid. No joke. For some women, doing a TV guy is the ultimate aphrodisiac, even if he is just a lowly pundit. While I had been doing these sorts of TV hits at an increasing pace for a couple of years and had grown pretty comfortable, I still needed even more exposure according to Jules. He thought this was an important step in "building my brand" and getting my radio program picked up in markets across the country.

"Syndication requires three things," he had told me. "First, you need big numbers in your home market. You have that. Second, these stations have to believe they can sell your show to advertisers, and the way to prove that is to read any script they put in front of you whether the product is gold or penile enhancement."

I wished he were joking, but I'd already done

both of those things. In fact, he'd just referenced two of my biggest advertisers.

"But you also need edge, something that distinguishes you from every Rush wannabe, and that is where TV gives you a chance to shine. Use cable to build your identity, Stan."

I remember the first time I got a call from a cable TV booker inviting me to provide a political opinion on then newly elected governor Chris Christie. I was a bit clueless about how the medium worked and how best to use it to my advantage. But I learned two lessons that night. First, I initially thought I would have to go to New York to appear. Little did I know that there was a satellite TV facility in a high-rise office building just two blocks from the WRGT studio. Modern Video, the studio where I have appeared countless times since, has a hokey, fake backdrop of a beach scene that may or may not have been taken in the Tampa area. What I remember from that first night was being surprised that the show was live at 9 p.m. but on the backdrop behind me, the sun was shining. "Who are we shitting with that?" I wondered.

My second lesson was substantive. Or maybe I should say, lack of substance. A major blizzard had hit the Northeastern states. It was so bad that the NFL took the unprecedented step of postponing a playoff game scheduled between the Eagles and Vikings for two days, which then became good talk fodder when Pennsylvania's Governor Ed Rendell complained that we'd become a nation of "wussies." (He later got a book deal and a TV contract out of that one comment.) Although the storm was predicted, some cities and states were caught flat-footed. In a snowed-under New York City, Mayor Michael Bloomberg lost his cool with a challenging media. And in neighboring New Jersey, both Governor Chris Christie and his lieutenant governor (whose name I can't remember) were both out of state at the same time. Christie was in Disney World with his family, and his proximity to my market might be why I got the call. Well, as the plows were still moving, I made my first cable appearance that night in a segment discussing the reaction of public officials to the snow.

"What about Chris Christie being in sunny Florida while his constituents need the roads cleared and the power back on?" I was asked.

"Well, there is a practical consideration and a political consideration," I said. "The practical consideration is that snow removal is primarily a responsibility of local governments. That's why in New York, the focus is on Mayor Bloomberg, not Governor Patterson."

I was staring into a satellite camera more than 1,000 miles away from the cold when I finished my thought.

"But the political consideration is that the optics

are bad for Governor Christie who is one of the rising stars of the Republican Party, and you can rest assured that in some future campaign a photograph will surface of him riding Dumbo the Elephant and be used against him in a commercial."

Phil watched the segment. He was pissed.

"Well you fucked up your debut, Powers."

"How so?"

"Too much hair splitting. Too much of you trying to be the smartest guy in the room. And not enough edge. Just way too much inconsistency." And he was right, at least in the world of cable TV. It was a long time before I was invited back.

"You should have just said that Chris Christie is working his balls off trying to bail out New Jersey after the disaster that was that liberal cocksucker Jon Corzine, and people need to get off his back while he recharges his batteries with his kids. Stress that he is with his f-a-m-i-l-y," Phil wisely emphasized.

Now, years later, I was getting much more face time just as Governor Tobias was touring the country in support of his now-official presidential run. A few days after his appearance on my program, I watched him speak to a rally at a shuttered manufacturing plant in Reno ("this is what Republican tax cuts do for the working class") with Susan and their daughters at his side. The Tommy Bahama in his Florida closet had been replaced with Brooks Brothers. But my eyes were fixed on Susan, looking positively stunning in a pair of Christian Louboutin black boots, tight-ass jeans and a turtleneck that ran up to those classic Princess Grace facial features. Fuck Tobias. Maybe my callers were correct. They hadn't let up from the moment he walked out of the studio.

"Hello, Stan? You were too nice to that European socialist Tobias. And his wife is to the left of Nancy Pelosi. Why doesn't she stay home and raise those kids?" said one who was typical.

"Well, some would say all you need to know about his wife is that she kept her name," I responded lamely. "Thanks for the call."

The Florida primary finally arrived, and to no one's surprise Tobias hammered Vic Baron and his other five opponents. The surprise was what happened on the Republican side. To my secret delight, Margaret Haskel barely edged out Colorado Governor Wynne James. It seemed that the conservative vote was getting divided between Haskel, Redfield, Lewis and Figuera, and the fringe threesome of Redfield, Lewis and Figuera was taking enough of the vote from Haskel to give an opening to the one candidate in that field with whom I was personally comfortable—but of course who my core audience distrusted.

With Florida behind him, Tobias' attention now shifted to Super Tuesday states. As he made his initial whirlwind tour, I saw Susan constantly at his side. But then one day she was missing, or at least missing from the camera frame. And that's about when I got another message from Wilma Blake, whose first call I had never returned.

Most days after my program ended, Alex and I would recap what had gone well and what had tanked, plan the next day, and sift through listener email and (old school) letters. These days, Alex would also review with me requests she'd received for print interviews from newspapers across the country (it seemed that everybody wanted the inside election scoop on Florida) and finally, we'd review the miscellaneous telephone messages left at WRGT's main number. It sounds like a lot, but we'd run through this list in five minutes, sometimes with Rod sitting in our suite pretending to be going through his own email. Like who the fuck was emailing him? NAMBLA?

"Some lady named Wilma Blake called again," Alex told me. "She's left two or three messages, Stan, and says you and she are old friends and she is anxious to speak to you about a confidential matter."

Confidential matter. That's another thing. Rare was the phone message or email from a random listener that did *not* concern a self-proclaimed confidential matter.

"Sure, give me that number," I said, trying not to attract Rod's attention.

I had avoided her initial message, and by now I was convinced that Susan would have seen me talking about her husband on TV. I know how presidential campaigns work—they monitor all the media, especially during an announcement week, to see how it plays and how their candidate is being treated in the different outlets. I envisioned Susan sitting in a Radisson in Virginia Beach watching tape of her husband's announcement, immediately followed by talking heads, including me, raising issues like whether he is sufficiently Christian to be elected president. I'd waited years to reconnect with Susan Miller, but as I prepared to dial the telephone, I was no closer to any kind of a plan as to what I was seeking from the interaction and how I intended to get there.

Convincing myself that I would simply be a good listener, I got in my convertible but kept the roof up like it was one of my Phil sessions where I actually wanted to hear his advice. And then, just as soon as I'd cleared the underground lot and had given my customary nod to the lone fisherman, I dialed.

"Look at you now," was how she answered the phone.

"No 'hello, it's been a long time'?"

"It's not a social call, Stan. I think you know that."

"You always were about getting down to business, Susan. What can I do you for?"

"Listen, I'm calling you as an old friend. I think you misunderstand some things about Bob. I'd like the chance to set the record straight."

"Sure. Come on the program tomorrow. You can pick the time, although I'd recommend the 7:30 segment."

"I'm not interested in being on your program Stan, and Bob won't be coming on again either. But I am interested in meeting with you privately to clarify some history."

"A history lesson would be nice," I awkwardly responded.

Susan said she was headed to a hospital fundraiser in Sarasota the next night and that she could meet me afterwards.

"It'll have to be private, Stan. I don't want this to sound harsh, but it wouldn't help Bob if we were seen together, and I am counting on you to keep this confidential."

I wanted to tell her there was a keg freezer where I could usually count on a little privacy but instead I showed some uncharacteristic restraint.

"No problem, consider it off the record," I said.

And then reflexively, I said:

"I have the right spot. It's seedy but safe."

"Sounds like old times," she said with a laugh that bore distant recognition.

"It's called Delrios," I said, and started to give directions.

But Susan interrupted me. "I know where it is. I'll be there around 8ish. Sit in the back. Bye, Stan."

The line went dead.

I drove along with the phone to my ear for a few more seconds before putting it down in a cup holder. How did Susan Miller know Delrios? The place was a mystery to many of the year-round residents of Clearwater. What I did know was that Susan Miller, Florida's first lady, was now acquainted with a numbnuts named Stan Powers, a conservative talk radio host, presidential kingmaker, and supposed right-wing ideologue. For all she knew, the skinny barkeep she'd thrown some snatch at in a cold storage locker many years prior had had a transformative epiphany that lead him on a holier-than-thou path which now included disparaging her husband. She'd have no way of knowing it was all about entertainment in the name of growing my career and lining my pocket—or did she? If she had any doubt, I could let Debbie enlighten her.

I also wondered what history she was coming to explain? Ours? Or that which concerned her husband's faith? Personally I didn't give a shit as to which altar he knelt at, and ditto for her. Religion was not something that had ever come up back at Shooter's. Nor did we discuss anything else all that personal. She'd always kept things close to the vest. And what I knew of her personal life thereafter was what anyone could learn by Googling her and Tobias. Susan Miller had returned to FSU for her junior year and seemingly never looked back. According to Tobias' official bio, the two of them met during his senior year (her junior) when he was the household-name quarterback of the football team. After her graduation, she followed him to Tallahassee where he was serving in his first job—as an assemblyman. No ordinary political freshman, Bob Tobias already had more name recognition in the state of Florida that just about anyone shy of Dan Marino. Two terms in the state House and two terms in the state Senate later, and he was ready to be elected to the governor's mansion.

The moment I hung up the phone something else occurred to me. I'd reflexively said Delrios without realizing that tomorrow was a Tuesday. I'd just agreed to a clandestine meeting in my usual haunt on my normal drinking night. The cone of silence at Delrios was about to be tested.

CHAPTER 7

WRGT never did bring anyone else to town for the early shift, other than me. To this day I don't know if Steve Bernson really tried to negotiate a deal that fell through, or if he always planned on trying to make a go of it with me. Maybe he was following Phil Dean's advice. All I know is that my 30 days became three months, which before I knew it, had become a few years and my position as a talk host was secure.

Phil was vital to my success. Whenever I start thinking that I could have become a talk host without him, all I need to do is think back to my first two weeks on air. At the moment when the station actually flipped formats, Phil was finishing work on another station makeover, so for my first two weeks in morning drive, I was flying blind. What I knew about the format was limited to what I'd heard and usually turned off when listening to pre-set stations in rental cars. Given that it was a talk format, I naturally assumed that the goal was to make the telephones ring. The more rings the more callers, the more callers the more listeners, or at least that's what I thought.

Bernson was temporarily my day-to-day manager, and he'd instituted a system whereby the guy ending an air shift would spend five minutes with the guy taking over. It seemed to make sense. The idea was to try to hold the audience of the guy who was leaving for the guy who was taking the chair. When I was getting started in the mornings, it meant that my cross-over time was with the guy leaving after doing the overnights, a fellow named Frank Sellers, who worked the graveyard shift. I can still picture him wearing a Madras sport coat and argyle socks, dressed like he was headed to a sock hop or something instead of a talk studio when most people were sleeping. At age 67, Frank was a veteran talk show host, one of the last vestiges of the era where personality mattered, not ideology, as evidenced by the fact that he was an old liberal warhorse who idolized RFK. We both thought we were placeholders, and maybe that's why we bonded. In his case that was true. His liberalism didn't fit with the station's new direction and he knew his days were numbered, but he wanted the paycheck and the station needed someone to hold down the fort. Frank was old school. He didn't own a cell phone and couldn't tell the Internet from intercourse. He read newspapers that were printed on paper and required turning the pages, and to him a newscast was one that began at 6:30 p.m. on one of the "big three" networks.

Well, in the wee hours of a morning during my first week on the job, we did our standard crossover at the shift change per Bernson's instructions. On air, Frank would ask me what I intended to discuss that morning, and I'd mention a few headlines from the *St. Petersburg Times* or *Tampa Tribune*. Frank would play along and tell me that whatever I said sounded interesting when I am sure, in retrospect, it did not. Then the "on air" light would go dark, and he would amble out of the chair, gather up his newspaper clippings from the console and make room for me. One morning, while a commercial played and I was plugging in my headphones, he said something that I haven't forgotten.

"Just remember, kid, these three things if the phones are dead. First, you can always ask whether social security will be there when you need it. Second, say 'Don't tell me where I can walk my dog.' And if you really get stuck, ask, 'How come two parents can raise ten children, but ten children cannot take care of two parents?' "

All spoken like an overnight veteran, but I had no idea what the fuck he was talking about. I just smiled and got in position and started my program as the sun was coming up.

About an hour later, I looked at a computer screen that was intended to display all of the calls from people wanting to get on the air. Only the screen was blank. No one was calling. Whatever I was discussing was tanking, at least in terms of calls. In my mind I equated silent phones with no audience, and so I desperately took Frank's advice and launched into a story about having taken my schnauzer for a walk on the beach the day before.

"There I was on a late afternoon walk, minding my own business when an old bat came along and told me that dogs weren't permitted on public sands. She was in one of those 1950s bathing suits that were a combination of dress and one-piece, standing under an umbrella that was the size of a parachute."

Then I said that when she harassed me, I'd responded, "Don't tell me where I can walk my dog."

It wasn't even 7 a.m. in Tampa, but the telephone lines suddenly exploded. I had never had more than two of the twelve lines illuminated at once and I was so panicked at the reaction that I quickly Googled "schnauzer" so I at least knew what one looked like.

Half the people calling were dog lovers who told me that I went easy on the old bag.

"Stan, you should've told her to pound sand. Anyone who disrespects animals is hiding deeper secrets. These guys like Jeffrey Dahmer always start out abusing pets."

The other half *were* old bags!

"Staaaaannnnn. How dare you speak to a seasoned citizen like that? How would you like it if someone spoke to your mother that way?"

And so for about two weeks, until Phil Dean got into position, I adopted old Frank's philosophy, and yes, it made the phones ring. When I got tired of the dog routine, or the social security thing, or wondering why parents could raise kids who later could not care for parents, I learned a few tricks of my own, like pulling out the DEFCON1 of talk radio: guns, abortion and the Church. It hardly mattered what I said, just so long as I mentioned any of those three, the phone lines melted. And after ten days as a talk show host, I was convinced I'd already learned what I'd need to know to succeed. It was like shooting fish in a barrel. Turn on the mic, breath the word "contraception" and sit back and watch the time pass.

But all that ended the minute Phil Dean came aboard. He quickly disabused me of any idea that this was either good talk radio or anything that would ever get ratings. And he went on to prescribe a program schedule and formula that he told me would work.

"Rule No. 1, Powers—there is zero relationship between the number of callers and the number of listeners."

Years later the only criticism I have of that advice was in calling it "Rule No. 1." Over the years Phil has given me dozens of Rule No. 1's.

Phil had a detailed thought process as to the role of the caller. He was forever telling me that the callers were there to be used as "stage props" for whatever I was delivering and that they were never to be looked upon as content in and of themselves.

"Let me ask you something, Stan. When was the last time you yourself called a talk radio program?"

"Never."

"Exactly."

Phil's next item of business was to prescribe a program schedule and formula that he said would work. I was enticed by the prospect of success, intrigued by the mystery man from Taos, and dutifully followed all of his advice. My hours were brutal and I worked my balls off, but I was having some fun with the challenge of reinventing myself. My day would begin when the first of my two alarm clocks sounded at 3:30 a.m. Not that any one alarm clock has ever failed; I just refused to take chances. This too was something about which I'd received advice from Frank Sellers. He'd said, "Kid, every morning guy has a strategy to overcome getting up at a God-awful hour. Some guys nap. Some guys go to bed early. Some guys try to catch up on week-ends. Well, let me tell you, none of them work. The human body is not made to get up in the middle of the night."

About this he was right.

So in the morning, I followed one cardinal rule: getting my ass out of bed the minute the first alarm sounded. The worst thing I could do, I soon learned, was lay awake and second-guess my need to get up. Better to get moving instantly and stay on schedule. The way I did it, every second mattered. While it took me 45 minutes to drive home after a program, the early commute took literally half that time. Drunks and DJs were all you'd find on the highway at that early hour (and I know, having been both). After driving through a Stop-N-Go to pick up some coffee, I was sitting in my studio by 4:20 a.m., staring across a conference table at Alex, who always managed to beat me to work. A television was on in the background, showing a local early morning newscast that had begun at 4 a.m.

Following Phil's advice, I never stopped preparing for the next day's program. All day long I stayed current in the news, and whatever my mobile device of choice was at the time buzzed and hummed constantly with headline updates and news with a conservative analysis. I never went to bed without knowing the lead stories in the nightly cable news world. Phil told me to take my cue from Fox News, which I did.

And as he instructed, sometimes I would watch MSNBC just to know what to avoid. Of course, I never told him that the latter often made more sense to me than the former. But mostly, I thought they were both full of shit. When Obama was president, I never took him for a European socialist antichrist, and neither did I think he was a savior. He was not the Kenya-born Manchurian candidate conjured up by Sean Hannity, just like George W. Bush wasn't the stumblebum that Keith Olbermann (himself a pompous horse's ass) suggested in his exhaustive rants. Then, unless it was a night dedicated to grab-assing at Delrios, at about 9:30 p.m., right before turning in, I would send an email to Alex and offer my nightly suggestions for her show outline, which we would go over, face-to-face, the following morning before sunrise.

The program itself always followed a loose formula outlined by Phil. I often started the 5 a.m. hour with a soft story, sometimes pulled from the front page of the *Wall Street Journal*, below the fold with one of those pixilated photos. The *Journal* has a habit of printing terrific, slice-of-life kinda stuff in that spot, often having nothing to do with the world of finance. I remember one day they had a great piece analyzing the number of times college basketball players bounce the ball before they shoot foul shots in games in relation to successful attempts. (Four times seemed to bring the best success, 77 percent of them went in the hoop, as compared to say, 60 percent if you only dribbled once.) Or another day I pulled something from the *New York Times* about how only seven people in the company that owns Thomas' English Muffins knew how the muffins got their distinctive air pockets, and how when one of the seven left for a competitor, his departure touched off a case of alleged corporate skullduggery. Phil thought these kinds of stories were a nice way to ease into the day before I got to the red meat. In my head, while determining my content, I would picture my typical listeners as they awakened to *Morning Power*. The guys were usually fortysomething masters of the universe in the midst of their early morning workout, having just gotten laid, pumping some serious iron and getting ready to drive a 7-Series or S-Class to work. The women were invariably 25-year-old grad students with giant hooters, listening to me via clock radio while lying in 1,000 thread-count Egyptian cotton sheets and wearing red thongs. (For some reason, both of my stereotypes were always seriously underrepresented whenever we did remote broadcasts or live events that our listeners attended.)

After the soft stuff, I'd begin the process of running through the main headlines of the day, a combination of the local and national. For the entirety of the 6 a.m. hour, I would continue with the rundown of the news, offering some commentary with every headline. For a while, we called this hour "Headlines Redefined" which I liked. Sometimes I would look to Alex for a female perspective, in which case she would always oblige with a pithy, albeit predictable feminist view with which I would invariably disagree. These were the talk equivalent of whacky morning radio bits where the music staples were kazoos, horns and fart machines. For us, it was trashing liberals.

"Breaking news from the Middle East today where Secretary of State Hillary Clinton is brokering peace talks," I once said with a mock, Ted Baxter–like voice. "Madam Secretary was actually captured on film by paparazzi wearing a dress."

I looked at Alex who took my visual cue and recognized it as her invitation to jump in, in this case, defending the sartorial choice of the former first lady.

"That is so sexist, Stan. And you never once commented on something Condi Rice wore."

"Why would I? *'Dr.'* (with great emphasis added) Rice always comported herself as a lady while representing the affairs of the United States of America."

The telephone lines would light up, and I'd be off into an eight-minute segment on whether a pant suit was ever appropriate dress for our secretary of state as she engaged world leaders. Of course, my view was that anything this secretary of state was doing was wrong, in contrast to her predecessor, the aforementioned "Dr." Rice, to whom I would invariably give a pass.

Things changed at the stroke of 7 a.m., prime time for morning drive radio. Now I would take it up a notch and hit hard on the front-page items of the day. The lead political story commanded my attention and this was where I tried to pack a punch. In campaign season, it was always something political. National healthcare (bad), illegal immigration (worse), and the federal deficit (atrocious) had been my stock-in-trade for the last few years. I'd spell out an issue, cue Rod to run some sound bytes that corresponded to that news, then offer my take, and finally go to the phones.

"Ignore those blinking lines until they serve a purpose," Phil would constantly drum in my ear. Still, it was hard not to be pleased by the instant feedback.

"Remember, those callers are your props. Nobody gives a fuck what that guy says except that guy. If his old lady cared, he'd be telling her not you. But she doesn't give a shit. So you're the only outlet he has. The only reason you let him on *your* air is that he gives you fodder to say more."

Phil also timed my callers like they were running the 40 at an NFL combine. I swear he would sit on his ass in Taos with a stopwatch and shout whenever any caller was on the air for more than two minutes. No caller was ever worth two minutes of airtime according to him. At first I didn't see any harm in letting someone ramble as long as I thought they were interesting.

"Isn't it supposed to be a talk program?" I would sometimes counter.

"It is . . . and *you* are the one who is supposed to be talking."

Over time, I saw his point.

"Callers are there to give you something to play off of, to give you material to say something and appear smart, or acerbic. And let me tell you something else—nobody wants to hear callers who say 'Stan, you are so right about this.' Booooring."

In no time we were routinely flooded with callers regardless of the subject, and it took quite a skill set for Alex to juggle 12 ringing lines at once. Her job was to not only get some bare bones information about who was calling and why, but also to type that data on her computer, which in turn put it on a screen in front of me. At the same time she needed to ascertain whether the callers could put together sentences and were younger than Stonehenge. Nothing sucks more oxygen out of a program that an old-timer who dodders when you punch up his call.

Our focal point every morning was the 7:30 segment, during which I would often do interviews with hard news guests. Newsmakers, like elected officials, or nationally known politicians or pundits or authors of right-wing screeds would usually be heard then. Again, with a short call segment to follow.

"Welcome back to *Morning Power*, on the line, it is my privilege to be joined by former Governor Mike Huckabee. Huck, thanks for being here."

"You're welcome, Stan, and good morning to all in the I-4 corridor. . . ."

In the final hour, having already covered the hard news of the day, I tended to do more shits and giggles. You know, some pop culture, sound from *American Idol*, and the other water cooler stuff that gave the show balance. This was the *Seinfeld* part of the program as Phil liked to refer to it, and handling these subjects came more naturally to me than politics. If you asked me to describe some of my favorite radio that I have done in Tampa, I would not describe my interview with Governor Palin in 2008, or Senator McCain in that same cycle, or my Scott Brown and Marco Rubio interviews in 2010, or Romney in 2012. Not even the time that I broadcast from a Tea Party rally surrounded by 5,000 listeners. Instead I would probably tell you about my tutorial on how to beat a speeding ticket (immediately fess up, "Yes officer I know I was speeding and boy am I embarrassed," cause it catches them by such surprise that they will let you go), or the time that Alex was driving her 12-year-old niece from a birthday party with her young friends and accidentally popped in a CD with Estelle featuring Kanye West singing "American Boy" with some highly explicit lyrics.

We did a half-hour on the issue of whether she was then obligated to call each girl's mother and advise them of what their daughter had inadvertently heard in the car. The telephone lines melted. Alex later told me Rod had asked who Kanye West was.

When the program went dark, I'd often record some post-show interviews, meet an advertiser or two and then begin planning the following day. Then I'd head home and try to catch a nap. All day long I'd stay in touch with Alex by email, culminating at night in my final missive of the day which contained my thoughts about what the nighttime cable shows had covered. I'd say that on a typical day, about 50 percent of the next program was set by the time I'd go to sleep, and the other 50 percent was determined before sunrise based on the morning newspapers, blogs and talking points from affinity groups like the RNC, NRA, and Human Events. Each of them had me on an email alert list, and not a day went by when they weren't alerting me to something sneaky that the Democrats were up to.

It took me about a year to get my mental grasp of the issues and feel comfortable spouting what Phil was telling me to say about politics. *Morning Power* didn't hit its stride in time for the 2008 presidential election, but things really clicked in the fall of 2010, a watershed election featuring the Tea Party which provided me with radio gold on a daily basis. Nearly two years into the Obama Administration, the "hope" hype had worn thin with listeners, most of whom never liked him to begin with. The economy sucked. Spending seemed out of control. The deficit was growing. And unemployment was nearly 10 percent. Our listeners were super pissed, and licking their chops for the chance to throw out of office the man many of them figured was born in Kenya and secretly a practicing Muslim. After all, that's what I'd told them. But at the time, we thought that would have to wait two years. So instead our collective sights were set on Nancy Pelosi, Harry Reid and anyone who had ever been in their company. The voter angst spawned the Tea Party movement, and I was there from the start. We all were—those of us taking our cues from Phil. It often made me wonder whether the whole thing was his creation.

Around that time, Phil came up with this ingenious idea for me to do a slew of personal appearances at businesses that promised to fly the Gadsden flag, the distinctive historical marker with a rattlesnake against a yellow background with the words "Don't Tread on Me". This publicity campaign was a huge hit. And WRGT's head of sales, Don Fortini was ringing the register every time I would venture out. For a payment to the station that was initially just $500, I'd show up in the afternoon, having mentioned the visit on *Morning Power*, and standing next to the owner of the business, I'd hoist the flag. At first, tens of listeners would show up to watch me hoist a flag and leave with one of their own with WRGT emblazoned across the bottom. Then the crowds started building, and the WRGT price for advertisers kept rising. Next it was $750, then $1,000. Eventually it would grow to $5,000, not chump change for a mid-sized market, especially when we were doing these daily. One day outside a gun show, we crossed the 1,000-attendee threshold. And by the time the election rolled around, I was routinely drawing crowds in the few thousands. These Gadsden flags were everywhere around Tampa Bay, and the beauty of the effort was that people gave the station, and my program in particular, credit for any yellow flag they saw, even if the flag's owner had never heard the show.

It wasn't long before the local network affiliates took note. Every time we did a hoisting, they were there with a camera. Eventually their film footage of thousands of Floridians demanding relief from the federal government made its way to nightly national newscasts, and the cable stations. And more times than I could count, I was asked for comment. The whole thing got a bit scary. I'd MC these rallies where crowds got worked into a frenzy with their opposition to the White House. The mere mention by me of words like "socialism" and "Obamacare" would rile the troops. Although they didn't run the same flag campaign, it was the same frenzy being created by Phil's guys across the country.

"We need to take back our country," I'd rail outdoors, never explaining exactly from whom or what I was talking about. It didn't matter.

"Maybe our president needs a history lesson. There is precedent for how the citizens of this country will act when confronted with a detached government which tramples on our God-given freedoms" was one of my standards from the flag events. The crowd would roar.

And people went crazy. Some crossed the line and said some nasty shit about the president while cloaking themselves in a misunderstanding of the Founding Fathers. Because I knew that I was partly responsible for inspiring them, I felt publicly obligated to defend their behavior, which only caused my stomach to turn. Good thing none of them was peering over my shoulder after I closed the curtain and cast my own ballot.

Not that I was thrilled with two years of Obama's change, if what it meant was that one out of ten Americans would remain unemployed and that entitlement spending wouldn't be reigned in. One thing I meant when I said it was that government spending was way out of control.

But what I firmly believed and didn't say was that eight years of George W. Bush's spending, including an unfunded drug mandate, with Republican concurrence, and the initiation of two wars without end were what put us in the economic crapper. That, and all those pinstriped thieves on Wall Street who took advantage of deregulation and caused the bottom to fall out of the banking business while continuing to pay themselves record bonuses. Yes, Obama inherited a shitstorm. But I didn't dare express that view, especially as the passion from the public outbursts continued to drive my ratings through the roof.

The most amazing part was that a guy like me, admittedly a quick study but still with a very limited understanding of government, could so quickly be taken seriously as a political commentator. Somehow the possession of a microphone in this country confers Ph.D.-like powers on its wielder, regardless of the subject. (What exactly did four years of high school in Ft. Myers, pouring beers at Shooter's and eventually spinning vinyl in Pittsburgh teach me about global warming? Thank Christ no one ever asked.) Think about the big names in the business and go online and check out their backgrounds. You're not going to find a depth of education and experience in the subject area for which they are now known. Instead, you're going to find individuals who didn't vote, did serious drugs, and worked construction. Don't get me wrong, I'm not making a holier-than-thou pitch. I'm just saying the minute you have a microphone in front of you, a portion of the public believes you to be eminently qualified to offer expertise on anything, and that's a scary thought. For my program, I had lots of help. Phil initially schooled me daily, and then at a reduced schedule of several times a week in the early months. Alex would email to him our show outlines in advance and he'd weigh in on what issues to drive, and which to avoid. His advice was consistently about consistency.

"Read the Huffington Post and Salon.com only so you know what *never* to say," he'd caution.

And he was forever drawing comparisons to my prior work as a DJ.

"Your job hasn't changed," I remember him telling me one day. "Just keep playing what they want to hear."

CHAPTER 8

My iPhone rang the moment I walked in my condo. I looked down, relieved to see that it was Carl and not Phil. The moment I said "hello" it hit me that I'd have to explain why I couldn't hang out with him and Clay tonight, even though I was hoping to keep a low profile at the same bar with an important guest. The call was awkward.

"What do you mean you're not coming to Delrios?"

"Well, actually I might be there, but I have some radio horseshit to deal with."

Weak. Clay and Carl knew I valued Delrios for the exact opposite reason. Because it was an oasis where I did not have deal to with any radio horseshit.

"Oh."

Pause.

"Everything okay?" Carl asked. "This will be the second time in a few weeks that you've ditched us."

"Yeah, it's some work-related shit about the election," I said, trying desperately to make it all sound uninteresting, and probably failing. But good guy that he is, Carl let me off the hook.

The usual drill was for Carl, Clay and me to meet sometime around 8 o'clock. That was when Susan was due to arrive, so tonight, I made sure to get there by 7:30 so as to increase my odds of grabbing a booth way in the back, which is where she told me to be. By 7:35, I was secure in a fairly private spot, clutching the first of many Buds and staring at an empty shot glass. I had my back to the rear wall with a clear view of the front door. The place was three-quarters full, which was typical for a Tuesday night because of the drink specials. And like clockwork, at the stroke of 8, the door opened and in walked my usual drinking buddies. They saddled up to the bar about 50 feet from me, which meant they had a clear view of the door and sightlines all the way to the men's room, near where I sat. There were plenty of people standing and drinking, so the view wasn't unobstructed, but it made me nervous just the same. I had no idea how'd I'd explain my guest if they spotted me and dropped by the table.

By 8:15, nothing had changed. But when my watch said 8:17, the door opened and in walked a woman who was trying desperately to look nondescript without success. She was wearing jeans and a baseball cap pulled down to her ears, with her dirty blond hair in a ponytail. She paused inside the door, presumably to let her eyes adjust to the dim lighting and then walked toward me with a sense of purpose pretending not to notice the eyes that looked up from the bar. My eyes immediately went to Clay and Carl. Lucky for me they were busy talking to two women I didn't recognize. Susan Miller had been all over the news but always in much different attire. The only person who I detected doing a double take was the bartender, Ralph, who never missed a trick. He looked at her, then looked at me, and then quickly averted his gaze like he'd seen something he wasn't supposed to have. Maybe I was reading into it. Maybe not. Either way, that was going to cost me an extra C-note at Christmas.

I watched Susan draw near with her fitted t-shirt and designer jeans tightly hugging her chest and thighs, and tried to act nonplussed as she slid into the wooden banquet. Holy shit it wasn't easy. Especially when the intoxicating green eyes I remembered so well settled in less than 24 inches from mine. Very lightly made up. Jesus, she was still beautiful.

I told her that I'd had a head start and she obliged by ordering a chardonnay. I couldn't help but ask if she'd had trouble finding the place, again wondering why she'd been so familiar with the neighborhood.

"Nope, not at all," was all she said.

I pushed.

"You've been here before?" I asked incredulously.

"Stan, I've been all over Florida," she laughed. "Do you know how many events I attend?"

Oh come on, I thought. There was no way she'd ever done a political event in this dive. If I'd offered to meet her at the Pinellas County Court House, a few blocks over, and she said she knew the place, that'd be understandable. If I'd said we'll grab a drink at Bob Heilman's Beachcomber, and she'd responded, "Oh yeah, over on Mandalay," I'd get it. There were plenty of iconic spots with which a Florida first lady would be familiar. But for her to say she knew Delrios, a place notable only for its cross section of bikers, hookers, and professionals looking to get lost, that was significant. In fact, the only thing noteworthy in this neighborhood was the Church of Scientology.

And then it hit me. That proximity could explain a lot. And maybe the proof had been staring me right in the face.

The item had come to me like so many other tidbits of information on which I had traded. Listeners were always handing me stuff when I would appear at events. All sorts of chatchkas: political buttons, bumper stickers, looooong type-written letters mostly about their legal plights, books they hoped I would read (both the published and unpublished), t-shirts advertising bars and restaurants, and lots of business cards were the norm. Same as the mail that came to the studio. In the mail, I'd also receive many birthday and Christmas cards from total strangers, a nice gesture from some who listened to *Morning Power* and felt a proprietary interest in the program and me. Sometimes nice, hand-written notes would arrive thanking me for particular radio segments. And there was always a steady stream of postcards with simple messages like "You are a jerkoff" or "I will always remember your name." Additionally, people were always mailing or handing me conspiracy stuff. There was always a tendency to just shit-can it all, but much like sorting through Phil's advice, it was important to pay attention to all of it, lest I miss a nugget of information worthy of discussion on air. After all, I need to fill 20 hours of content per week, so I always need to be on the lookout for new material.

So after every live appearance or mail inspection, I'd do the sifting in a hurry and then find some hand sanitizer. The craziest stuff I'd give to Alex and she'd pin it on a bulletin board in our WRGT studio office. That bulletin board now takes up an entire wall, and on it, you'll find some insane stuff. I never mention this on air because if I told people they could end up on my wall just by mailing nutty things I'd probably need a storage locker.

But a few years ago, I'd read and saved something that was stuck in my hand by someone at whom I never got a clear look. It was at a WRGT Gadsden flag rally in Pinellas Park. As was often the case, after I spoke, I posed for a few pictures with listeners and signed some flags. And before I knew it, I found that I'd accumulated a stack of nicknacks given to me by attendees. Anxious for a quick exit, I tossed the stuff in my car and forgot about it until I arrived home. There, I scooped it all up and headed into my condo where I figured I would toss most, if not all of it, right down the garbage chute.

When I got inside, I saw that the stack contained a nondescript, white, No. 10 envelope with no return address. My name was emblazoned on it in block style *handwriting*. Strangely, *typed,* it then said "PERSONAL AND CONFIDENTIAL." I figured it was a crank. Make up your fucking mind. Who writes *and* types? If you'd have asked me before I opened it, I would have guessed that it was another of Obama's Kenyan birth certificates, or maybe an image of him "refusing" to salute the flag. Once, I even received what was supposedly Obama's transcript from his brief time at Occidental College, where he had excelled in a course on "black liberation theology" overlooking, of course, that no such course had ever been offered. All fake. But like

I said, every now and again I'd be handed something of value in such missives. Like the time I got a state senator's DUI paperwork, or when somebody handed me a vintage ticket stub to Woodstock! And besides, even the stuff from crackpots was usually good for a few shits and giggles, which I'd either show to Rod Chinkles acting as if we were co-conspirators, or to Alex just to get a rise out of her, before it'd get pinned up.

But this particular item purported to be the notes from an "audit" of a member of the Church of Scientology. I'm not talking IRS audit. I mean a Scientology audit, as in the sort that members of the church routinely undergo that is akin to another church's confessional—only in Scientology the person being audited isn't inside a booth speaking to a priest through a screen. Instead, the person is holding two cans connected to a lie-detector type of device called an E-meter.

The document had a date, time and location, but the name of the person who had been audited was blacked out. In paragraph form, it was a summation, not a transcript of what they'd said— namely that they feared a fellow Sea Org member was married to a "Potential Trouble Source." That's Scientology speak for a possible turncoat. The auditee was concerned that this PTS, whoever she was, would seek to convert her husband away from Scientology, because she was worried that her husband's affiliation with the church would "jeopardize his political career." Neither the politician nor his PTS wife were named.

I remember that when I first saw the document, I had no idea what I was looking at. I had never heard of audits, E-meters and potential trouble sources. But Alex was in the loop. Her roommate had first come to Clearwater as a member of Sea Org, the most loyal of Scientology followers, but had left the church because she found it to be intolerant of her lifestyle. Alex deciphered what I'd been handed at the event. We thought it was sufficiently whacky to make the bulletin board, where it had remained to this day.

But now, sitting across from Susan, a light bulb went off in my head. Suddenly I desperately wanted to get to the studio and pull that crackpot piece of paper down off the wall and examine it. Could it be? If the reference was to Tobias, it would sure explain a lot about his reluctance to toe the line on religion. But then again, it seemed farfetched. Too farfetched. Why would I be in possession of such information without a whiff of confirmation elsewhere? Rumors are a dime a dozen online and while there was plenty of speculation that Tobias was not a man of faith, I'd never heard anyone even hint that he worshipped at the altar of Tom Cruise and John Travolta.

"To Willy," I said, when her wine arrived.

Susan didn't respond, nor did she take a healthy sip. In fact, while I was always game for a refill, she nursed one drink the entire time we were together. Her lack of libations was a quick sign that while I was hoping to close a few old loops, the woman in front of me was all about the future. But at least her silence didn't last. And what unfolded was more substantive conversation in 60 minutes than we'd had in our 60 days as fuck buddies.

"I never figured you for a Tea Party guy," she told me.

I quickly debated whether or not to explain to her the difference between Stan Powers and Stanislaw Pawlowski. I passed. For now. She didn't wait for an answer anyway.

"I'm sure you have your reasons, but the nation's fucked up right now, Stan, and as you well know, the outcome of this election is going to be settled right around here."

Her casual dropping of the f-bomb gave me instant wood.

She told me she'd become aware of my new persona in 2010 when I was getting all the visibility with the Gadsden flag events sponsored by WRGT. That mystery was now solved.

"Quite a change from getting 'Stanned in Pittsburgh,' " she said with a wry smile.

Part of me loved that she'd either been following my career or had recently looked into it, but I wasn't sure what to make of that comment. Maybe she did have the whole thing figured out. Or perhaps that statement was a bit of a threat, I didn't know. But I stayed in character, assuming that she figured that she was in the company of a true believer, a conservative ideologue, who must have had some epiphany in life after getting high and getting laid in redneck bars. Besides, I was too embarrassed to say otherwise.

Anyway, this was not a night for nostalgia. In fact, every time I tried to steer the conversation in a personal direction, she resisted. She was all business. All campaign business, that is. She rattled off the upcoming caucus and primary dates like they were family birthdays.

"Winning Florida was big, but not a big surprise. The next 30 days will be key. Vic Baron is getting lots of support in Nevada but we will take Colorado. A state that votes for Wynne James as its governor can live with Bob Tobias."

"James is impressive," I offered in an effort to suggest that I was no crackpot.

"Impressive? He's the one Republican no Democrat can defeat." Then she continued with her assessment of the field against her husband. "Vic Baron is a very successful governor, but his slick, trial-lawyer image is just too smooth to have broad appeal outside New York.

"Evers is going nowhere, and I think we have

a real shot in Pennsylvania—our polling shows that Coleman Foley is winning *only* his congressional district. Nice guy, but zero nationwide appeal. Same with Roy Yih in California. No one in Congress has even heard of the guy.

"Bill Brusso is a blowhard; there's a reason that despite his $5 million in contributions to the party he was appointed to Luxembourg and not the Court at St. James.

"And while Laura Wrigley could take her home state, she could never win outside of Vermont.

"So you see, Stan, this thing has really broken our way. It's a crowded field, but not a strong one. Apart from Bob."

She ran through the recent polling data like a pro, and when she finally shut up long enough to take a meager sip of her drink, she revealed a supreme confidence in her husband's ability to get the Democratic nod and that the campaign was already looking toward a general election.

"November is far more tricky," she confided.

She then proceeded to give me a tutorial on the numerology of presidential politics that would have made Tim Russert proud. She spelled out calculus after calculus by which Bob Tobias could receive the requisite 270 electoral votes, assuming he was the Democratic nominee. In one scenario, Tobias capitalized on his relationships with Cuban Americans and turned it into a

Hispanic juggernaut that enabled him to capture the Southwest: Colorado, New Mexico and Nevada. In another scenario, he was the Robert E. Lee of the cycle. In other words, it was all about the South, or more specifically, what the pundits called the New, or Upper South: North Carolina and Virginia. Still another scenario had Tobias winning the Midwest, including Indiana and Ohio. By the time she finished spouting off states and electoral votes my head was spinning. But in every scenario she offered, the critical mass was Florida. And to win Florida, she knew they had to win the I-4 corridor. And to win the I-4 corridor, they needed to win—or at least neutralize—me.

After playing a hot, female version of David Axelrod or James Carville, Susan shifted gears and became a policy wonk. She launched into a diatribe about Keynesian economics and why austerity wasn't working for the Europeans before trashing the Republican weaknesses when it came to de-fanging Iran. She spoke with such specificity that I just sat there, drowning in shots of Jack, and not wanting to reveal the superficiality of my views.

"You can tune in tomorrow if you want to hear what I have to say about that," I mumbled a time or two like an idiot.

Susan also confided her husband's worst fear: that if and when he'd eventually disposed of

Vic Baron, he'd have to deal with Molly Hatchet.

"She'd play well down here, Stan. Your hardcore types love her. And those good looks will go a long way toward masking her far-right positions."

Even as she spoke about Margaret Haskel's attractiveness, I couldn't help sizing up Susan's features. Still flawless skin. High cheekbones intact. A perfect nose. And the eyes. The years had been kind to Susan Miller. All of her political banter was wasted on me, because I was more interested in erection than election strategy. Like a sophomore in high school, I sat planning my next move. A hand on her knee under the table? A touch on her hand as it cupped her drink? What the hell—why not a flat-out suggestion of a "freezer run" for old time's sake? I'd had years to prepare for this moment but sadly, no plan.

"Of course, the candidate we'd struggle the most with is the one they're working so hard to bury. Wynne James is a friend of Bob's. They met at some gubernatorial retreat and really hit it off. We just cannot understand why the Republicans cannibalize the guy at every opportunity. How do they not see that he is the best shot they have?"

On this we agreed but I wasn't about to tell her so.

"You think Wynne James is the Mike Castle of this race?"

"Exactly, Stan. Mike Castle would be in the Senate today if he hadn't lost a primary in the midst of all that Tea Party craziness stirred up by your brethren."

Mike Castle was a moderate governor and congressman from Delaware. A couple of cycles ago, he had been opposed in a primary by an opponent with a checkered financial past who couldn't hold a candle to his qualifications. The most attention she'd gotten previously was by telling Bill Maher she'd once dabbled in witchcraft. But in this campaign, she'd kept her broom in the closet, spouted off all the Tea Party bullshit and upset Castle when virtually no one showed up to vote in the primary. The few who did were fringe-worthy and they managed to retire a pretty good public servant in the process. It was the first of a string of similar defeats of Republican candidates who could have won general elections, but had not survived the primaries. Wynne James was shaping up to be this type of a candidate on a national level.

"He could have a shot if the other four split the conservative vote."

"I doubt it Stan, there is nothing left in your party *but* the conservative vote."

She had a good point. I went back to undressing her with my eyes and trying to plot my next move. While I dithered, Susan checked her phone, noted the time, and said she had to get going.

"Good to see you, Stan. I'm very happy for your success." She smiled. "And we both know who told you your future was behind the microphone."

I smiled back, but I was baffled. There was no ask. No "Lay off, Stan," or "Trash Margaret Haskel." Nothing requested.

She stood up to leave. I looked at her from head to toe one more time. And like a clumsy bastard, I half rose from my seat, just as I'd done in the studio a few weeks prior when she visited with her husband. But I still didn't get it quite right.

I watched her walk past the bar. With some kind of sixth sense, Ralph looked up and met her gaze as he was pouring a draft. Clay and Carl paid her no mind. And then she vanished. Susan Miller was gone.

I sat there for a few minutes wondering, "What the fuck just happened?" Then I joined the boys for another round.

CHAPTER 9

"That loony bitch from Texas wants to come back on, this time in studio."

This was how Alex greeted me the next morning, before explaining that she'd been contacted by Margaret Haskel's advance staff. She would never speak that way in front of anyone else, especially not Rod unless she deliberately wanted to annoy him. But privately, she and I were way beyond trying to uphold some kind of façade.

The second she left our office to get coffee, I moved swiftly toward the bulletin board and spied the item I was looking for. It was pinned between a photograph of Obama with a hammer and sickle emblazoned on it and a photograph of Hillary Clinton in the form of a Wanted poster with a purported connection to the death of Vince Foster. I removed the tacks holding it in place and slipped it into my satchel.

That Margaret Haskel wanted to come in studio was no surprise. Colonel Figuera had taken Iowa, but Haskel had won New Hampshire.

The only real upset of the season thus far had been in South Carolina where Wynne James came out on top. Still, Margaret Haskel had been dismissive of the loss.

"What do you expect?" she'd said. "Hilton Head is the last outpost of country club Republicans."

She'd gone on to win Florida, and even though James was a close second in that race, the conventional thinking was that he'd hurt himself in a recent debate when he'd refused to commit to never raising taxes.

"The only everlasting pledge I've made is to my wife," he said. "How can I possibly anticipate what financial situation I might one day encounter and tie my hands as to how I'd handle it?"

Too nuanced, as Phil might say. That his comment made perfect sense to me and probably to a whole lot of other people was beside the point.

It was still Haskel's race to lose. That she could split the very conservative vote with Figuera, Redfield and Lewis—and still not be trailing James—was a testament to the exodus of moderates from the GOP. She was a guaranteed daily headline on the stump just as she'd been in Austin, and had a firm grasp on conservative women in Middle America. Those women wanted to be her, and conservative guys wanted to do her. She was both blunt-spoken and hot, a more cerebral Sarah Palin, and therefore a serious candidate. I got the impression she was deliberately dumbing it down to appeal to the base.

Although we'd done several phoners in the past, she'd never actually been in my studio, and her sudden desire to pay me a visit was yet another sign of my growing stature, or at least the importance of the territory I reached. No doubt her staff had taken note of both the Baron and Tobias interviews, not to mention the time I'd afforded her Republican opponents. On air, I'd been an admirer. Even when she'd made gaffes, like when she interchanged the word "impotent" with "important," I somehow found a way to give her support.

"Who hasn't?" I'd offered weakly.

Professionally speaking, I had no choice but to have her on. WRGT's P1s absolutely loved the governor who'd never met a government program she wasn't willing to cut, and with the economy in the crapper and people demanding fiscal accountability, she was in the right place at the right time. Hell, she made Mitch Daniels of Indiana seem like a big spender back when he'd been governor of the Hoosier state. She was, as a candidate, what Phil desired in a talk show host —a down-the-line conservative, with no exceptions. In fact, if she were not already employed, she'd have made a great talk show host because only phony politicians and fake media personalities like me portray everything in such black-and-white terms. Both groups get rewarded for simplicity and lack of independent thought.

It's true what Debbie said: Talk radio ratings are based on the unwavering allegiance of a small but committed group of conservative listeners who are drilled to see things entirely in black-and-white terms. The libs are the same with their cable television station of choice. Those Republican listeners turn out in primaries and nominate candidates like Governor Haskel, and it's the same on the other side of the aisle. Passion drives the primary voters, and who holds the most passion? The most conservative or the most liberal candidates, of course. So even though Independents are the fastest growing segment of the electorate, they often don't get a say until the general election when they are forced to vote for the lesser of two evils.

Just about everyone I meet in the real world outside the studio, whether I'm having a couple of beers in Ybor City, or shopping at Publix, or playing a game of pick-up at the beach, says that the guys on the right and left are fucking us equally. They don't want to be associated with either of them, and if they are even registered to vote, more and more it's as Independents.

"Maybe you should go back to bartending, Pawlowski," Phil once told me with derision when I voiced my skepticism about the parties.

Anytime he used my real last name, I knew I was in the shithouse.

But he had to know that what he was suggesting I say was completely illogical. Before I came to Tampa, I wasn't even a registered voter, and would never have even considered giving a political contribution. I had no idea what separated a liberal from a conservative, or what united the views of those who called themselves either. But Phil had directed me to web sites that put the issues of the day in a form that was easy for me to understand and parrot.

For me, there was nothing complicated about being a human megaphone on individual issues. All I had to do was memorize a series of rote responses:

Same-sex marriage? "Adam and Eve not Adam and Steve."

Guns? "If they were outlawed only outlaws would have them."

Global warming? "The biggest hoax perpetrated upon the American people."

And so on.

"If you are ever stuck for content, go online and rattle off whatever Bill O'Reilly's Talking Points Memo is peddling. And if you have more time to fill, log onto Salon.com or Daily Kos and take the opposite view," was another Phil-ism I followed.

The hardest part for me had been wrapping my

head around what supposedly united conservatives or connected liberals, because frankly, much of the time I could not see the linkage between the different issues. Sure, there is some symmetry to party platforms, but there is also a complete disconnect between certain Republican and Democratic tenets. Say you believe in the power of private enterprise. Chances are you are also going to stand for lower taxes and fewer government programs. Ok, I get that. And at the other end of the spectrum, if you believe in the necessity of creating a safety net for the disadvantaged, that will translate into support for things like unemployment benefits. Or welfare. Maybe universal healthcare. That makes sense. But why did it necessarily follow that if you were pro-choice, you also thought the Iraq war was a mistake? And that if you supported the death penalty, you probably hated trial lawyers? What does opposition to abortion have to do with whether we waterboard Mohammad? Where was the philosophical or intellectual connection between these issues? Beats the shit out of me. But that's the way our political discourse has evolved. Certain positions are associated with others solely because over time, they have come to be known as conservative or liberal. Independent thinking is discouraged. It was all or nothing under one label or the other, and it drove me nuts.

Of course, if my radio listeners even heard me ask these questions they'd think I was a closeted left-wing pinko, which wasn't the case. Because I did genuinely hold some conservative views. Now that I was making a decent six figures, I *didn't* want to hand it all over to Uncle Sam. I truly believed that our interrogators should stop at nothing to save American lives if some al Qaeda asshole had information we needed. And I thought that our borders were porous. But some of my thinking would definitely be classified as liberal. Personally, I don't give a shit if two guys hook up, any more than I want them involved in my bedroom. I'm also for legalizing pot and prostitution, and I really don't care what a couple of scientists do in a petri dish—in my definition, that's not life. I'm Stanislaw Pawlowksi and I approve this message!

But Stan Powers would disagree. And right now, Stan Powers was enabling Stanislaw Pawlowski to have a view of the Gulf from his high-rise apartment, wear custom-made sport coats, drive a new model convertible and have his iPhone tab paid for by mobile-phone advertisers.

"I'm not really a wingnut, I just play one on radio," was the way I always explained this dual existence to Debbie, especially when I was negotiating to see her naked.

"The real you would be just as entertaining," she'd say.

But I doubted it.

And it was the same with the politicians. What gets a member of Congress elected in a hyper-partisan district is offering a consistently conservative or liberal, if sometimes illogical platform. Those views that served me well while entertaining similarly benefited someone like Margaret Haskel when trying to reach voters because they engendered loyalty from my listeners and her constituents. Just like her nighttime raids with the self-described Minute-men who patrolled the Texas/Mexican border, or the changes she'd made to Texas law to more easily enable parental takeover of public schools, or the YouTube video recorded at a backyard picnic of her saying "Yes, Jugdish, I believe in protecting our borders." Liberals were repulsed. But her fundraising skyrocketed.

Although Margaret Haskel was in her late 40s, attractive and successful—like Susan Miller—that is where the commonality ended. Texas's heavily styled governor flaunted her femininity alongside her conservative credentials, and derived great pleasure from titillating her more manly constituents. In a bygone era, she would have earned the moniker of "brick shithouse" with a personality to match the looks. How else to explain the interview she'd given a few years prior in *Texas Monthly* when she was being recognized as the first female Speaker of the state House? The interview was printed as a direct question and answer, without analysis. The questions were pretty standard stuff. But one of the answers was out of the box.

"Madam Speaker, who among famous Texas females do you most admire?"

"Well of course I have the highest regard for my friend Laura Bush. Ann Richards was from a different party but I acknowledge her independence and achievement. And although she was before my time, what I know of Lady Bird Johnson makes me hold her in the highest regard. But judging by the way she ran her house, I'd also have to put Jerry Hall high up on the list, too."

That answer must have gone over the head of the candy-ass who was writing the article, because there was no follow-up. Instead, came another inane question. Something like:

"And who would you say you most admire from the world of Texas sports?"

It only took about two seconds after the magazine hit mailboxes for Democrats to remind voters of what the former wife of Mick Jagger had once said:

"My mother said it was simple to keep a man. You must be a maid in the living room, a cook in the kitchen and a whore in the bedroom. I said I'd hire the other two and take care of the bedroom bit."

But the liberals overplayed their hand when they dug up the quote. The conservatives weren't offended by her, they loved it—both the men and women. She was a more intelligent Michele Bachmann. And momentarily caught off balance were these self-described progressives, who now found themselves at odds with a sexually liberated . . . conservative!

Margaret Haskel was the hottest commodity in the GOP and it was to my benefit that she wanted to be in the chair where just weeks prior I'd questioned Bob Tobias.

Still, when she arrived in the studio a few days later, she was not what I'd anticipated. Appearance-wise, she was as advertised. Pretty. Well put together. Properly made up in a California sorta way. Big hooters. Tiny waist. A 45-year-old MILF.

"I'm Molly Hatchet," she'd said, actually introducing herself to me using her nickname, as she extended her hand. I shook it with not just a little sense of pride. I was almost getting used to this. Here I was again, hosting a presidential candidate in my Tampa studio with a horde of media in the house. I saw Rod Chinkles ask her for an autograph on his side of the glass, and took note that Alex did not so much as raise her head.

For the second time in less than a month, the other side of my studio was crammed with national cameras, there to witness my face-to-face with someone who was potentially the next president of the United States. But the minute we got into the interview, I could tell immediately that she was not about to reveal any intellectual depth. Haskel said not a word without visually surveying her staff for approval, and the result was an antiseptic conversation yielding plenty of coverage but no real headlines. We each played our respective roles.

I asked about terrorism.

"We need to continue to fight them over there so we don't have to fight them here."

I inquired about the economy.

"Small businesses are the economic lifeblood of the United States."

I raised the Second Amendment.

"If guns were outlawed only outlaws would have guns." (She used my favorite line; I had no retort. Actually, she said that line with a straight face, like it was a creative thought. I might have been more impressed had I not seen it about 500 times previously on bumper stickers, or if she would have added another standard: "gun control means using both hands.")

It was as if I said "x" and she slid her finger to "y" and read me an answer. The way she rattled off her responses was disappointing but I couldn't be too indignant—after all, that's what I said!

But the audience, at least as indicated by the

callers, ate it up. From the minute our conversation began, every line was lit with nothing more substantive than "Joe from St. Petersburg" who wanted to know "how fast Governor Haskel will repeal Obamacare?"

"Just as soon as I sit down from my inaugural address," was the answer. And judging from the calls, it was the perfect response.

But I didn't get seriously distressed until the conversation turned to social issues, even as I told her I "admired the conviction of her views."

"Governor Haskel, let's do a lightning round on the non-economic issues. When I give you the problem, please try to offer me a solution in a short sentence if possible."

"Lay it on me, Stan."

"Ok, what about the repeal of Don't Ask, Don't Tell?"

"The Bible speaks of Adam and Eve, not Adam and Steve."

"Abortion?"

"It's time we had a president willing to stand up for the rights of the unborn."

"Prayer in public schools?"

"If Congress can begin its day in prayer, why can't our schoolchildren?"

I had a Stepford candidate across from me and nothing I raised would shake her from her script. And if I'd been keeping score, she would have batted below the Mendoza Line with me personally. Tobias, by contrast, would have been spot-on with my views. But, of course, the Tobiases didn't control talk radio ratings. The Margaret Haskels did.

Then it was time to take comments or questions from the audience.

"God bless you Governor Haskel, we are counting on you to take our country back!"

"We know where you were born Governor, Godspeed."

And:

"I know you won't apologize for our nation."

When the "on air" light went dark, my program was over, and Governor Haskel said she'd like to have a word with me.

All of her aides except one left the studio. Haskel got up from her side of the console and walked around to where I'd been seated.

"Stan, I admire the courage of a man willing to say that which needs to be said to protect his country, even when it gets controversial."

I said some shit like, "I consider it my duty, governor."

"Well of course you do, because you are a great American."

I wanted to say, "Why, because I questioned the beliefs of the Democratic frontrunner with that old canard about Judeo-Christian principles?" But instead I remained silent. Her next statement told me that was exactly what she was thinking.

"You have to keep on it. Some of my people have looked into your governor's faith and believe he's not a Christian," she whispered. "Or worse."

That took me back. What could she possibly think was worse?

"Stan, this is Jackson Hunter," she said, introducing an aide who had been a flowerpot during the interview. "He's going to give you his business card. And any time you should need to reach me, about anything, all you have to do is call him. If he speaks to you, he speaks for me. I want you to have that kind of access, okay Stan?"

"Thank you, Governor."

Jackson Hunter was a 6-foot, late 20s, handsome guy with blue eyes and the full political uniform: blue suit, red tie, white Oxford cloth. He was a bit too perfect. Nothing was out of place.

"And Stan, I understand we might be seeing a bit more of you out in California in just a few weeks. Perhaps you and Jackson will speak before then?"

I had no idea what she was talking about, but I smiled and nodded my head affirmatively like I was in the loop. She left, and my revulsion lasted only so long as it took the telephone to ring with a new round of cable TV requests for me to discuss how I thought the Texas governor would play in the I-4 corridor against a homegrown Florida legend.

On the drive home, Phil said he was pleased with how it had gone. Then I picked up a long voice-mail message from Jules in which he said that some cable outlet had inquired of him as to when I would be announcing my endorsement for president. That was a first. No one had ever cared before. He also said that a web site with "red state" in its online address had speculated that I was in line for a West Wing position should Governor Haskel win the White House. Some kind of communications position. Like what, I thought, Deputy Senior Advisor for Horseshit? An endorsement was not something I had ever formally offered, nor ever considered, and the fact that anyone would be interested in a formal nod from me was indicative of just how crazy things were getting. I made a mental note to call Phil back and find out what his talk radio text-book had to say on the subject of endorsements. But Jules closed with one more line:

"Stan, your word is worth more right now than any member of the Congress."

The way he said it made it sound obvious. But I still had trouble computing the fact that whereas just a few years ago I'd be getting my rocks off by interviewing rock stars and debating whether Roger Hodgson or Rick Davies was the true voice of Supertramp, I was now in a position to play kingmaker. Things were changing for me faster than I could comprehend.

And it was beginning to impact my day-to-day lifestyle. Whereas the anonymity of radio had previously enabled me to fly below the radar, now wherever I went, there were hints of recognition. It's not that people would stop me to say hello, or that paparazzi would jump out of bushes and snap my picture with some scantily clad model (much as I would have loved it), but rather that there was a glint I would detect in the eyes of the people who saw me going about my normal routine. Whether filling my gas tank, walking down the beach, or sitting at the bar at Delrios, if my eyes locked with someone else's, I could tell that they thought they had seen me before. And it might take them a step or two after crossing my path before they put it together, but they were putting it together. Even though they rarely said anything.

"That was Stan Powers, the host of Morning Power, *the guy that all the presidential candidates are trying to befriend."*

Nobody ever said that. But some were thinking it. Or so I was beginning to suspect. Maybe not.

But I was thrilled anytime I heard from Jules. The increasing frequency with which he was reaching out to me (instead of me trying with futility to command his attention) was yet another sign of my success. In a heady moment, I almost called him back and told him with whom I had recently shared a private drink, but I caught myself and said nothing. Not to him. And certainly not to Phil.

CHAPTER 10

So odd was the inconsequential way in which Susan and I had parted at Delrios, that I wasn't sure whether I'd ever hear from her again, much less when. Obviously she was busy. Heading into Super Tuesday, Tobias had won Florida and Colorado like Susan predicted. Baron had won Nevada, and the two of them had split a few additional states, namely Minnesota (Tobias), Maine (Baron), Arizona (Tobias), and Michigan (Baron). President Summers had won virtually all of the Iowa, New Hampshire and South Carolina votes because new ballots couldn't be printed in time, and he was now promising that his delegates would be released at the convention in August. Ambassador Brusso was proving to be irreverent in the debates but a nonstarter at the polls. And at the rate they were going, I doubted whether congressmen Foley and Yih would last to see their own state's primaries in Pennsylvania and California, respectively. Their only role was that of potential spoiler if they lasted that long, but all seemed to be enjoying the limelight. Ditto for Senator Wrigley, who if she took Vermont on Super Tuesday, would count it as her only win.

On the Republican side, Governor James won his home state of Colorado as predicted and was getting a free ride from the media whose members both genuinely liked him and wanted to make sure that Margaret Haskel didn't wrap up the entire nomination before they could milk their advertisers. A good underdog story was always a winner. But while the mainstream media built up James every chance it could, it didn't go too hard on Haskel for fear that they'd help elect one of what I was privately calling the "triple threat" of Figuera, Redfield and Lewis.

Phil and I had strong disagreements about how to handle Wynne James, who was the surprise candidate in the field. While his competitors concentrated on Michigan and Arizona, he'd focused on Minnesota and pulled an upset. And where Figuera, Redfield and Lewis couldn't win, they were denying Haskel a blowout and put James in second position.

"He's in second position, Phil," I argued. "I've had virtually every other candidate on recently, why not him?"

"Nobody who would vote for him matters to you, Stan. Your P1s are a combination of Haskel, Redfield, Lewis and Figuera voters. Take any of the four anytime they'll do your show. You cannot lose with any of them. They are walking sound bytes who will say what your listeners want to hear. But James is a RINO. I'd rather you go kiss Tobias' ass again than welcome him with open arms."

"And where am I if James pulls a Romney, Phil? You and I know that the only way Mitt won the nomination is that Ron Paul, Rick Santorum, Newt Gingrich, Michele Bachmann, and Herman Cain were all trying to out-credential one another with their conservative bona fides. And Romney slipped in. If it happens again and I've treated this guy like shit, where am I?"

"That's not happening. There aren't enough country clubbers left in the party to enable this guy. South Carolina was a fluke. Of course he won Colorado, the land of the pot smokers. And fuckin' Minnesota? They elected Al Franken. What more need I say? That Haskel is beating him even with Redfield, Lewis and Figuera in the race is a testament to her strength."

On the eve of Super Tuesday, Susan surfaced again. I was in the big conference room at WRGT post-show, when Alex entered and handed me another "Wilma Blake" message that had been logged at the main number for "Stan Powers." One fake personality calling another. I figured that my appearance on *Hardball* the night before had drawn her out. Funny thing was that Phil had actually suggested that I use the appearance to trash Susan Miller ("she's the Jane Fonda of the New Millenium," he'd intoned). But I'd resisted and gone hard on Tobias' religion instead. If he'd known that Susan was now the one person about to give me feedback on the segment, he'd have had a conniption.

At the moment, her message felt like a lifeline. After completing my shift, I had holed myself up in the room where WRGT usually serenaded potential advertisers. But today was no dog and pony sales pitch. Instead I was now in the middle of taking a one-hour, mandatory, online decency test and ready to blow my brains out. A holdover from the sale of WRGT from Star Channel to MML&J, this obligatory, annual, cover-your-ass, broadcast ethics exam forced me to grapple with the likes of the following:

QUESTION #3:
Which of the following statements, if aired, might expose a broadcast station to the risk of an FCC indecency forfeiture? Please consider all options before answering.

ANSWERS:
1. "His testicles are, like, down to the floor, you could use them as bocce balls."
2. "He's a complete bullshitter!"
3. "He really seems like a dick to me."

Normally I would have pitched a fit to Steve Bernson and told him I had better things to do than waste an hour so that the company could later answer a lawsuit by saying, "Well, we gave him his training, so there was nothing else we could do to prevent him from spontaneously slandering someone." But right now I was in no position to complain. The fact was that I'd had a potential indecency violation right after the Margaret Haskel interview, and Bernson and the MML&J suits were in an uproar. I had uttered an f-bomb during weekend programming. This was a speed bump I could ill afford, because right now things with the show were really popping. The WRGT listeners were keenly interested in the Tobias campaign and there was rampant speculation as to why he would not offer me a more customary answer when I'd questioned him about his faith. It was almost as if they themselves had raised the issue, and they kept it going long after I brought it up.

"Stan, I heard Tobias is a Wiccan."

Or:

"You do know, Stan, that his wife was once in a Satanic cult."

And even:

"They're sympathetic to Sharia law."

I could tell that Alex hated it when callers would spread those sorts of rumors on air, but she knew her role, and dutifully punched up the calls and one-line summaries without any editing. Rod, meanwhile, was in his glory, and seemed to be choreographing the bumper music he played to suit the anti-Tobias sentiments embraced by the callers. One day a caller went on a tirade about Tobias' failure to embrace the Ten Commandments close to the top of the hour, when we had a hard out. Rod was supposed to start a music bed 30 seconds before our time was up, giving me and whomever I might be speaking with an audible signal to wrap it up. Well, in sync with this guy's tirade, Rod cued up the Rolling Stones' "Sympathy for the Devil." I admit it suited the brand of *Morning Power*, but it made me feel dirty to be the ringleader just the same.

The ratings suggested that this passion, most of it driven by anger, was translating into new highs for our listenership. That sense of purpose was measurable in other ways too, including my Twitter followers, Facebook friends and the deluge of anonymous postings on the *Morning Power* page of the WRGT blog. Although I'd always believed that if I could trace who wrote them, I'd find myself circling back to Rod's computer.

Now, seated in the conference room with my face getting tanned from the blue hue of a company computer, I suddenly found myself no longer thinking about Susan Miller, Governor Tobias or Governor Haskel, but about whether I'd even hold onto my job. Don Fucking Fortini.

It was truly his fault. He'd tried to squeeze too much gold from the goose. If he hadn't gotten me involved in recording some infomercials disguised as programming, I would never have been in this mess.

Fortini was our head of sales, and he had suggested to Bernson that we look for new revenue streams to capitalize on my increased ratings. The PPM ratings' data for *Morning Power* proved we were on fire. And with the additional ears came new advertisers and WRGT's ability to raise rates. I was doing as many as five live reads per hour that were wreaking havoc on my voice. But even with the sharp uptick in cost per point, we lacked inventory because of increased demand among advertisers. We were sold out even after raising rates. For starters, all the political campaigns wanted to reach my audience in the I-4 corridor, but the trouble was, the law required they be offered available time at the lowest rate for which it had been sold in the prior year. The second and fourth quarters of the year are big for radio advertisers, but there are some lean weeks in January and February and again in July and August. Whatever the lowest rates the program commands in those months now had to be offered to the political campaigns in what was already a busy time of year. The resulting demand for advertising airtime created a daily scrum to see who we could clear and I desperately resisted any effort to increase the commercial allotment beyond 16 minutes per hour. Well, that's when Fortini pitched Bernson with an idea.

In a bid to increase the WRGT bottom line, Don Fortini came up with the notion that I would host infomercials disguised as programming that would run in the weekend overnights. This would accomplish two things: we'd be able to soak some local physicians willing to buy time during a graveyard shift, and we could circle back to advertisers wanting a piece of me so they could be associated with my voice, albeit in off hours.

There is a constant tension in the business between a host like me who tries to protect his on-air reputation and brand, and a hungry, commission-driven sales staff like Fortini's that is looking to sell any and everything. I think his people have a more difficult job than me. Truly. I could never sell radio time. But that doesn't mean I was pleased to host these whorish interviews with physicians. I went to Steve Bernson and told him it would undercut my brand as a presidential interviewee and ultimately cause us to sell at a lower rate, but he wouldn't get involved. Even when I said:

"Steve, if you haven't noticed, I'm spending my time these days interviewing potential world leaders and I'm a little short of time to sell ass cream."

Despite my success, enhanced profile and ratings spike, WRGT was not in the beer money. We didn't get that kind of scratch, which went to the jock station. Our advertisers continued to be entrepreneurs and not advertising-agency-driven businesses, which had little regard for talk radio. Nor did we have a base of national advertisers, primarily because they were afraid to be associated with spoken-word programming for fear that they'd have to endure a flap like when Rush called that Georgetown coed a "slut." They were always worried that they'd get tied to a host who would say something stupid and then they would have to contend with a national boycott and angry consumers. It had happened with Glenn Beck, too. Just when he caught fire on Fox News, largely because he called President Obama a racist (whose advice does that sound like?), his TV show was the subject of a protest that caused him to lose dozens of advertisers. So in this climate, Fortini had come up with an idea to tap a new revenue stream—local physicians—and sell them half-hour blocks of time for a "show" that they would call *Doctor's Hours*.

I had learned to keep my eye on Don Fortini from my first few days at WRGT. I just knew he was capable of getting me into a shitstorm. In a different life he'd have been the maitre' d at a Vegas showroom, the kinda guy who would know exactly where to seat you based on your shoes, the size of your wife's handbag, or how much you squeezed in his palm. But Fortini seemed ill-suited for Tampa. He was consistently overdressed wearing suits and ties in a town where the "players" wore designer shirts open at the collar with sport coats and jeans. The thing he had going for him was that he spoke the language of the small businessmen who were our economic lifeblood. Medium in height and build, and darkly complected, Fortini was a radio veteran who earned his stripes first selling specialty programming like Saturday morning real estate shows and Sunday night soothsayers. Trouble was, he didn't know when to stop selling. He would sell absolutely anything.

In my first year in Tampa, he'd hatched "The Right Way to Eat," a one-day smorgasbord where WRGT commandeered the entire St. Petersburg Times Forum, a giant arena that normally plays host to Ringling Brothers, concerts, and the Tampa Bay Lightning. For an advertised flat fee of $20.00, listeners could come and sample the fare of more than 300 food vendors and restaurants. The concept was great. Listeners got to eat good food on the cheap. Restaurants got a ton of promotion. And the station made a ton of money. It would have been win-win-win had Fortini capped the event as planned at 2,500 attendees, but he could not bring himself to stop selling admissions. So when 7,500 listeners showed up, causing every restaurant provider to run out of chow, we had a near riot on our hands and most of our P1s went home hungry. Every successful station had a Fortini, usually held in check by somebody from programming, but at WRGT, that person was Steve Bernson, who was under pressure from his corporate bosses to turn some coin from their foray into talk radio. Apparently the boys at MML&J could preach a good game, while also knowing how to count the collection basket. In the end, the collection basket was more important, and now my tit was in the ringer because of this corporate greed.

"Stan," Fortini had once said to mollify me, "these docs are not the Marcus Welby or Doogie Howser type. They are businessmen. Entrepreneurs. Just like our roofing and gold clients. They are all about business and we need to work with them."

So twice a week I'd have to interview the docs on everything from plastic surgery to sciatica. It was a forum for them to sell their businesses, thinly disguised as legitimate, albeit boring, programming. The interviews were then bundled in twos and run at a time when only insomniacs and some guy getting up in the middle of the night to take a piss would hear them. Still, if you tuned in at any time after the broadcast began, you'd miss the disclaimer and instead of knowing you were getting a paid-for infomercial, all you knew was that you were hearing God-awful radio. And with me as the voice—even though I went out of my way not to introduce myself.

To my amazement and disappointment, WRGT never had a shortage of physicians willing to pay thousands to hear their own voice on air. Most of these guys just did not translate to radio. They could remove your appendix, but answering a set of basic, health-related questions in a manner that a radio audience could follow was a challenge for them, to say the least. It probably took longer to edit these interviews than record them, just so "ums" and "ahs" and boring-as-hell answers could be made barely listenable.

So one day a rheumatologist was sitting across from me in the middle of the morning. I was already cranky from having gotten up at 3:30 a.m. to do my own program and now this, and he was talking like he was the walking dead.

On mic, I told him, "Doc, you gotta wake the fuck up."

I shouldn't have said it. I should have just thought it. He looked temporarily shell-shocked. But my comment did the trick; we finished up the discussion and I forgot about it. Like I said, these were taped segments that required heavy editing.

The following weekend, some rookie technical

producer (not Rod) was running the master board when his computer crashed just before *Doctor's Hours*. When he rebooted, he clicked on the wrong mp3 file, and instead of the edited version, he played the raw version with me telling the man with the stethoscope to wake the fuck up—the "wtf" up version as I liked to call it.

But he didn't get fired for that.

He got fired for his second mistake: filling out an internal MML&J report of some kind and thereby bringing it to the attention of Steve Bernson, which forced WRGT to fire the geek, lest anyone could ever say that management learned of what happened and didn't act. Unlike talent, the technical folks weren't forced to take the online broadcast ethics training, or maybe MML&J could have invoked the "well, we trained him not to" defense. Instead, Bernson had no choice but to alert the Atlanta parish and they demanded that he take defensive action in case the house of cards started to tumble. Typical corporate bullshit.

I heard about it the following Monday morning from Alex.

"How many complaints?" I asked.

"Just one, so far," Alex said. Oh shit.

"From the rheumatologist who stayed up to hear his own interview!"

Which was a great relief, but we were not out of the woods. I was nervous because now I was suddenly expendable under the morals clause of my contract. Dropping an f-bomb was a fireable offense, even if I was hot as a pistol because of the campaign. And it was the sort of thing that could follow you from market to market. Especially with some of the religious or self-described family-values groups that now made a habit of charting personalities nationwide. Every station I've worked for has lived in fear of the FCC and their humongous fines, even when court decisions suggested the standards of what was indecent were getting permissive. My owners were un-persuaded by the mixed court precedents.

U2's Bono has done more to clarify those standards in my professional lifetime than even George Carlin did with his seven dirty words uttered close to when I was born. (Shit, piss, fuck, the c-word I will not say, cocksucker, motherfucker and tits, in case you are wondering.) In 2003 Bono got up during an NBC broadcast of the Golden Globes (he got something for *Gangs of New York*) and said it was "fucking brilliant!" Bono didn't mean fornicating brilliant. He meant fucking brilliant. Like, hey, how terrific. Still, the FCC called that a fleeting expletive, for which broadcasters could be fined.

Saying fuck, the FCC decided, had an "inherently" sexual connotation in all contexts, and was therefore indecent speech that was subject to limitation, meaning fines. In other words, even if you said "fuck," but didn't mean the act of fucking, you were still on the hook, or the broadcaster was. (Can you tell that I paid attention to this battle?)

Eventually a federal appellate court tossed out the fleeting expletive policy, saying, "By prohibiting all 'patently offensive' references to sex, sexual organs and excretion without giving adequate guidance as to what 'patently offensive' means, the FCC effectively chills speech, because broadcasters have no way of knowing what the FCC will find offensive." Then the Supreme Court said the FCC could fine for this sort of thing but left the door open as to whether the law was unconstitutional.

What does it all mean? Beats the shit out of me, and apparently, my employer, MML&J. Nowadays, nobody knows what the rules are. Which is why before I even read the possible answers on the quiz, I knew I'd look for the one that was most encompassing. If the choices were: "A) only 1; B) only 2; C) only 3; D) Both 1 and 2; E) Both 1 and 3; or F) Each one of these statements is potentially indecent," I always checked "F" and kept moving.

Needless to say, when Alex interrupted me, I jumped at the chance to excuse myself from the "training." Wondering what it was all about, I returned Susan's call.

"Next time, wear a tie," was how she answered.

So it was about *Hardball*. Clearly she was referencing my attire on TV the night before.

She was probably right. When I went for that more casual look I felt like I was imitating the pseudo terrorism experts who popped up post-9/11 all wearing mock black turtlenecks and looking like they just finished accompanying Seal Team 6 while killing bin Laden before heading into the studio to offer some analysis. But of course, they weren't accompanying Seal Team 6. They were warm and cozy inside a television studio. I made a mental note to follow her advice.

I was never sure when Chris Matthews was finished with his own thoughts and it was time for me to jump in, but I appreciated the visibility that came from appearing on his program which was a staple for politicos on both sides of the aisle. Of course, on *Morning Power*, I'd forever mock him for once having said that watching Obama gave him "a thrill up his leg," but in every one of our TV encounters I was reminded that he had no equals when it came to his institutional knowledge of electoral politics. The guy started as a cop on Capitol Hill and worked himself into a position of power and influence. Of course, nothing good would come from my saying that on radio.

"Hello, Susan," I said. "What can I do for you?"

"Stan, I think we are on our way. The advance polling from Georgia, Ohio and Virginia all looks good," she said, referring to the biggest prizes on Super Tuesday. "Vic Baron just can't match our field organization."

I waved off Alex who suddenly appeared at the door to the conference room, and let Susan keep talking.

"Congratulations," I said. "But why are you calling me?"

"I'm calling because I'd hate for you to be on the wrong side of this."

I wasn't sure what she meant. But it was a far more direct point she was raising now than anything she'd said at Delrios.

"You know I could never be for your husband," I said softly into the phone.

"Of course not. We all have to play our roles. But there is a difference between opposing someone on the merits and leading a crusade."

I hardly thought her word choice suited what I'd told Matthews the night before. I'd repeated my usual mantra about Americans being "distrustful of someone they can't picture sitting in a pew next to them." Susan must have taken that as a dog whistle.

"I really don't know what you think you know, Stan," she went on. "But I'd welcome the chance to discuss it with you."

"Can you call the show tomorrow at 8:05?" I

209

said. "I'm happy to move whatever we already have booked."

"I don't mean publicly, Stan. I mean privately."

I felt some wood.

"I have no idea where I am being sent next. But I will call you as soon as I know." Click.

If it were possible, I now had even less interest in my online ethics training.

Study hall was over; it was time for me to get back to class. I wrapped up my online session and headed for home not knowing the outcome and wishing I had that hour of my life back. What really pissed me off is that even after the online course, I remained on pins and needles because of *Doctor's Hours*. Bernson told me he was waiting for the final word from Atlanta, and that in the meantime, he was putting a "letter of reprimand" in my HR file where it was to remain for one year. Unless Atlanta intervened, he said that so long as there were no more infractions (and no formal FCC investigation), it would be expunged. That's the sort of thing they use to hang you with if your ratings tank, but in my case, I had ratings and revenue, and a clause in my contract that said I could only be fired "for cause." Of course, they now had one, and could can me at any time. I hoped I didn't need the full seven months remaining on my contract before I was playing on a bigger stage. Before the end of the year, I was hoping Tampa would not be my sole station, but would be one affiliate of a string of many on which my program was broadcast. In the meantime, I needed to keep the platform I had.

CHAPTER 11

"I'm coming to Florida, Stan, and would like to see you."

My first thought when I heard Jules DelGado say those words was that I was getting shit-canned. I suspected he'd gotten wind of a formal FCC investigation for my "wake the fuck up" comment to Dr. Kervorkian.

"What brings you to town?" I timidly inquired.

"You. What kind of question is that?"

I quickly evaluated how much of a pussy I would be if I said something like "What about me?" and decided against it.

Forty-eight hours later, we were having dinner at Bern's Steak House, not too far from the studios of WRGT. Bern's was a legendary joint started in the '50s by a guy with that name. It offered the finest steak and the most expansive wine list in a setting where you figured dessert would come after some buxom madam called your name and said, "Sonny, you are about to get blown in bedroom No. 45." Seriously, the place looked like a brothel out of a John Wayne western. But more deals got cut at Bern's than any other place in town, so when Jules said he was coming for dinner, there was no hesitation on my part as to where to take him. If this was an execution, I was going to be the equivalent of someone getting their hand cut off in an Iranian soccer stadium.

Jules DelGado was a great barometer of where my career stood. I was used to competing for his attention. For a few years, I had been his least important client, often wondering why, given his unresponsiveness, he'd ever undertaken my representation. But now, when we spoke, there were fewer interruptions on his end of the line where his male assistant, Philippe, was always a third wheel in our conversations. During so many previous calls, Philippe had barged in with something like, "Mr. DelGado, you have a conference call holding," or "Mr. DelGado, I have Ben Sherwood waiting from ABC to begin your call." At last, *I* was the subject of the conference call. Hell, Jules was actually calling me for a change, instead of the other way around. I was fighting less for his attention. And struggling to keep up with his emails seeking updates on my show plans and cable appearances. Now we were meeting, and on my turf.

Fearing that he was the bearer of bad news, I decided to invite Debbie along, on the theory that it'd be more difficult to deliver a blow if a guy's significant other were at the table. Of course, I'd shared nothing with her of my concern for the fallout from *Doctor's Hours*. Yeah, I'd told her a bit about the incident, but I'd deliberately underplayed it, lest it spark another lecture.

"Stan, you really need to grow up. You talk live, on radio, for 20 hours a week without cursing. Don't you find it interesting that you couldn't hold your tongue when you were recording an interview, in the same way you can't seem to hold your tongue when you aren't on air?"

She didn't say that. But I figured she would have if I'd told her the full story. It's funny how many conversations I'd had with her in my mind like that—conversations she never even knew had taken place. I figured it saved time. Multitasking by Stan Powers.

To my pleasant surprise, I could tell Jules was in a good mood from the moment we were seated. The three of us sat with a view of the kitchen while we put a dent into a bottle of Peter Michael L'Espirit Des Pavot Cabernet Sauvignon while devouring steaks.

"Stan, I want you to know how much I value our relationship. I'm sorry if in the past you've felt that you had to compete for my attention. Those days are over."

Jules had never spoken to me with such an

attempt at sincerity. Maybe that was for Debbie's benefit. She looked terrific which is no doubt why, even when he was speaking to me, Jules was mostly looking at her. I loved hearing the words roll off his lips, not that I was fully buying it. Until then, I knew I was always the low man on his totem poll, somewhere after about a dozen other talk and cable personalities, and his wife and kids. But I'd always calculated that I was better off being on his second team than anyone else's first squad. He'd been representing me since I negotiated an extension of my afternoon program back in Pittsburgh. Star Channel had made me an offer that I thought was weak, and so I called Jules up cold to ask him to represent me and try to do better. It worked. We never met and hardly spoke to discuss the deal. But the mere involvement of his firm had added at least ten percent to the deal, which is exactly the amount he took of my annual salary.

"I'm getting calls about you, Stan, calls from people who are contemplating whether to give you a larger platform."

Hallelujah.

"Your name is coming up more and more often as the big syndicators survey the landscape to see who can be the heir to Limbaugh, Beck and Hannity."

He said that the overtures had been increasing since my Tobias and Haskel interviews and the resulting cable appearances. As Phil had predicted, there was a great demand on the part of the television broadcasters to have someone on camera who was in the thick of the I-4 corridor and could give good ear on Tobias' political prospects, and I was doing my best to keep up. Gore Vidal once said, "You should never miss a chance to have sex or appear on television." Well, Vidal only told part of the story. GOP dirty trickster and Vidal acolyte, Roger Stone was the one who correctly explained that doing the latter would facilitate the former. The more you appeared on television, the more opportunity you had to get laid.

And never before had I had the opportunity that was now around me. It was everywhere, even though I wasn't taking it. Chicks from sales whose names I didn't know were suddenly delivering my live copy to the studio early mornings, instead of just leaving it in my *Morning Power* mailbox as they had done for years. I had broads introducing themselves to me at supermarkets and gas stations. Of course, my newfound fame had the reverse effect with Debbie, who took every opportunity to tell me how disgusted she was by what she called my "Sybil situation."

"There is now medicine for schizophrenics like you, Stan," she would say.

While Jules continued, I was sure I saw Debbie rolling her eyes.

"I have an offer for you, Stan. One of the cable outlets has invited you to be an official, paid contributor."

"What does that mean?"

"It means they will put you on the payroll, commit to so many appearances per week, and will ask for exclusivity in return. No more appearing on whatever channel happens to ask. Now you will be tied to one."

He reached for his wine before adding:

"Which is why I don't think you should take it."

I had often heard others whom I was appearing alongside introduced as "contributors" and was never sure about the distinction, but it seemed like a credential worth having. When I was introduced, they usually said "Stan Powers is joining us now from Tampa, where he is the host of a daily morning radio program on WRGT." Or, "Stan Powers is a conservative radio host based in Tampa." Those who were introduced as "contributors" had a level of validation I envied, even if there was no serious coin attached. I was happy to hear that they wanted me on that team, and surprised that Jules was seeking to curb my enthusiasm.

"It's meaningless, Stan. Chump change, really. We are playing for bigger stakes now."

I was rapt. Debbie was frowning. We both remained silent.

"It's only worth $250 per appearance, and while I'm sure you'd like the ego stroke of the contributor title, it's not worth tying your hands. I'm duty-bound to present you with all offers, but I think you'd be making a big mistake by taking it."

He then used a baseball analogy and explained that this was a bona-fide invitation to play pro ball, but that I was being placed in triple A ball, instead of being called up to the big show.

"They see you are on the come, but they don't yet know what to do with you. I've seen this move before. They want to take you off the board before someone else can come along and make you a real deal," he reasoned.

I wasn't sure. The only thing that registered was that we'd just drank a week's worth of cable TV contributor fees with our appetizers.

"You flew down here to tell me *not* to accept a title for $250 an appearance?"

"Hell no. I flew down here to tell you that you're on a fast track, that people are noticing you in a way that you have long wanted to be recognized, and to share with you an opportunity far bigger than a horseshit title on a cable station that during most of its hours, has fewer eyeballs watching than you currently have ears listening."

The waitstaff from Bern's commenced carting off the carcasses while Jules caught his breath and prepared to lay out his plan. Debbie said she was going to freshen up and I ordered a pair of Remy Martin Cognac Louis XIII Grande.

"Stan, the goal here is national syndication. The only thing cable TV can do for you professionally is gain you recognition with PDs across the country, so that when they get a call from a syndicator who wants to know if they'll clear your show, they don't say, 'Never heard of him.' Remember, there are more than fifty guys who are syndicated in this country, but only about five who have made it work. When I cut your deal, I want you to be one of the five, not one of the fifty."

"I'm listening."

"Well, you're in demand by the B-list of syndicators, but the A-team is still not paying enough attention."

"Maybe they need to see more of me on television?"

"Horseshit. You've already done that part."

"Then what do I need to do?"

"Participate in a debate."

We both stood at the table in a perfunctory manner to welcome Debbie back to the conversation.

Jules speculated that the GOP nomination fight might not wrap up before California voted, and there was an important, upcoming Republican presidential debate being planned for the Ronald Reagan Presidential Foundation and

Library in Simi Valley. This would be the final debate between Haskel, James, and the others, assuming they stayed in the race until the end. Super Tuesday hadn't been decisive on either side of the aisle. For the Republicans, Margaret Haskel had only barely edged out Wynne James in Ohio. The real upset that day was in Virginia where James was the victor, officially moving him from the dark-horse category and turning the GOP contest into a competitive race. Every time Figuera, Lewis and Redfield grabbed a few points in each state where they competed, they were cutting into Haskel's conservative vote, a fact not lost on the Lone Star governor. "My three amigos" she began referring to them on the campaign trail with a smile that could cut a rib eye. Without fanfare, and certainly with no advance warning to pollsters, every remaining moderate Republican was casting a ballot for Wynne James. Haskel was fortunate that this was a year when the Texas primary, often superfluous when finally staged in late May, would have real value. Still, it was doubtful her home state would put her over the top. That distinction could come in California. The Democratic race was no less interesting. It too had divided along the lines of an A and B tier, with Tobias and Baron sharing the top shelf while Evers, Foley, Yih, Wrigley and Brusso vied for attention on the second level. The governors of Florida and New York had traded states along the eastern seaboard tit-for-tat, reminiscent of a Civil War divide. Georgia (Tobias), Massachusetts (Baron), Ohio (Baron), Tennessee (Tobias). Baron had the Empire State primary on the horizon, but Tobias was showing strength in the Midwest and West. Texas was also polling well for Tobias, and his numbers in California were looking particularly strong. Most surprisingly, none of the second-tier candidates in either party were showing signs of fatigue or interest in dropping out. Such was the tumult and uncertainty caused by President Summers' surprise withdrawal, and the abundance of free media supplied by a 24/7 news cycle, that each appeared content to stay in until the end of the primary season or even the conventions, assuming no one locked up the requisite number of delegates. There was true strength in numbers. If any of them folded, it might set off a domino effect, but for now, all were standing pat. The visibility for me as a panelist would be huge. The GOP debates had been ongoing for more than a year, although it seemed that only now were people paying attention. Not only had President Summers' announcement created a scramble on the Democratic side, it made Americans want to pay attention to the GOP race, too. Jules said that another of his firm's clients, a big-name network anchor who he would not name, was about to be announced as the moderator of this forthcoming debate, and that he'd be accompanied on the debate stage by a pair of questioners drawn from other media outlets.

"Stan, what if I were to offer you the chance to be a debate questioner? How would you like to sit on the stage under Ronald Reagan's Air Force One, with the entire nation watching while you ask any question to any Republican running for president?"

I was stunned.

"Are you shitting me?"

"Nope.

"The party thinks it's important to give the talk community a seat at the table because of the importance of the format to the base of the GOP. They want a new face, preferably from a swing state. I had my guy suggest your name, and the party approved you. So too did the network brass. They think you'll add some edge."

There was that word again.

"Who will the other panelist be?"

"Probably a newspaper reporter from a regional publication, more along the lines of the *Orange County Register*, than say the *New York Times* or *Washington Post*."

I moved my snifter toward him looking for a celebratory clink, but Jules didn't reciprocate; he wasn't finished.

"I don't know if you appreciate the power you

have in this presidential election, Stan. While your focus is on expanding your reach, others are looking at the value you could bring to them with the following you already have."

The cognac settled in my stomach, chasing my wine, which had already pursued a gin martini. I was starting to feel too fucked up to follow.

"I'm talking about the party, Stan. The GOP. It's their debate. The RNC calls this shot, although the network has final approval. And their national leadership is pushing for your involvement harder than I have. I'd like to take more credit, but you were an easy choice, Stan. Everybody knows the importance of the area you reach, and they like that you are playing hardball with Tobias who looks like he'll take down Vic Baron and win the nomination."

In the midst of my cognac fog, I suddenly remembered Margaret Haskel telling me she'd be seeing me in California. Now her comment made sense, but the fact that she'd known well before I did made it seem a bit unsavory. I could only imagine what Debbie would say if I told her. So, of course, I didn't.

"They view you as a power broker, Stan. The only guy with a command of the I-4 corridor in what the experts all see as *the* swing state, with or without Tobias. More than Ohio. Bigger than North Carolina. The Republican Party desperately needs you, so much, that I think after the debate they will consider a role for you at the convention."

"What kind of a role?"

"That remains to be seen and negotiated, but some kind of a speaking role for sure."

Now our glasses met. We both sipped and smiled, and then remembering Debbie's presence almost as an afterthought, we looked in her direction. There was no reaction.

"This debate is big. Don't fuck it up. Make an impact in the debate and you will assure yourself a role at the convention, maybe in prime time. You do both, and I can guarantee you a syndication deal worth signing. I'm sure Phil Dean can offer some thoughts. How is that sack of shit? Oops, sorry Debbie."

"Don't mind me while you plot the destruction of the country," she said, her first words in 30 minutes.

Jules smiled in her direction but said nothing, no doubt pondering what was going on in her head.

Fucking Phil. It hadn't occurred to me that he was a part of this new dynamic. I could only imagine what he might want me to do in a debate, although the drill would be different than the normal carpet-bombing of liberals. Only Republican candidates would be on that stage in California, and there was only so much fellatio permitted in prime time.

I was feeling no pain by the time that Jules paid the bill and jumped in a cab. Debbie and I said so long to him outside the valet stand, and when they brought my car around, she directed me toward the passenger side and announced that she was driving. I could tell that she was upset and knew better than to challenge her.

I was nevertheless in a celebratory mood as we headed to my place, but she would have none of it. She started up just as soon as the valet closed her door.

"You have got to be shitting me," said the normally proper Ms. Cross. "Stan, I know you. At least I think I know you. And you're building an entire career based on a fiction. The Stan I know isn't a guy who would voluntarily spend 10 minutes with Margaret Haskel even if it were in the Oval Office. The Stan I know doesn't give a damn about what church Bob Tobias kneels in, or whether he kneels at all. Maybe because I happen to know that my Stan hasn't walked into a church himself since I have known him! He gets more intellectual stimulation trying to decide what Roger Waters was writing about when he composed *The Wall* than he does from the *Wall Street Journal*, and would rather smoke pot with his buddies Clay and Carl than sit in a smoke-filled room with political windbags."

Through bloodshot eyes I could see her carotid artery pulsing and knew she wasn't finished.

"Just how far are you going to take this? You're not just some guy spinning records. You aren't influencing a top 10 playlist anymore. People look to you for guidance thinking you are honest and sincere in your views. The future of the country is at stake. There is no way this ends well for you if you keep it up."

All of which is kinda what I'd expected her to say. Maybe on some level, it was why I'd invited her along to begin with. She was my sanity check. She grounded me. She spoke to me in a way the sycophants I'd been collecting in my orbit never would. Whether I was prepared to heed her warning was another story.

CHAPTER 12

A few weeks later, it was announced that I'd been chosen as a panelist for the GOP debate at the Reagan Library. Not long thereafter, Alex got a phone call from a Bill Maher producer. The debate at the Reagan Library was set for a Monday night, the night before the California primary. The stakes were big for Haskel and James. She could finish him off with a win in California. But a James victory in California meant the GOP battle might be settled in New Jersey, New Mexico, Montana or Utah—or not until the floor of the Republican National Convention. So of course, Haskel was going all in for Cali. And on the Democratic side, there was a similar sense of finality between Tobias and Baron. The seven-way sprint that began with the surprise withdrawal of a sitting president's candidacy, looked likely to wrap up with a Tobias victory on the left coast. Funny thing, the more I'd questioned his religious conviction, the higher his numbers seemed to rise among the core of his party—the exact opposite effect

I'd had among Republicans. I might be killing his chances in a general election, but I was actually helping Tobias secure his party's nomination, not that I thought Susan would be giving me credit anytime soon.

The Maher producer wondered whether I'd be willing to be a panelist on Maher's HBO program, *Real Time*, the Friday before the debate. For me it was a no-brainer. Here was a great opportunity to expand my visibility in left-wing circles on the eve of the GOP debate. Jules, too, thought it suited our objective because Maher was watched by anyone who mattered in the world of punditry, even those who would never admit it. He said it was all about enhancing visibility for potential program directors.

"Everyone on the left and right watches him, Stan. The only difference is that the conservatives pretend otherwise. It's a great opportunity to build your brand with syndicators and potential affiliates."

Phil disagreed.

"You're getting sandbagged, Stan. The only reason he's invited you on is because you've embarrassed Tobias by questioning whether he's a conventional Christian. Maher loves the idea that Tobias might be what your audience loathes."

Phil was more animated about this than anything we'd discussed since my in-studio interview with Tobias. He was insistent that before I commit, I first watch Maher's movie about religion, which I promised to do, but never did. Big mistake. It would've let me know what was coming.

"And I'll tell you another thing. That audience will fucking hate you. He'll put you in the wing-nut chair alongside two Hollywood types, and nothing good comes from getting heckled by Bill Maher in that lion's den."

I could tell from Phil's detailed analysis that he was among the regular viewers, just as I would have suspected. Still, as I protested, he remained firm.

"Remember, he gave all that money to Obama. Our audience will think you are pandering to Maher unless you cold-cock him. I say don't take the risk."

This was the first time I could remember there being such a sharp difference of opinion between Jules and Phil. Then again, they had separate roles and it might have been the very first time their interests had collided. Jules' job was to increase my platform and cut deals. Any notice on a national stage was going to help him make the case to syndicators (and thereby to potential station affiliates) that I was a sufficient radio star to warrant a national rollout. Phil's role was to ensure that I was always saying the right things to cultivate support from the talk radio base, thereby enabling Jules to grow the platform. In this case, Phil's argument was that Jules' efforts would be hampered by any association between Maher and me since he was viewed as a pariah by the program directors of conservative talk stations. Jules' response was that the PDs didn't have to like me—they just needed to be able to see my name in lights. Phil and Jules had a healthy respect for one another, but they never actually spoke, and this time was no exception. Instead they made their independent arguments to me and left the decision in my hands.

My brain agreed with Phil, but my ego sided with Jules. I found the idea of flying to California early for the debate and being a big shot on HBO intoxicating. If unpredictability was the issue, I rationalized to Phil, then how different could it be from the risk of taking a live call on radio and not knowing what the person was going to say?

"On any given morning, I never know what might happen when I answer the phone," I said to him.

"Stan, the only difference amongst your callers is their shade of red," he answered. "This live audience will be a sea of blue and we can't afford a YouTube moment."

What I didn't tell either of them was that I was myself a pretty avid Maher watcher. I didn't always agree with him and thought he was pretty acerbic, but I liked the politically incorrect nature of the program and certainly sided with him on legalizing pot. Maybe I should wear short sleeves, I wondered? Of course, Maher didn't know what was emblazoned on my forearm—and even if he did, I was still an unlikely ally. The only thing he'd know was that I was a conservative talker from Tampa with an increasing amount of influence on the other side of the aisle in the midst of the presidential race. And, he'd surely know that I had raised questions with regard to Tobias' faith. Which is why Phil was worried that I would be a particularly attractive candidate for a Maher ass-kicking on national TV just a few nights before the debate. So one more time, I circled back to Jules for some confirmation.

"Phil's right to be cautious," he said. "But if you think you can handle Maher, the payoff in visibility could be enormous. The timing is perfect. I wasn't going to tell you Stan, but today I spoke with Chuck Schwartz from Panache Broadcasting and he has room on his roster. You are on that short list, although you may have to change time slots because it's tough to syndicate a morning show."

That was the only encouragement I needed. I flew to LA as HBO's guest on a Thursday right after *Morning Power* and checked into the Beverly Hills Hotel, all on HBO's dime. Pulling into the driveway off Sunset Boulevard I saw the iconic, pink outline that I first came to know as the cover art for the Eagles' *Hotel California* while studying the vinyl in my Ft. Myers bedroom. I felt that my career had come full circle. Then I wondered if it was an omen as the title track's lyrics popped into my head with a sense of foreboding.

I spent the late afternoon sipping bloody marys at a cabana, and watching a pair of thongs swim laps in a pool that played music through underwater speakers. Later that night, I drove a rental car a short distance to the Whiskey A-Go-Go to see some live rock. The room that had once hosted the likes of the Doors, Guns and Roses, and Van Halen was filled with twenty-something headbangers listening to a Scandinavian band that looked like they were from Spinal Tap, only they were too young to have known what I was talking about if I'd asked whether their amps where turned up to "11." Maybe I'm too old for this shit, I thought. Anytime I wore my old concert t-shirts around my condo, Debbie would say, "Time to retire it, Stan."

The next day I ate breakfast at a diner-like counter in the basement of the hotel while sitting next to a starlet who was famous for being famous. She'd either shoplifted or had one too many DUIs. She may also have recorded a few songs, but I was sure that in ten years no one would remember her name unless she OD'd in a room upstairs. Then again, maybe if she knew who I was she might say the same thing about me.

At noon, I was scheduled to have a conference call with the Maher producers who wanted to review the show's agenda. The proposed issues were all political and the same as what I'd spent the previous couple of days discussing on air back in Tampa, so I felt no need to cram on any current events. They told me they'd send a limo to the hotel at six, so I decided to head back to the pool, which is when I looked at my iPhone and recognized Phil's number.

"Dress the part," he said when I called him back.

"What does that mean?"

"No open-collared casual. Be loyal to your persona. You are not playing to his base, you are playing to your own. Your audience will respect you only if you step into the lion's den and stand your ground. Fuck those Hollywood phonies. And put a flag on your lapel."

So much for the short sleeves. I went to a souvenir shop a few blocks off Sunset and bought a flag pin, following Phil's instructions. He may not have wanted me to do the show, but I was still taking his advice on how to best pull it off.

Back in the room, a bottle of champagne had

been delivered with a cheese tray. It was from Jules. With the hour drawing near, for the first time, I began to feel nervous. It happened when I started thinking about the road from Shooter's to Pittsburgh to Tampa to Hollywood. Never, while spending way too much time in my bedroom during high school wearing monstrous headphones, could I have envisioned that I'd end up here.

Maher's program is done live from a soundstage that doubles as a game show set. The audience of a few hundred are there because they share his liberal political views, and during the pre-program warm-up with a producer, they get worked into a frenzy while loud, thumping music plays over the house sound system and previous show highlights roll on video monitors. It feels like a political disco by the time the show starts. I arrived about 45 minutes before we went live, and was sent to make-up and then to my own green room. That's when the show's executive producer stopped by for a final run through, during which he told me my seat location.

"You'll be in the chair nearest the audience."

I felt a bead of sweat pop out of my forehead. That was just what Phil had predicted. Phil had said that location was a "tell," a tip to the audience to recognize me as the evildoer on that night's program from the start. On this night, it also meant that to my immediate left would be a guitar player who most people knew for his music, but whom I recognized for his once having headlined a benefit concert for Mumia Abu-Jamal, a convicted cop killer. In Pittsburgh, I had refused to play his music. To his left would be a B-list actor who'd appeared in a number of films that had earned the respect of those who bestow Academy Awards, but not of the Americans who actually go to the movies. What they had in common was an unyielding liberal ideology. I was no closer to them on the issues than I was with my talk radio brethren. In my mind, both extremes were full of shit.

After his monologue and brief interview with some environmentalist, Maher joined us and immediately zeroed in on me.

"So Monday night is the final Republican debate of primary season, right here in California," he began. "Margaret Haskel and Wynne James are ready for a steel cage match at the Reagan Library where you will be a debate panelist. My audience might recall that several weeks ago, it was you who put the faith of the Democratic frontrunner, Bob Tobias, in play. In fact, you're the guy who criticized his failure to publicly adhere to a particular faith. What was all that about?"

"Well, I simply wanted to clarify what beliefs he holds," I responded. "I think it's important to know . . . ."

I was just getting started on Phil's talking point when Maher interrupted.

"Who cares? What does faith have to do with anything?"

Maher suddenly sounded like Debbie quoting me on my drunken drive home from Bern's. Only this time, there was applause from a live audience. The studio suddenly felt warm and I could feel the television cameras bearing down on me.

"I think it's legitimate to ask presidential candidates about the depth of their beliefs, to know from where they draw guidance, and to understand whether they recognize the country as having been founded on Judeo-Christian values."

The Judeo-Christian line was pure Phil. Only this wasn't a studio audience of talk listeners, it was the antithesis. And I wasn't finished.

"I think all of us want to know, Bill, whether candidates attempt to live their lives in accord with the Ten Commandments."

Well that did it. It was as if I'd pushed a nuclear launch code. The last part caused a core melt-down.

"Wait a minute. You mean you believe in the Ten Commandments?"

The combination of laughs and groans from the audience were audible to me on stage, and I was sure they were at home as well.

"I do."

"You think that if some creator of the universe were sitting around and came up with a list of ten rules for humans he'd put on the list relaxing on Sundays, but would leave off rape and child molestation?" Maher asked incredulously.

The audience reaction was a combination of laughter and applause. I feared that the vein shooting out of my forehead would be visible on TV as I tried to maintain my footing. Phil had anticipated this and told me to disregard the assholes in the studio audience, and think only of those in flyover country who comprised the crowd I was seeking to reach. While it was true that he hadn't wanted me to do the show, as soon as he realized I was going on anyway, he had patiently schooled me on how to create a controversy which would put me at odds with Maher over God, and rejuvenate interest in Tobias' faith all at the same time. And I have to say that his strategy was genius.

"I absolutely do, Bill. And I would think that even a nonbeliever like you would recognize the virtue of leading a life free of killing, stealing, and sleeping with another man's wife—even if those things are the lifeblood of this town."

That was part two: A direct assault on Hollywood. Phil had made me repeat the line about "this town" incessantly before I flew to

California, and he'd done it again in his final pre-show prep that afternoon.

Now I heard outright hissing. I had gone and launched an assault on the entertainment industry, right here in the heart of its capital. And, caught up in the role I was playing, I relished firing off that sound byte. The rock star to my left wanted in on the action. So too did the actor whose awards to date were only critical acclaim. What they said, I cannot recall. I only know that Stan Powers and Phil Dean had thrown a stink bomb into the studio which was going to live on long after the stage went dark. By the time the conversation turned to the way America's standing in the world was still suffering from the way in which the Bush Administration had fought al Qaeda so many years prior, I was totally in character and ready to keep firing.

"We deserve whatever comes from the Muslim world when our uniformed representatives resort to tactics such as waterboarding," said the actor, two seats away, to great applause. Maybe I'd have let that pass if I hadn't already been ridiculed for supporting the Ten Commandments. But not tonight.

"Wait a minute," I protested. "Only three al Qaeda—three!—were ever waterboarded. And that was after our efforts to get information by offering them a latte from Starbucks failed. And for all the criticism leveled at Bush, not even Obama ended the rendition program, or even closed Gitmo. And so while it's nice to sit here in Hollywood and talk about a world of peace, love and harmony, I think it's more important to first ensure that we're around to experience it."

That comment went over the head of the two jerkoffs on the panel, but I think I actually heard two or three people in the audience clap.

And so went the rest of the program. When it ended, I passed on the after-party, deciding I'd rather drink alone in the Polo Lounge than with these left-wing assholes. I had as much desire to hang with them as I would to hang with the sacks of shit who dominated my industry from the opposite end of the ideological spectrum. To both sides, everything was black and white, and the other side was sinister and always wrong. Fine. I'd hang alone.

In an SUV, being driven back to the hotel, I looked at my iPhone for the first time in hours. There were a few hundred new texts and emails. I was surprised the device hadn't overheated from the volume. It seemed like everyone I'd ever known had watched the show and had a reaction. I looked at the texts first. There were so many that it took quite a bit of scanning to even find Debbie, Jules and Phil. And, of course, I wondered if I'd hear from Susan.

Debbie: "Everything you believe was said

on that show tonight. Just not by *you*." Damn.

Phil: "I told ya so. You should have kneed him in the balls and walked off. But on balance, we'll take it. The only YouTube moments you created were in defending God and country—the P1s will love it when it gets replayed on cable."

Jules: "Proud of you. This will help us. Try to get some rest Stan. Monday is a big night."

Holy shit. Monday. It had almost become an afterthought. In three days I'd be a panelist for a presidential debate for which I'd hardly prepared. Until now I'd had a great game plan: The news cycle was changing so rapidly that I'd convinced myself I need not prepare until the weekend lest I'd waste time crafting dated questions. But suddenly, with *Real Time* behind me, I regretted that approach.

There was no message from Susan, but I knew that her preferred mode of communication was to leave a telephone message at the station. Maybe I'd have to wait until Monday.

There was, however, another text that caught my eye. It was from Jackson Hunter asking that I call him tonight, no matter the hour. The name didn't even register at first. And then I remembered that he was the advance man who traveled with Margaret Haskel, the guy she'd made the point of saying I should regard as her eyes and ears and use as a personal conduit. I wondered what he wanted, but there was no way I was calling him, at least until I'd had a Jack or two and cleared my head. Crawling down a busy Sunset Strip on what was now an active Friday night, my phone rang with a blocked number. I hoped it was Susan and so I answered. It wasn't. It was Jackson Hunter instead.

"I don't know if you got my text, but I'm in town and the Governor would really appreciate your giving me five minutes."

He left me little wiggle room.

"I'm not sure I can do that because I'm already back at my hotel for the night."

"That's perfect. I'll meet you in the Polo Lounge in a half-hour."

Kinda creepy. I hadn't told him where I was staying.

I needed a head start, so 10 minutes later I was seated in a booth at the iconic watering hole awaiting what was already my second drink when Hunter approached my table and sat down, looking like he'd just stepped off the pages of a J. Crew catalogue.

"Great job tonight, Stan. The Governor loved the way you didn't take any shit from Maher."

"Somehow I didn't figure she'd be in the demographics I was reaching."

"Don't sell yourself short, Stan. I'm sure there were many on our side who tuned in tonight specifically to see whether *Morning Power* could play in the big leagues. And you certainly silenced any doubt."

Our side. I didn't even find that objectionable. Not after the way the rock star, actor and comedian had tried to gang bang me in front of a national audience.

Someone downed the dimmer switch in the bar, and a piano player began his set. Hunter was now drinking a Coke with a lemon slice. I was ravaging a dish of nuts.

"Stan, this was just a warm-up for what's to come in three nights. You have an enormous opportunity to shape the fight for the nomination on Monday night, and the presidential race overall. The governor is sure you will be up for the task. And she hopes you will not be offended if I leave you with a few thoughts."

I said nothing. I just sipped my drink.

Hunter reached inside his coat pocket and pulled out a nondescript white envelope. There was no addressor or addressee. It was just a white envelope that, judging from its width, held only a sheet or two of paper. It reminded me of listeners handing me packages at Gadsden flag rallies. Like the one that purported to be a Scientology audit.

"Just for your consideration," he reiterated, placing it on the table.

I didn't immediately retrieve what he was handing over. I just let it sit in front of us and took another sip of my drink.

"You know, Stan, once Tuesday's primary is behind us, Governor Haskel will shift her focus to planning the summer convention. And that includes the roster of those who will be invited to speak in a supportive role in prime time while the nation watches."

This must be what Jules had referenced. Damn, this young guy was smooth. Nothing that was happening could be proven in a court of law, but it was pretty clear to me that there was a quid pro quo. Something in that envelope could help determine the outcome of the debate. And my willingness to use it was directly tied to a speaking role at the GOP convention in Tampa.

For the second time since my arrival the previous day, the foreboding lyrics of "Hotel California" popped into my head: "You can check out any time you like, but you can never leave."

Hunter excused himself and told me he'd see me Monday night. I watched him leave and ordered my third drink. Then I pulled out my iPhone to go through a mountain of emailed reactions to the program that by now was finishing its second airing of the night. As I thumbed through the lot, I thought about the education I had gotten in just the past 24 hours. For starters, I'd learned that a former DJ could, within a few years, be a presidential power broker in the United States. Others might see a

Horatio Alger tale. I suddenly felt like I was living in a banana republic. I'd also confirmed that prime time at a national convention was something that could be negotiated in a back room, or at least the Polo Lounge of the Beverly Hills Hotel. I looked at the envelope and wished I'd told the pretty boy to shove it up his ass. Instead I slid it inside my coat pocket and took another sip of my drink.

CHAPTER 13

I awoke late Saturday morning in California to the sound of a knock at the door from a waiter delivering coffee that I had ordered with one of those hanging chads on my doorknob the night before. A fellow dressed in a white linen version of the Beatles' suits on the *Sgt. Pepper's* album cover greeted me by name and poured my coffee for me. As soon as he left, I took my java, my iPad and my monstrous headache out onto a patio shaded by palm trees and began to scroll through a boatload of email messages, each calling my attention to the online treatment that my smackdown with Maher was receiving. In conservative circles, I was being hailed for having stood up for God and country. In liberal quarters, I was, well, a douche.

Drudge: Tampa Talker Trashes Tinseltown

Huffington Post: Maher Eviscerates Evangelical Host

Evangelical host? They obviously had me confused with Pat Robertson or Benny Hinn.

But maybe this was a good thing. I made a

mental note to have Steve Bernson send a link of the latter to the suits at MML&J in Atlanta, who were still being pissy and had refused to clear me for the f-bomb. Before I left for LA, Bernson had told me that the owners of WRGT were pleased with my newfound national success but suspicious as to how a God-fearing man could have so casually dropped "an expletive" in front of an open mic.

"Obviously he has said that word before," their missive supposedly read.

No shit Sherlock.

Bernson said they had peppered him with questions regarding my behavior off-air, including whether or not I was "living in sin" with Debbie. I saw Rod Chinkles' hand in that one. The truth was that we lived separately. But it sounded like the sort of horseshit he'd feed his old man to prove his intelligence-gathering capabilities. I told Bernson that the next time they asked if I was "living in sin," he should tell them, "Every night he can." Bernson did not smile. I liked him, but was reminded that he was still a suit.

Those who knew me best condensed their email reactions into just a few words in the subject line, understanding that the likelihood of my reading anything longer was pretty dim. First was a follow-up from Debbie that struck a note similar to what she'd texted the night before.

Debbie: "What did he say that you haven't?"

Ouch.

Alex: "Wow."

Rod: "Amen brother."

Carl: "You're buying Tuesday night."

Count on it.

Clay: "So what's it 'Mr.' Cocksucker now?"

Like me, Clay knew all the lines from *Wall Street*.

Phil: "Fallout as I expected (and hoped)."

That sounded promising.

Jules: "Ur on fire. Break a leg Monday!"

Monday. As in, the day after tomorrow.

Not that I had completely forgotten, but getting through the previous night had been just about all my attention span could handle. With the *Real Time* appearance now behind me, I was 48 hours away from going back on national television, this time to question the Republican presidential candidates in their final encounter. And only now did I remember the still unopened envelope given to me by Jackson Hunter last night. I retrieved it from my sport coat and slid it open. It read:

"Governor James: Many voters in tomorrow's California primary wish to vote for a candidate who shares their family values. Can someone who once told his own spouse that he desired an open marriage be that candidate?"

The suggested question was worse than I could

have imagined. That was some pretty nasty shit right there, I thought. Somewhere, Donald Segretti would be smiling. Molly Hatchet wanted me to take out the Colorado governor with a question that purported to be about family values, but was really about wife swapping, or so it sounded. I could just imagine conservatives hearing that and conjuring up an image in their minds of Governor James walking into some party and throwing his car keys in a dish, anxious to find out whose wife he'd be driving home (in more ways than one).

Attached to the page with the typed question was the purported justification for asking it: a page from the deposition James' first wife had given in the midst of their divorce many years ago, where she claimed that the now Colorado governor had wanted a threesome. Regardless of the reliability of the source, it was just the sort of thing that would serve as chum in the shark-infested debate waters, one night before the final primary vote. The prospect immediately sapped any sense of pride I'd had in pulling off the appearance the night before.

I suddenly needed to clear my head and break a sweat. I put on a pair of sneakers and asked the hotel concierge, who had the same name as a famous comedian (but not his appearance), where to go for a hike. He suggested Runyon Canyon and handed me a map. Twenty minutes later, I parked my rental car on an incline on Franklin Avenue and headed for the trek. While Van Halen pumped through my buds, I weighed my willingness to prostrate myself on national TV for Margaret Haskel. She currently led Wynne James in the latest California polls, but only by a narrow margin. A strong performance on Monday night would presumably keep her on that perch and finish off any chance James had to win the nomination.

I figured things could be worse. At least I hadn't been asked to stack the deck by someone who looked like a loser. If I asked the question, and James fumbled, I would not only be facilitating Margaret Haskel's victory, but also cementing myself in her good graces as attention shifted to the convention being held in my hometown in just two months. Such a relationship with the nominee could only be beneficial. So professionally speaking, it was all net. There is no such thing as going too far in my business. Rush had called Sandra Fluke a "slut." Imus had referred to female college basketball players as "nappy-headed hoes." Beck had called Obama a "racist." That kind of crazy talk could actually help your career, no differently than it did in Congress. South Carolina's Joe Wilson had raised a fortune in fundraising after shouting down Obama in a joint session of Congress with a cry of "You lie!" Same on the left with

Alan Grayson when he'd said that the Republican healthcare plan was that they "want you to die quickly." The more heated the rhetoric, the further you got. In the talk world, even the guys who got fired for being outrageous never stayed fired for long.

Personally, however, the decision was not so simple. I had little regard for Governor Haskel and could never see myself voting for her. The only reasonable guy on the stage was the one I was being asked to undermine. Frankly, all of the other candidates scared the shit out of me. Colonel Figuera not only still supported the war in Iraq, he was also saying that we should have stayed and seized the oil. Senator Redfield's invoking of Biblical reference convinced me that there was little difference between his approach to government and that of the Taliban. He seemed oblivious to the fact that we were governed by the rules of man, not God. Then there was William Lewis, who supporters liked to tout as a hybrid between two other businessmen-turned-politicians, Ross Perot and Herman Cain. He had Perot's all-American story, and Cain's personality on the stump, but he lacked any depth whatsoever on any subject to which he could not apply his entrepreneurial instincts. During one of the earlier debates, he had firmly stated that "Israel should be allowed to develop a nuclear capability."

You'd think one of his high-priced advisors would have briefed him on the fact that they already had.

As I climbed higher above the City of Angels the view became increasingly spectacular. Finally I paused on a bench at a spot that gave me a terrific, 180-degree view. Straight ahead was downtown LA. To my left, the iconic Hollywood sign. Off to the right lay the Pacific Ocean, which I had a desire to visit. And around me— walking, some marching—was a mismatch of Holmby Hills housewives in designer spandex and twentysomethings whose sociological ancestors would have best been described as beatniks. There were dogs on leashes, dogs off leashes, and a couple of photographers smoking pot who looked like they were disappointed that a starlet hadn't kept her promise of a "spontaneous jog." A better place to people watch I hadn't seen since a night I spent on the Atlantic City boardwalk. Stan Powers had used California for plenty of fodder over the years, but now, caught up in the scenery, I was thinking there were plenty of worse places I could be. The hum of my iPhone ruined the solitude. I answered reflexively, without first looking at who was calling. A voice said:

"What are the five questions?"

It was Phil. Even at a nearly airplane altitude, there was no escaping his reach.

The only item of substance on my Saturday agenda was a late afternoon conference call with the other debate participants, and I had been requested to be ready with five potential debate questions. Not surprisingly, Phil had strong feelings as to how I should conduct myself. I myself hadn't come up with anything, figuring that something would pop from the morning headlines. But I had forgotten to even look at them given what was now on my plate.

"Remember, this time you're officiating a Thanksgiving Dinner dispute, Stan. Unlike last night, your role is not to take sides."

Easy for him to say—he had not been visited in the Polo Lounge by the aide to the front-runner with a request to throw a hand grenade into the tent of the runner up. But Phil was adamant that I play the part of party elder and not be perceived as having a favorite.

"They are all family," he said. "Escape without a YouTube moment and you cement the next step at the convention."

That was the total opposite of what I was contemplating. And it convinced me that while Phil was almost certainly tied into the Haskel campaign, he was out of this particular loop. Jackson Hunter hadn't needed to say "don't tell anyone," it was implied. So instead of telling him about the envelope, I told Phil that I would be finished with my preparation later in the afternoon and would email him my five intended questions. I suspected that if he knew what I'd been asked to do, he would have argued for dropping the bomb on radio first, something that was not possible anyway because, due to the time difference, I was not scheduled to be back on air again before the debate.

My Saturday call was set for 5 p.m. Pacific Time, which left my hands idol for some devil worshipping. The pungent smell from the paparazzi made me want to get high, and I figured I could combine a beach trip with a reefer run. Venice was a 35-minute drive with no traffic on a Saturday, so I retrieved my rental and headed toward the 5 without stopping at the hotel. Upon arrival, I quickly experienced what Governor Schwarzenegger had once bragged was a great "contact high" near Muscle Beach. I had my choice of dispensaries that required only a prescription from a walk-in "clinic" where Mr. Pawlowski showed his ID while feigning back pain.

"How long have you been suffering?" asked the quack.

I was tempted to say, "Since I walked past the guys getting high in Runyon." But I didn't.

Back at the hotel, I toked on the private patio and used a notepad from under my room phone to make notes. Try as I might, I just couldn't come up with five questions to send to Phil for clearance. Instead, I took a nap at the pool and woke up just in time to log onto the call.

The conference call was a circle-jerk led by the debate moderator, Barry Earl, another one of Jules' clients, who the press had nicknamed "Mr. Wonderful." If you wondered why, you need only ask him and no doubt he'd be happy to explain. He spent a full 20 minutes pontificating to me and Penny Wire, the other panelist, about why this debate was the most significant since Kennedy/Nixon. He finally came up for air only to ask us if there was anything we wished to ask him. The guy was so caught up in himself that never once did he ask us what we intended to ask the presidential candidates, much less attempt to nail down our five specific questions. Which suited me just fine.

Starving, I next headed for Dan Tana's, a classic Italian restaurant not far from my hotel. I was flying solo and had no reservation, intending to discreetly saddle up to the bar and enjoy some pasta before going back to the Polo Lounge. The place was small and built inside a classic California cottage that would look nondescript to the uninitiated, but it had a street-smart maitre d' who was old school, and made it his business to know faces. Several people were waiting to be seated but when he saw me, there was a glimmer of recognition along the lines of what I'd been getting at home in Florida, and he quickly found an open seat for me at an otherwise crowded bar. I don't think the guy could have identified me as Stan Powers. But I *do* believe that he'd seen me somewhere and figured he'd cover his bases in case I was somebody important. Well not yet, but I was working on it.

Since I wasn't doing *Morning Power* on Monday, my plan was to relax at the pool for the next two days before being picked up late Monday afternoon and driven to Simi Valley. I would take my luggage with me because immediately after the debate, I was catching a red-eye back to Tampa so that I could host the radio show on Tuesday morning. If things went according to plan, I'd land at about 5 a.m. and get to the studio just in time to host the second hour of the program. Steve Bernson had already texted that the local network affiliates appeared interested in sending cameras to the studio to record me taking calls and offering a debate recap.

Sunday brought a reminder of how big my participation in the debate was back at home. The *Tampa Bay Times* had a morning story titled "Power in the Morning" previewing my role in the debate and what they described as a "meteoric rise in the GOP power circle." There was a quote in the story, which I read online, from state party chairman Herb Barness, who said he viewed me as "a committeeperson without portfolio" who could "single-handedly drive the vote in the I-4 corridor." Not bad.

He even said, "Stan Powers might elect the next president."

The notoriety was building, not only back home, but even here on the left coast, and not just at Dan Tana's. On Sunday at lunchtime, a Swede named Sven who ran the pool at the hotel approached me in my cabana saying, "Mr. Powers, is there anything you require for tomorrow night?" Not for today. Not for the pool. He meant for the debate. I made myself at home there for the rest of the day and returned on Monday morning to read the papers poolside on my iPad. Enjoying the sun and star treatment, and eating eggs Benedict at a cabana while watching a model swim laps, the idea of hitting Governor James below the belt with a question about his open marriage didn't seem so awful anymore.

Reagan Library made me actually want to be a Republican in more than name only. The place was magnificent, built on a hilltop, and it featured the actual Air Force One that had carried both Nixon back to San Clemente and Ronald Reagan to his meeting with Mikhail Gorbachev in Reykjavik. This Boeing 707 had been flown to California, disassembled and put back together inside a glass pavilion that made you feel like you were coming in for a landing when you stood next to it and looked outside. It was an awesome sight and with the airplane as a backdrop, it made a wonderful setting for a presidential debate. We panelists were to be positioned with our backs to the audience of a few hundred wealthy donors and party activists, facing the candidates.

The debate was scheduled to last 90 minutes. There would be an opening sentence, not really a statement, for the candidates to introduce themselves. Then, 20 minutes of questioning by Mr. Wonderful, followed by a question each from myself and Penny Wire. This was the first time I'd gotten a look at her. She was a thirtysomething hottie from the *Orange County Register* who'd probably gotten the gig because of her eyewear. She fit the bill for what was needed—easy on the eyes female from a California conservative oracle, but she wore a pair of designer glasses that were the equivalent of lipstick on Fox. Then we'd repeat that drill three times. So I'd be asking three questions but had to have more at the ready in case any of my material was preempted either directly or indirectly by the other two.

I figured there would be some last-minute coordination among the three of us regarding what we would ask, but there was none. As the hour drew near, we still had not shared any thoughts with one another. And there were no limitations as to what I could ask—at least none that anyone had brought to my attention. This was much more seat-of-the-pants than I would have imagined. I guess that could be attributed to journalistic integrity, but I had none. And I was committed to dropping the hammer at my first opportunity. My thinking was that by asking the question early, I would create a ripple effect. And if they chose to, the other candidates could come back to it, no matter what James responded.

I took my place at a desk which would face the candidates with my back to the crowd. Mr. Wonderful was at the other end. Penny Wire sat in the middle. The red lights of the cameras went on and Mr. Wonderful welcomed the national television audience to raucous applause from the live crowd. By now the packed room had the feel of a political rally, not a serious debate, and not too different from what I'd experienced three nights prior at *Real Time*.

"And now," said Mr. Wonderful, "let's meet the Republican candidates."

Out they walked, one at a time, taking their places at their respective podiums.

"Texas Governor Margaret Haskel."

There she was looking pretty damn hot in a fitted white dress with a blue scarf.

"Colorado Governor Wynne James."

I couldn't even look him in the eyes. Partly

for what I'd failed to do in support of him over the past few months, but mostly for what I was planning to do to him tonight.

"Georgia Senator Laurent Redfield."

Redfield got huge applause, but only from a handful of people. I figured they were whatever's left in Southern California of the John Birchers.

"Businessman William Lewis."

He hadn't won a single state so far, but if you'd landed from Mars, turned off the sound on your television and judged the debate solely based on confidence and charisma, you'd have scored him a winner. As usual, he was perfectly coiffed, sporting a bespoke suit, probably from Saville Row, and a striped shirt that I was sure had been made for either him or Prince Charles at Turnbull & Asser.

"And Colonel George Figuera."

Figuera gave what was by now his signature salute. He did it every time he was introduced at debates or at his rallies. His supporters would return the salute whether they'd actually served or were chicken-hawks. But he was no chicken-hawk. Figuera was the real deal: a hawk's hawk. At some level I had to respect that. He'd been there. He just wished we hadn't left, and I couldn't fathom why.

They each shook hands with one another and got comfortable. The order from left to right was: William Lewis, Governor James, Margaret Haskel, Senator Redfield and Colonel Figuera. The idea was that James and Haskel would share center stage; they'd earned this prominence through their performance in primaries thus far. The three others would flank them. Many things were odd about this crew, not the least of which was that none of these five had dropped out even though only Haskel and Lewis had a shot at capturing the nomination. The two had traded victories in some delegate-rich states. Illinois had been a big victory for Haskel. Wisconsin, too. But James had responded in kind with a win in New York. In Pennsylvania, a strong James showing in the Philadelphia suburbs gave him a decisive victory. North Carolina went to Haskel. And of course, Haskel won big in Texas, putting her within striking distance of securing the nomination. It was a marathon and they were all still standing. Something else the Republicans had in common became obvious from the very first question: no one was going to leave anything off the table tonight!

The crowd had come for red meat, a fact not lost on the five candidates. The more extreme the answer, the better it played with the live audience. Logic be damned, theatrics mattered. It was hard, I'm sure, for the candidates to refrain from feeding on that instant gratification and think instead about those watching from home in California. Or even Middle America. As the night progressed, I knew that the mainstream media would have a field day in lampooning everyone on the stage, including me.

"I wonder if I'll end up as SNL material," I thought to myself.

William Lewis set the standard for the night with his very first response.

Mr. Wonderful: "Mr. Lewis, you've yet to win a single primary, and yet here you are tonight. Why would anyone vote for you in the California primary tomorrow where your sole role is that of spoiler?"

Lewis, without missing a beat: "I happen to know you get paid seven figures to essentially work one day a week hosting a Sunday morning show. How about you and I make a wager. I'll bet you $10,000 that I win tomorrow's primary and if I don't, that money will go to a charity of your choice. All you need do is match my offer."

The crowd went absolutely crazy.

"Do it, do it, do it!" erupted the audience in a chant.

I sat there loving the fact that Lewis had completely turned around an embarrassing question with a preposterous wager. Mr. Wonderful was now a seven-figure pussy. Temporarily forgotten was the fact that Mr. Wonderful was correct—

Lewis hadn't won a single primary but had nonetheless stayed in the race until the end.

A question or two later, Mr. Wonderful turned to a giant video screen to welcome a YouTube submission, where a military veteran had a question for Colonel Figuera.

"Thank you for your service, sir," the questioner began innocently enough. "I am Brian Meyers, and I honorably served my country on two tours of duty in Afghanistan."

There was polite applause from the audience as the tape of the questioner continued.

"I share your view that we dishonored the sacrifice of those who never came home when we bid a hasty retreat."

I tried not to show any facial expression, but found that idea to be absolutely crazy. Hasty retreat? After a decade of war? What wouldn't be hasty? Twenty years? Fifty? I looked at Figuera who was standing tall and smiling, obviously enjoying the attention.

"But there is one area in which we disagree, sir. I am a gay American, and I would like to know why you opposed, and still oppose the repeal of Don't Ask, Don't Tell?"

Figuera frowned. The audience immediately turned sour. What had been polite applause for a young veteran was now a smattering of boos. It wasn't a majority of the audience. It wasn't even half. But it was a noticeable number, and the boos would certainly be audible to television viewers. A soldier who had fought in Afghanistan and wanted us to remain there—but who happened to be gay—had just gotten a Bronx cheer. It was the equivalent of Philadelphia Eagles fans once booing Santa Claus, and now, on top of Lewis' $10K wager, this too would make news.

Figuera proceeded to mishandle the question. He gave a substantive response which would have been appropriate had there not been the boos. He ignored that reaction completely. Big mistake. Had Colonel Figuera confronted that outburst, he would've been the hero, at least in my book, and gotten some positive media play for the GOP. But instead he gave a rote reply about "maintaining discipline in a battlefield environment."

"Wow," I thought. This thing was quickly turning into a clusterfuck.

As the questioning continued, with the exception of Governor James, the candidates were each trying to out-right-wing one another as they had been doing for more than a year. And nary a question was answered without someone invoking Ronald Reagan's name. But in my opinion, if the Gipper were alive he would never have passed the litmus tests this group heaped upon one another.

After Senator Redfield repeated his mantra

that he'd remove every last vestige of Obama-care from the federal regulations, Mr. Wonderful asked him, "What would be the fate of an illegal immigrant who walked into an emergency room lacking insurance?"

Redfield's reply that "His care will be left to God" drew a robust round of applause.

Three thousand miles from Florida, I thought I heard Debbie vomit.

Margaret Haskel took a question from the woman at the *Orange County Register* regarding her opposition to an assault weapons ban (big applause) and turned it into an opportunity to highlight her signing of 17 death-sentence warrants (even bigger applause).

Poor Governor James. He'd done far better in the actual primaries than anyone would ever have guessed from the crowd's reaction. His supporters never seemed to be represented in these venues; perhaps they preferred to leave their McMansions, draw a curtain closed, and vote for him anonymously before heading to Starbucks. The more he made sense—at least to me—the more he was heckled by the crowd. When Mr. Wonderful asked him whether he'd enforce federal drug laws in states like his that had decriminalized marijuana, you'd have thought he'd embraced reprieves for child molesters, not Americans who chose a joint instead of a martini.

Molly Hatchet took every opportunity to go after him.

"I run a border state. I know what it's like to have these marauding illegals come across the border and to take our jobs, prosperity, and women. You should ask Governor James why he wants to send all their kids to college in front of ours."

The line didn't make sense, at least as I had heard it, but it didn't matter. The audience ate it up, hearing only, I am sure, that James was for the illegals (bad) and Haskel was not (good). And when James offered an explanation about "extending American opportunity to children who themselves had not sought to break any laws," his answer drew catcalls from the crowd.

That's when Mr. Wonderful came to me.

As the debate had progressed, so had my dread. On a legal tablet in front of me, replete with the insignia of the Reagan Library and my idiotic doodles (including the prism from the jacket of *Dark Side of the Moon*), sat the paper with the typed question that Jackson Hunter had handed me in the Polo Lounge. To ask it could potentially ensure Margaret Haskel's victory in tomorrow's primary, her nomination, and my syndication. But when those words left my mouth, so would every ounce of dignity I had left.

Could I do it? Should I do it? I heard Phil's

voice in my head as I had so many times before: "Don't be a pussy, Powers." I took a deep breath, grabbed my sack, and let it fly.

"Governor James. Many voters in tomorrow's California primary wish to vote for a candidate who shares their family values. Can a candidate who once told his own spouse that he desired an open marriage be that individual?"

For the first time all evening, there was rapt silence. The gay soldier had been booed. A preposterous $10,000 wager, death penalty talk, and the idea that God was a better answer than modern medicine had been cheered. But now the hall stood frozen. It was as if everyone at the Reagan Library inched forward in their seat, not wanting to miss a word of James' reply. That the governor was on his second marriage was not news. That his first had ended badly was also the subject of rumor and speculation, but not something that had ever been publicly addressed. His first wife had died from breast cancer after their divorce and before he married his second wife, or perhaps she would have spoken for herself. And while the divorce records of the parties were supposedly long sealed, Jackson Hunter's question had a seemingly credible attachment: a page from Evelyn James' deposition in which she stated that a young Wynne James had come to her with a proposition for an open marriage for reasons that were not identified in the transcript. Now, tonight, on the eve of the final primary, I had just rolled that stink bomb right under Air Force One.

I'm sure Wynne James had been prepared for hundreds of possible questions tonight. There had been enumerable debates over the last 18 months, and by now, the candidates were largely on autopilot. They were like wind-up dolls, capable of spouting off an answer to any issue the moment someone pulled their string. But it was painfully obvious that he was not ready for my low blow. He took a second or two to compose himself, which in comparison to the tempo up until that moment seemed like an eternity. His face reddened. He clutched the podium. And he stared right at me.

"Mr. Powers, I will not elevate your scurrilous accusation as I seek the most dignified elective office in the world."

That was it. One sentence. He fucking shot me between the eyes. And I deserved it.

The crowd remained silent. No one was sure how to react. And the debate continued. More crazy talk was offered. But I knew that no matter what had preceded that exchange, and regardless of what came after, I'd just uncorked the debate equivalent of the legendary anti-Goldwater TV commercial which showed a young girl picking daisies over a sound bed consisting of the doomsday countdown clock.

Knowing the way Molly Hatchet played, I was sure that the deposition question was being put online as I still sat in my debate chair, and all I wanted to do was get on the airplane and fly home. The rest of the debate was a blur; I don't even remember my other two questions.

Finally the red light on the floor camera turned off. The candidates shook hands and welcomed their families onstage before being released from the camera shot to depart as their aides scurried to get into the adjacent spin room where they would offer themselves to the amassed media. There was a group of reporters now gathering at the foot of the stage, and they all wanted to chat with just one candidate: Wynne James. I tried not to notice as I quickly gathered my notes, mindful of needing to hustle to catch the red-eye to Tampa in time to host *Morning Power*. I made it off the stage and was headed outside where I hoped a Town Car sat ready to shuttle me to LAX when Jackson Hunter appeared out of nowhere and asked for a quick word. He shook my hand, congratulated me, and said that Governor Haskel was still in the building and had specifically asked to see me. Having begun the night as frontrunner, she would no doubt be upgraded to "presumed nominee" in the morning's newspapers. I was in no position to object.

"Breitbart just posted the deposition excerpt,"

he said under his breath. I was hardly surprised. In the spin room, I was equally sure that Haskel's representatives were claiming their hands were clean and that they were as surprised as James about the question. That's the way these things work.

Hunter escorted me to a private, second-floor, hideaway office at the library that he said had been used by the Gipper himself before his passing. There, sitting on a loveseat in a room filled with the personal possessions of Ronald Reagan, surrounded by major donors and a half-dozen aides, was the Governor of Texas, studying her iPhone. The fact that of all the candidates, she had been allotted this as her green room told me a great deal about her status within the party. As I walked in the door, there was a smattering of light applause from the 20 or so people. Margaret Haskel looked up and said, "There he is, the great moderator, Stan Powers!"

Then she pulled me close and dropped her voice.

"Stan, I want to thank you for your courtesy tonight."

My courtesy? A more honest statement might have been, "I want to thank you for kneeing Wynne James in the nuts tonight."

"It was my pleasure, ma'am."

Ma'am? I never spoke like that. If Debbie

had heard me say that I'm convinced she would have slapped me. Maybe even harder than she would have slapped me for asking the open marriage question.

Governor Haskel moved in closer. We were face to face now. The others in the room knew to give us a moment and resumed their conversations. The governor remained standing and lowered her voice.

"I was just talking about you today with Herb Barness."

Barness was the state party chairman, the same guy who'd just said nice things about me in the Sunday newspaper.

"He agrees that you'd be a perfect representative of Florida to cast your state's delegate votes for me in the roll call at the convention, especially if Tobias is our opponent, which I think he will be after we both win tomorrow. You know the normal drill with the roll call—every state gets a minute to say a commercial about their home, but I've been thinking that it wastes a valuable TV moment. If I'm running against Tobias instead of Baron, I would like Florida to be the state to put me over the top and I don't want a damn commercial for Florida being the last thing people hear before I am formally nominated. We have something else in mind. You seem to work well with Jackson. He will be in touch."

I said nothing and tried to process exactly what was being offered, if anything.

"It could be a very big, highly watched moment, Stan. I'd like you to think about that. Assuming it's Tobias, I'm offering you the chance to address the party convention and the nation, from your hometown."

"Well, that would be an honor, Governor."

"Good. It'll be a critical time, Stan, just as people are starting to focus on their November choice. And there are a few things they need to know about the Florida governor sooner rather than later. Things you'll be happy to share, I'm sure."

"You can count on it."

Margaret Haskel shook my hand again, more firmly than most guys I know. Somebody suggested we pose for a photograph together, which we did. And then I was shown the door. I scrambled to juggle my luggage as I hustled out to the curb and my car for the 50-minute ride to the airport, all while wishing I had more time to go back to Venice Beach for medicinal purposes. Alone, in the back of a Town Car, and for the second time in almost as many days, I scrolled my iPhone for reaction to the spectacle that had just occurred.

By that point every news outlet—large or small, left or right—was all about the election. Summer's withdrawal had stirred the pot and generated interest like never before, and both parties' nomination contests had started to feel more like *Survivor* than *American Idol*. America was hooked. The excerpt from the James deposition many years ago was now getting the siren treatment at Drudge. Huffpo remained focused on Tobias and Baron going down to the wire, which was more of interest to its readers. I thought of Susan and hoped she'd had bigger things to do tonight than watch the circus on the other side of the aisle. The Democratic debates were over and tonight Tobias and Baron were both holding their final rallies of their abbreviated primary campaigns.

Having surveyed the blogosphere to see how big the open marriage question was playing (Answer: Big), I was ready to see how my role had been received in my inner circle. In my mind, texts were like exit surveys, emails more like election results. Via text, friends could only give me the bottom line, but if they were so motivated, could tell me more in an email. I started with the exit surveys.

"U should have told me. Homerun," was Phil's take.

"Important that you call me tomorrow," from Jules.

"Atlanta extremely pleased," from Steve Bernson.

"You had to have been high," from Alex.

"Asshole."

That was the one word that was texted to me from a phone number I recognized as Debbie's. That's about what I'd expected from her. And I didn't disagree. Suddenly I lost my appetite for reading the longer-winded emails.

That night I learned why they call those flights red-eyes. Given all that had happened over the previous couple of days, you'd think I'd have slept like a baby, but I hardly caught any rest. Instead I tossed and turned under a blanket in seat 3C replaying in my mind everything that had happened since Thursday. But the critical timeline extended further back than that. Phil had been adamant that I push Tobias on religion. Even though I'd soft-pedaled it on account of Susan's unexpected presence in the studio, there was no doubt that I was the one responsible for making it an issue in the election, at least amongst those on the right. The Haskel campaign had noted that I'd raised something hot while advancing my own interests, and appropriately concluded that I was game for bigger assignments, namely taking out Wynne James. And now, anticipating that they'd vanquished James, they were hoping I would do likewise for them with Tobias. How exactly they expected me to do this hadn't yet been explained. Molly Hatchet had said there were things people needed to know about Tobias sooner rather than later. Flying home solo, I thought about the people I could possibly call for advice by running through in my mind what I knew they would say. Phil? He'd have me throwing that Molotov cocktail on radio air immediately, not waiting until the convention. Jules? He'd tell me the convention speech would guarantee syndication and that everything should be focused on that moment. Debbie? I doubted she'd even speak to me. And if she did, she'd say I had finally, officially sold my soul. Susan? Holy shit. My head was spinning.

Putting aside my complicated feelings for his wife, I liked Bob Tobias and thought he'd done a decent job as Florida's governor. And of course, I didn't give a shit whether he was a person of faith. How could I? Debbie was correct in saying that I hadn't exactly set church attendance records on fire. But if the path he'd chosen was a religion founded in the twentieth century by an American science fiction writer based on some intergalactic horseshit, not even I could ignore that. Frankly, given the fantastical basis of Scientology, I couldn't believe that the IRS gave it tax-exempt status. The audit summary that hung in my office alleged that a spouse was challenging her husband's adherence to Scientology and that he was an elected official. Assuming that Tobias was the public figure referenced, Susan Miller was the one who'd tried to drive that wedge.

It might be total bullshit. The idea that such a secret could be kept from Florida voters for so long made it dubious. And even if the audit was truly related to the Tobias/Miller marriage, it was unclear whether Susan had been successful. I also considered the possibility that she too was or had been a Scientologist and that perhaps she was trying to get her husband to ditch the church with her. How the fuck should I know?

What I thought I *knew* was: Tobias had a long-standing refusal to say the usual bullshit about our nation's religious roots while running for office; I'd had something stuck in my palm at a Tea Party rally that purported to link an unnamed elected official to Scientology; Susan had an uncanny awareness of a hidden dive bar that was located within spitting distance of Scientology's headquarters; and Molly Hatchet was now insinuating that Tobias had a deep dark secret that voters needed to know. All that, and the fact that Susan was mysteriously interested in keeping me close to her as the campaign unfolded.

Ever since she had left me that first message after my in-studio interview with Tobias, I'd wondered what her motivation was. Of course, I hoped it was sexual, that she thought about me over the years, and that now, recognizing the career I'd built for myself on a path that she'd paved, she wanted to rekindle an old flame. Whether she'd come to the studio that day to be the dutiful political spouse, or because she'd figured out that she knew Stan Powers, I wasn't sure. But she came, we saw one another, and then she called. That was followed by our odd encounter at Delrios, a night that had seemed to lack any purpose. Or did it? I hadn't raised religion in the offensive manner prescribed by Phil, but I had raised the subject in a cursory way face-to-face with her husband and countless times on the radio thereafter. Maybe her purpose in coming to Delrios had been to take my temperature, to see whether my questions and comments were based on anything substantive or whether they were just the usual drivel from her husband's detractors. After all, if I were onto the fact that he, or he and she, were followers of a faith that Middle America found cult-like and preposterous, wouldn't I have brought it out when we were alone? This seemed plausible. Maybe her only interest was in finding out whether or not I knew she was a Scientologist. And for all I knew, she'd done it with Tobias' blessing! Somewhere over the Grand Canyon I fired up my Kindle and began to read Janet Reitman's *Inside Scientology*.

CHAPTER 14

Rod Chinkles seemed legitimately happy to see me when I dragged myself into the studio on Tuesday morning. Alex, not so much.

"I don't get you, Stan."

"I don't get me either."

Thankfully, our listeners agreed with Rod. I received a hero's welcome from the many callers at WRGT who wanted to praise my exposure of Governor James and throw Bill Maher under the bus.

"Stan, you spared us another Clinton fiasco with James. He'd have sullied the Oval Office if not for you," Kyle from Riverview told me.

"Maher's the same guy who called our soldiers cowards. Way to go, Stan," said Walt from Winter Haven.

I only had a vague recollection of Walt's reference. No doubt Maher had said something stupid when comparing the relative cowardice of the 9/11 terrorists to our military's use of drone technology, but I wasn't about to jolly-stomp on the statement. It wasn't something I would have said, but I thought I understood what Maher had been trying to say at the time. I was too tired to get worked up about it. And besides, a guy who does what I do every day is always a seven-second delay away from temporary unemployment.

I spent an hour on air recapping the *Real Time* appearance and played sound bytes that Alex had edited, and another hour rehashing the debate.

"Thanks for outing that bigamist," said another caller, regarding James.

By the time I signed off and headed for sleep, the campaigning for the nomination was finally over. Californians were headed to the polls and when I'd return on Wednesday morning, the combatants for the general election would be set. On my way out the door, Alex handed me another message from Wilma Blake. This time she said:

"Funny name. I don't think I've ever taken a call on air from a Wilma."

Clearly she had noticed that this wasn't the first call from Wilma, and I'm sure she was looking for my reaction. I tried to offer none.

My convertible top was up when I cleared the parking garage and gave a nod to my fishing friend. Then I dialed. Every time I had returned her calls, they had been to a different number. This time it was a Los Angeles exchange, suggesting she was still in California to watch the returns later tonight. Obviously Tobias thought he was winning the state or he'd be moving on before the votes were tallied.

"Good luck tonight," I said when she picked up. "Win and you'll be just one step away."

Susan didn't even so much as say thanks. Nor did she offer any thoughts on today's primary, including the buzz created by my question to Wynne James. She was all business.

"You really need to give this a rest, Stan. I saw the Maher show. You're embarrassing yourself every time you talk about Bob's faith. Haven't you noticed that no one else shares your obsession?"

"Maybe that's because they don't know what I know."

"And what is it you think that you know?"

It was really the first time she flat-out asked me what I had on her husband. I partially obliged.

"I know that for your husband this is far more than a semantic debate."

I wasn't prepared to drop the S-word yet since I was far from having the goods. All I had were a few threads that raised a suspicion, but nothing that warranted an outright confrontation. Plus, who knew what kind of *News of the World* scum was tapping her phone calls these days. Still, she seemed to get my meaning.

"I think we should meet to discuss this."

"I assume you're not talking tomorrow at 7:35 on *Morning Power*?"

Susan ignored the suggestion.

So I said, "Okay, how about Delrios again?"

"I'm flying back into Tampa tomorrow. Meet me at 7. The Clearwater Hilton right on the beach."

I was surprised that she'd pick such a public spot, a hotel no less, but I said, "Fine."

"Ask for Wilma Blake at the desk. They'll know."

The line went dead.

I wasn't sure how Susan intended to meet with me at the Clearwater Hilton without getting noticed. Her husband's visual ID was about 100 percent in Florida, and now 98 percent in America—and hers was climbing just as high. She had already been on every regional television program, and in every regional magazine and newspaper. And come tomorrow, she would be the wife of the Democratic nominee for president.

I had ignored an incoming call while speaking with Susan and now saw that someone had left me a voicemail. It was Carl.

"You sure as hell better be at Delrios tonight. Three strikes and you're out," he said.

All I wanted to do was go home and go to sleep, and the last thing I felt like doing was tying one on with my buddies. I erased the message as I headed for a nap, deciding that I'd see how I felt if and when I ever woke up. Then I drove home, showered, pitched the blinds, and turned off my electronics.

When I awoke sometime later in total darkness, I'd been in such a deep sleep that I didn't immediately recognize my surroundings nor the day, much less the time. Both of my digital alarm clocks said 8:40. I didn't know if that was a.m. or p.m. My first fear was that I'd slept through an air shift. Elated when I figured out that wasn't the case, my next thought turned to my empty stomach. And remembering my looming meeting with Susan tomorrow, I suddenly felt the need for a drink. It was then that I decided I'd hightail it over to Delrios to meet Clay and Carl, less they voted me out of our triumverate. By the time I caught up with them, standing exactly at the bar where I expected to find them, they were hammered. And, happy as hell to see me. Of course, it was my round. I waved Ralph over to pour us a few shots and so that I could ask whether there was anything edible in the kitchen.

"You sure do spend time with interesting people," he said with a bottle of tequila in his hand.

I smiled and reached for a shot, trying to comprehend what he was saying. Was that a reference to me being on Maher? Participating in the presidential debate the prior night? Or was he subtly telling me he'd figured out with whom I'd shared a drink in the back a few weeks ago? I wasn't sure. And he was way too street-smart to let me know which it was. Bastard. Two C-notes were now coming his way at Christmas.

The television above the bar—the same set on which I'd watched President Summers' shocking announcement six months prior—now showed the election night coverage from California. The polls had just closed, and the exit surveys showed Margaret Haskel beating Wynne James by four points, cementing the nomination. The sound was muted on account of the jukebox, and the closed captions for the hearing impaired were crawling along the bottom of the TV. I caught enough to know what they were talking about:

". . . credibility was hurt when the divorce deposition was revealed. . . ."

Meanwhile, on the Democratic side, Bob Tobias was expected to handily defeat Vic Baron. That would make it official. As I had long suspected, it was going to be Haskel and Tobias fighting for the presidency. The three of us just stood there with our drinks, temporarily speechless as we watched the screen. Normally Clay and Carl would never bring up anything that involved my work, but I was in the midst of a pretty amazing run and therefore not surprised when tonight of all nights, they crossed that line. Of course, at the top of their list was Margaret Haskel.

"That is one presidential hottie," Clay said. "She's had my vote ever since she told the women of America to be like Jerry Hall."

I was surprised he was even aware of that quote, but it was proof of Haskel's ability to generate buzz well beyond the political sphere. But his next statement tempered my belief that he had any interest whatsoever in policy.

"Heaven would be that Texas broad and Florida's first lady in my hot tub at the same time," he hooted.

Carl had his own area of interest.

"Stan, sometimes I don't get you. I watched last night when you gave that guy a workout because he told his old lady he wanted a threesome. The Stan Powers I know might not have asked, but would have been thinking the same thing."

Clay laughed. I smiled but did not respond. Instead, I nervously clinked shot glasses with the two of them just as Ralph brought out something he said was a Philly cheesesteak but bore no resemblance to anything I'd ever eaten in Philadelphia. I felt like I was being fed a tourist special, but that didn't stop me from eating it, further fucking up my body clock which was already confused by my sleeping eight straight hours during the daytime.

After I got home, the combination of too much rest, booze, and the remnants of something disguised as a cheesesteak sitting in my stomach made for a restless night before what promised to be one of the more interesting days in an already crazy week. I tossed and turned trying to decide whether I should show Susan the audit summary when I met her at the Clearwater Hilton the following day. And, whether I should tell her the Haskel campaign wanted me to do to her husband what I'd done to Wynne James. By the time my two alarm clocks went off at 3:30, I'd made up my mind to take the audit with me and confront her with it.

I was still a bit fucked up when I went on the air. Fortunately, given the interest in the outcome of the California primary and the finality of the nomination contests, it was an easy show in which to coast. Listeners wanted to talk and I stepped out of the way and let them. Frank Sellers would've been proud. Then I went back home and tried to get some rest. When I left my condo later that afternoon, I was wearing my usual uniform: Bruno Magli shoes/no socks, jeans, Oxford cloth and sport coat. Only this time, tucked inside the left breast pocket were the purported notes of a Scientology audit, perhaps concerning a younger Bob Tobias.

I did as I'd been instructed. I arrived at the hotel at 6:45 p.m. and tossed my keys to a valet.

Adjacent to his stand sat a pair of dark Town Cars, idling, that I thought had official state tags. But tinted windows prevented me from getting a look at the drivers, much less at any passengers. I slowed my gait wondering if Susan would emerge from one of the rear doors. Nothing happened, so I continued inside and up one flight of stairs to the lobby. It was overrun by baseball fans who were in town to participate in one of those MLB dream weeks at the nearby spring training home of the Phillies. Two guys in pinstripes stopped me in my tracks and asked if I would take their picture. I obliged, and then one of them said:

"Hey, aren't you the Tampa talker?"

This was the last place where I wanted any recognition or notoriety but what choice did I have?

"We're Lancaster County Tea Partiers," he confided before asking his buddy to take his picture with me.

I took a moment to survey the lobby. I knew better than to think that Susan Miller would be prominently seated and waiting to chat with me in the lobby of a fucking Hilton, but I felt unsure about what to do. Then a 40ish guy in a suit standing behind the check-in counter made eye contact with me and stepped around the desk with an envelope in his hand. He spoke in a quiet voice.

"Thank you for joining us, Mr. Powers. Mrs. Blake's assistant has left you your key."

Smooth. Her assistant huh? I wondered who else was in the loop. And, I had never even mentioned any name to this guy so he clearly knew to expect me.

"Thank you," I responded, hoping he hadn't taken note of my lack of luggage.

The open envelope had "505" written on it and one of those magnetic keys inside. I thanked him while trying to act like I was used to this level of service, then got on the elevator and pushed 5.

My chest was thumping as the elevator climbed, and then the doors opened and I walked along the corridor heading west. Whatever was about to unfold, it was going to go down in a beachfront room. Tucked inside my sport coat pocket was the purported audit, but I still had no idea of how I was going to raise the subject. I rehearsed a few lines in my mind as I put the key in the lock, but it didn't matter. The room was empty.

It was a standard-sized unit with a king bed and balcony facing south and offering a partial view of the Gulf. The bed was made. There was no luggage, and no clothes hung in the closet. Instinctively, I reached for the minibar, delighted to find it unlocked. I poured a miniature bottle of Jack into a glass I found in the bathroom after removing its paper lid.

After about 10 minutes, there was a knock on the door. Nervously I walked over and peeked out of the keyhole. Seeing nothing, I nevertheless opened the door into an empty corridor. It took me another moment to realize that the sound had not come from the entranceway, but from the connecting door to an adjoining room. Fumbling with the bolt lock, I finally opened it, and there was Susan Miller.

I'd been afraid to study her features too intently when she'd accompanied her husband in studio. And the light here was much better than it had been at Delrios. But now I could see her clearly, and she was no less attractive to me than she had once been while wearing a suede skirt and cowboy boots at Shooter's. She stood before me wearing a white, tight blouse and an equally snug khaki skirt and matching pumps. We were two feet apart and I suddenly felt those green eyes seeing right through me. Envy was back.

Then she turned her back to me and walked a step or two into her room, which I interpreted as an invitation to follow. Hers was a one-bedroom suite better angled toward the water.

"Thirsty?" she asked.

She picked up a glass of white wine from a tabletop and motioned me toward the minibar. I helped myself to another mini Jack. We were in a small parlor which had a couch and love seat, and open French doors leading to a bedroom where I could see a king-size bed. As in my room, the bed hadn't been touched and I saw no luggage. I sat down on the sofa and noticed that the TV was tuned to a cable news station with the sound down low. I saw some B-roll footage of Bob Tobias and Margaret Haskel and a couple of talking heads who were having it out. I turned to Susan. Small talk was never my strong suit. But there was an obvious question burning inside me.

"Does your husband know you are here?"

"Bob knows we are acquainted."

That was a very interesting but incomplete response. Part of me was disappointed that he was in the loop, but an even more prominent part of me didn't give a shit. That same part had always felt that it was inevitable that we'd cross paths again one day, no matter who she'd married, and was just damn happy to be here. I wondered how she'd explained me to him. Did she tell him that we'd been summer fuck buddies years ago? Or that we'd simply worked together? Women must have a language for this sort of thing, but I was clueless as to what it was. Anyway, Susan seemed more interested in politics than the past.

"Bob's not angry with you so much as he is disappointed, Stan."

I said nothing. It sounded like a guilt trip.

"He thought he had you figured out. He told

me the night before our studio interview that he thought you were different than the rest of those guys. Since then you've proved him wrong. He never took you for a zealot."

In our first reunion, it had been all Red State/ Blue State analysis. But this time, Susan was making it personal. I bit my tongue and felt for the exterior of the breast pocket of my sport coat, seeking the assurance that the document was still in its place.

She was thinly smiling now, sitting opposite me on the sofa, and not exactly at the other end. She was leaning forward, clutching her drink, and staring right at me with those eyes.

"It was actually Bob's idea that I come to your studio that day."

I would spend a long time afterwards trying to unravel his motivation. How much did he know? I wanted to ask but she kept talking and I kept listening.

"You ought to be proud of what you've accomplished, Stan."

"And you as well."

"I just never took you for a Tea Party guy."

"So you told me at Delrios."

She was so close to me that once again, I was aware of her scent. It was the same as I'd remembered, sweet and clean and natural, and it was all I could do not to reach out and touch her. The situation was surreal. Here I was sitting in a beachfront hotel room with a woman for whom I'd pined for more than two decades. In the intervening time, I'd built a career for myself largely based on advice she'd given to me. And now, she was married to a presidential front-runner.

It was enough to make me quote Don King's *Only in America*. Instead I raised a glass and invoked another name.

"To Willy Blake and American exceptionalism."

She reciprocated with that same trepidatious smile and continued on.

"Look, Stan. About the religion issue. Bob's Florida detractors have been calling him an atheist for years. He shouldn't be harmed politically just for understanding the Constitution better than his opponents. The easy thing would be for him to just spout out the same bullshit the others do, whether he meant it or not. But instead he's remained intellectually honest."

Damn she was good. No wonder she'd been a superstar lobbyist. But I spoke up.

"You didn't need to run the risk of meeting me here or at Delrios just to tell me that."

Susan sipped her wine before speaking.

"Perception matters more than reality in the political world, and if you persist with rumor and innuendo, you're going to do greater harm than you could ever have imagined."

I said nothing.

"He's a good man, Stan, and I'm here to ask you to focus on something else. Call him a socialist. Crap all over his cancellation of the high-speed rail. Say he's a philanderer, I don't care. Do all those things that guys like you do. But the one thing I'm asking you not to do is challenge his faith. The country can handle the rest, but that will kill him, strange as it sounds."

The part about "doing all those things that guys like you do" was a kick in the nuts. She was right, of course. But I didn't like hearing it. That was something Debbie would say. Christ, they both saw me in the same light.

So I drained my Jack mini. Then I said something that seemed to suck the oxygen out of the room.

"I'm thinking there is more to all this than some esoteric debate about the Establishment Clause."

Her expression changed, and her dismissiveness was suddenly replaced with a clenched palate that told me I'd struck a nerve. Those green eyes drilled down on me with an intensity that made me nervous, and I scratched my chest because I wanted to confirm again that I held the goods.

"You hinted at that on the phone," she said. "Cut the crap, Stan. What is it that you think you've got?"

"Well, I don't really give a shit about whether your husband repeats some senseless sound byte about Judeo-Christian roots," I began, temporarily stepping out of Stan Powers' persona. "But if someone has made an intellectual investment in a belief system that is beyond fantastical—some might even say crazy —that would seem to reflect on their fitness for office, no?"

Susan did not immediately respond. But her body language told me that this was not the same confident, political gunslinger who'd sat across from me in Delrios. Instead I was increasingly convinced that the document inside my pocket was legitimate and that she knew her husband could never sustain its publication. America might have elected its first Catholic president and its first black president, but the election of a Scientologist was 95 million years away—coincidentally the same amount of time that the universe has existed according to L. Ron Hubbard. While Americans were willing to suspend disbelief when it came to their own faith or even other, conventional faiths, I could see no evidence that they were ready to entertain the precepts of Scientology. On the flight home from LA, I'd immersed myself in Janet Reitman's *Inside Scientology*, which pieced together lots of stuff I'd heard over the years but never fully understood. I'm not sure I understand now. But the basic tenets of Scientology—in which humans are believed to be descended from an ancient alien race ruled over by a guy named Xenu—make a virgin birth and resurrection seem staid.

According to Hubbard, we should all forget Adam and Eve because the real story of life on Earth began 95,000,000 years ago when Xenu, the leader of the Galactic Confederation, had been forced to solve an overpopulation problem by mass implanting. He had his hands full with opponents, so he put them inside volcanoes on the prison planet of Teegeeack—what we now call Earth—and wiped them out with hydrogen bombs leaving only the thetans, or souls, of his captives behind. These thetans were badasses. When millions of years later life began again on Teegeeack, the thetans attached themselves to human bodies. Scientologists believe they are the root cause of human problems, and that the only way a man can be saved is by freeing himself from the implanted thetans.

Bob Tobias needed the support of blue collar, Reagan Democrats in places like Ohio and Western Pennsylvania to defeat Margaret Haskel. And there was no way these folks were ready for that kind of culture shock. I'm not sure that people who live in glass houses and believe in things like the parting of the Red Sea or turning water into wine should necessarily throw stones, but still. This would be the death knell for Tobias' presidential hopes if word circulated to Duluth and Portsmouth.

Instead of addressing what I'd said, Susan's demeanor changed. The self-assured political wife disappeared and she seemed more like the girl I'd known years ago. And suddenly, she was anxious to fill in a few blanks.

"You know, I thought of you when I went back to FSU. I knew you'd left Shooter's because I called after you were already gone. They told me you'd gone to be a DJ and I was thrilled."

She was speaking more softly now, and looking straight into my eyes.

"I knew you'd make it, I just never thought that politics was your thing."

I toyed with telling her the story of the format change from classic rock to talk, but decided not to interrupt her. This was the most forthcoming she'd ever been with me and I'd waited a long time for these doors to be unlocked.

"I lost track of you after a while. Then I found out about your success in Pittsburgh when I Googled your name a few years ago and found a mention in the *News-Press*. Only then did I understand that you were working under a shortened name."

"It's a rock thing," I mumbled.

"Then I lost you again. I had no idea that you were doing talk as Stan Powers until the rise of the Tea Party when I saw you on TV. I'd actually heard about Stan Powers long before I realized he was you. All the politicos in Florida are familiar with *Morning Power*. You've really come a long way, Stan."

"So what happened?"

"You mean back then?"

"Yeah."

"I had some growing up to do. It really wasn't about you. I don't regret a minute of those nights at Shooter's, but I am sorry for how I handled it at the end. You were a good guy. You were owed better than that."

For years I had felt certain that she didn't even remember, that the abrupt ending of our brief relationship had been something inconsequential for her.

"My one consolation is that I gave you the career advice. I just never thought you'd put your talents to work like this. Someday you'll have to tell me how you went from making the pistol fire to picking presidents."

The sudden, jarring ringing of her cell phone interrupted the discussion. She looked down, and the nervous expression on her face told me that I should let her handle this in private. Tobias? Maybe he wanted to know what was taking so long. Or what I knew. A media person? I wasn't sure. But I walked back into my room without saying a word, and quietly closed the door. I sat on the one club chair and looked out at the Gulf, toward Sand Key in the distance. In my mind's eye, I was back on Rt. 41, inside Shooter's, pouring drafts and playing something like Pure Prairie League's "Amie" while trying to track the movements of a younger, smoking hot Susan Miller. So lost in my thoughts was I that I didn't hear the door opening and the footsteps behind me.

"Is it cold enough in here for you, Stan?"

Susan was behind me, buck naked, and apparently prepared to negotiate my silence.

CHAPTER 15

You'd think I'd have been elated to settle that decades-old score with the still gorgeous Susan Miller at the Clearwater Hilton. Actually, I was miserable in the weeks that followed. First, I'd betrayed Debbie. It was one thing to mind-fuck an old flame. It was quite another to actually do it. No, Debbie and I weren't married, but she deserved better from me than that. She was smart. She was sexy. She had a great career. She came from a nice family. And as far as I knew, she'd never betrayed the trust I'd placed in her. I was proud to walk into any room with her and was always aware of the roving eyes of the many guys who'd immediately cast their gaze upon her. She wasn't deficient in any demonstrable way. I was. I'd been walking around with a 20-plus-year hard-on that wasn't worth it. Never is. And I'd allowed that and my obsessive desire to get syndicated to let me take her for granted and discount her advice, which I knew to be valid. Because even though Debbie wasn't in the loop about most of my day-to-day decisions, everything she had warned me about was coming true.

She had long been telling me that I would not be able to maintain the Sybil-like existence between real life and radio.

"I don't get it, Stan. You're plenty engaging in real life. Why not let your audience see the real you?"

"Because this audience has no time for a slacker from Ft. Myers who likes to blow a few bones and thinks most politicians are full of shit, especially those who live on the fringe."

"Great. That makes you like everyone else."

"Everyone *except* those who listen to talk radio. The 'everyone else' you describe is too busy earning a living, raising their kids, and watching over their elderly parents to sit, fixated, listening to my brand of communication. You don't fucking get it. I work as the caretaker at a clubhouse for conservatives. These are people who once had no place else to go and now have found a home. I might as well try peddling vegan burgers at a Mickey D's. It won't sell."

We'd go round and round like that. Debbie's perspective was always the exact opposite of whatever Phil Dean recommended and I was convinced hers was a professional death sentence. But now, with the nomination battles over and the summer slogging on, and the spotlight turned on me full bore, my misery escalated.

And the conventions were coming. The

Democrats would have their Mardi Gras in New Orleans and the Republicans would follow the next week in Tampa. That left me with little time to sort out a lot of things. For starters, I'd logged a call to Jules to ask him to get the suits at MML&J off my back. The disciplinary action was still outstanding, and if I was selling my soul for the sake of ratings, I wanted resolution. Despite their pleasure with my defense of the Ten Commandments on *Real Time*, not to mention my takedown of the wife swapper in the GOP field, they still hadn't taken my reprimand out of their file. It was a total passive-aggressive thing that only made me distrust them more. It would not have surprised me to learn that Rod Chinkles had impressed upon his father the need for leverage to keep me ideologically in line until the election was over. After I waited two days, Jules finally called.

"I need you to come to New York in two days," he said.

It was a Wednesday morning and I'd stayed too long at Delrios with Clay and Carl the night before. I tried desperately to clear the cobwebs from my head as he spoke. I knew immediately that this was important. I'd never even seen the inside of his office. Still, with all that was on my plate, I hesitated at the idea of making a trip just to get him to log a call.

"Jules, I really just need you to call MML&J

about the complaint. I don't think it warrants a trip to New York City," I said.

"Stan, put that out of your head. You're the hottest commodity in AM radio right now. You think those guys are going to fuck with you for saying fuck? Stop beating yourself up. The good book they care most about is the ledger! I need you up here in two days. We can talk about it then."

"Can't we do whatever you need to do by conference call?"

"Stan, are you fucking kidding me? It's all happening. Chuck Schwartz will be in my office on Friday afternoon at 2 p.m. to meet you. Fly up here on Friday after you get off the air, or better yet, take the day off, you've earned it. Schwartz wants to eyeball you before we do a deal."

Chuck Schwartz was a self-made guy who'd started with one station back in the days before syndication kicked in and the conglomerates gobbled up everything. He'd built a radio network one station at a time and was now the president of one of the three biggest radio syndicators in the country. There were more, but only three that mattered. And he was among the most influential in the entire talk business. He had a stable that included some of the best-known names, all of whom (of course) were very conservative and likely Phil protegés. Jules went on to say that Schwartz was deep with talent in all day-parts except mornings. That was by design. Radio stations across the nation tend to offer local news and traffic in the morning and then rely upon syndicated talent from mid-morning until afternoon drive. This was partly because, as with WRGT, the local advertisers who want that hometown product during morning drive are their bread and butter. Which has always made syndicating any morning program a challenge—but that seemed about to change.

"He's willing to take the risk and roll you out in mornings, Stan. WRGT will be your flagship, but I think he has another major market, with a 50,000-watt clear channel signal, in his hip pocket. That'd be a great base on which to build."

This was the call I'd been waiting for. All those mornings—nights actually—of getting up early and delivering four hours of talk had been with the dream of this in mind. But now that it was happening, it didn't feel like I'd imagined. I should have been fist pumping the sky and reaching for champagne. I wasn't. But I told Jules I'd be there nonetheless.

No sooner had I hung up than I took a call from the Turd of Taos. All my demons, it seemed, were coming home to roost at once.

"This thing has really broken your way, Stan," Phil crowed.

"How so?"

"You got the Republican candidate eating out of your hand and you own the Democrat in his own backyard. I've got a lot of guys who'd give their left nut to be you right now."

Phil made me wonder why it's always the left nut that people refer to. I felt like asking him how many guys would give their right nut, but my head hurt too much to even razz him.

"It's time to plan for the convention, Stan. You're going to have a shot on national TV, with the world watching, to say something about Tobias and it's got to be right. It's got to be strong. It's got to be a knockout."

"They haven't formally asked me."

"Well, Haskel told you they would. It'll happen soon."

Phil seemed certain that Margaret Haskel's people were about to call regarding my representing the state of Florida in the roll call vote at the convention, but I hadn't heard another word in the month since the debate at the Reagan Library.

"They can't win without Florida, and you have as much clout as any statewide officeholder. And Stan, unlike them, you can be counted on to do what is necessary when that spotlight hits you."

That was the other part. In the eyes of Molly Hatchet, I was someone who'd be willing to play dirty if need be, as I had done with Wynne James. No one else could fill both roles.

My knowledge of the roll call process was limited to what I remembered from watching conventions with my parents when I was a kid. I had a vision in my head of somebody standing up on the floor wearing a donkey or elephant hat and a chest full of campaign buttons, and saying something like: "Madam Chairwoman, I'm pleased to report that Florida, the home of Mickey Mouse, the Miami Dolphins and Tropicana Orange Juice, commits all of its delegates to the future president of the United States . . ."

But I was absolutely sure that *wasn't* what they had in mind for me.

Debbie would have loved it if that was all it was going to be. I had told her there was something in the works. But even though I hadn't told her where the Wynne James wife-swap question had come from, she predicted things would get even nastier.

"They're using you, Stan. You are their lackey."

She'd always predicted that whoring my way to the top would get me in trouble, and now it looked like it just might. Margaret Haskel was a boob who I'd have definitely voted for as Miss America a few decades prior, but who was ill-equipped to run the country. Wynne James seemed like he possessed the type of level head best suited to run the nation, but I'd ruined any chance he had to win California and hence, the nomination. Not that I was so keen on the Democrats either. Bob Tobias seemed like a decent guy, and I couldn't give a shit where he prayed, but now it seemed like there might be some truth to this Scientology thing. I was increasingly put off by the idea that the guy with his finger on the nuclear button would be someone who thought there had once been life on the prison planet of Teegeeack! And beyond the religion question, part of me thought I was being manipulated by both him and his wife.

My reunion with Susan Miller hadn't lived up to the fantasies. It wasn't quite the length of "Stairway to Heaven" (8:02), nor was it "Good Times Bad Times" (2:48). When it ended, the extent of our conversation had been reminiscent of the way we'd often parted on those nights at Shooter's. We both got dressed and left after a few words of small talk. Frankly, the whole encounter hadn't felt much different than that night at Delrios. I didn't show her the audit or tell her that the Haskel campaign was hell-bent on making her husband's faith, or lack of it, the mainstay of their fall campaign. She already knew that. Nor did she ask me to do anything specifically to help her husband's campaign, although maybe that was implied by her behavior. Walking out of the hotel, I had no more of an idea of the purpose of the tryst than when I'd walked in, but the fact that it had all happened after she took a call made me wonder if she'd been following instructions.

But it turned out that Susan wasn't done with me yet.

We hadn't spoken or seen each other since the Hilton. Then, the day after I spoke with Jules, just as soon as the "on air" light dimmed, Alex came into the studio and handed me another phone message from Wilma Blake.

"It's your lady friend," she said this time, once again watching me for a reaction. I tried to offer none, but Alex was intuitive and had probably figured out by now that this was more than a random listener. Whether she'd figured out that it was the Florida first lady I had no idea, but I suddenly remembered that when Susan and Tobias had come into the studio all those months prior, Alex had shot me a look of warning. Did she know or suspect something? I couldn't be sure. But I put it out of my mind for the moment.

I returned Susan's call as soon as I cleared our office tower.

She picked up after one ring. "Hi, Stan." Whatever she said these days, I found myself wondering who was really doing the talking— Susan or Tobias.

"Susan."

"How is the man with all the *Morning Power*?"

"Just doing my job."

"This thing is about to heat up, Stan. We'll be in New Orleans soon. Then it's showtime for you folks."

Referencing the RNC like it was my gathering sounded like the set-up for a fishing trip. I sensed she was looking for any informational crumb I might be willing to share. I still hadn't heard from the Haskel campaign so for the moment was just going about my day-to-day routine of hosting the program and taking what was offered in cable TV hits. Both were keeping me busy at a time of year when I usually sought an escape from Florida's summer heat. The midsummer polls were showing the race deadlocked between Haskel and Tobias, and it was hard to discern who was undecided. Both bases were solid and energized. The left viewed Haskel as a Lone Star version of Sarah Palin with similar deficiencies on the issues. To the right, Bob Tobias was a heathen, something other than Christian, what exactly no one knew. A former jock who'd gone soft after marrying a commie who insisted on keeping her maiden name. So divided was the electorate, that by mid-July, pollsters were admitting that they were having trouble assessing the size and leanings of any undecided voters. For that, we could thank our polarized media, myself included, who were busy whipping both ends of the spectrum into a lather and ignoring the middle in the process.

"Is there a reason you called me?" I asked.

"Well, I was thinking that maybe we could get together before I head for the Big Easy. I'll be in touch."

Click.

On Friday morning I flew north and took a cab from Newark Airport to Midtown Manhattan. Jules' office was located high in a building on East 57th Street. The waiting area had three flat screens each tuned to a different cable television news channel, an enormous window with a commanding view of Central Park, and on the adjacent walls, framed notices of big deals that had been negotiated for the firm's clients from all the major trade publications. I scanned the clips and realized that every A-list host and anchor was represented by Jules or one of his partners. It made me wonder how his firm could represent all of them at the same time without any conflicts. Surely they were competing for the same slots? This was a visual reminder that despite my ascending star, I remained one of the smallest fish in this particular pond. But hopefully that was about to change.

"Stan Powers, meet Chuck Schwartz," Jules said after Philippe had ushered me into a mammoth conference room where there was a tray parked with coffee and sandwiches. I wished I'd worn a tie as I stood shaking hands with an immaculately dressed man who was the boss of some of the biggest names in radio.

"Jules has been speaking highly of you for quite some time, Stan, and of course, I've been following your career. I'm pleased we are finally able to meet."

We shot the shit for a couple of minutes. Schwartz was anxious to hear my assessment of the presidential race, and in particular whether Susan Miller would be Tobias' Achilles' heel. He'd have been shocked to know I'd been chatting with her the previous day. As the conversation flowed, we seemed to hit it off. He did express to me the concern that syndicating a morning program was difficult for the reasons I had discussed with Jules.

"Mornings are tough for terrestrial radio, Stan. Stern was an exception before he jumped to Sirius. These local affiliates, they need a local guy who can tell them about school closings and read live spots from the local car dealers."

I didn't interrupt. Jules had anticipated this concern but said Schwartz was willing to move forward despite his worry about the time slot.

"Stan, there is one thing I'd rather address than leave unsaid."

Oh shit. I felt like Pandora's box was about to

open. Here it comes, I thought. I could only imagine what he was about to say.

"We understand you're a pothead, Stan."

"We heard you fucked the next first lady."

"Our spies tell us that you get pretty hammered every Tuesday night in a dive bar."

"We heard you asked a dirty question at the GOP debate that was given to you by one of the other candidates."

"We hear you are willing to take a perfunctory moment at the convention and use it to advance a presidential candidate and your own personal ambitions."

"We have reason to suspect you don't believe half the shit you say on radio."

But it was none of those.

Instead he said: "Vernon Chinkles from MML&J is an old friend. He told me there is a possible indecency complaint pending against you with the FCC."

I looked at Jules. Dammit. I'd told him to get the suits in Atlanta to back off. Jules started to speak to deflect the issue, but I interrupted him.

"Well, Mr. Schwartz, I don't blame you for being concerned. That utterance was unfortunate and inexcusable. I don't know where it came from, and I am embarrassed that it came out of my mouth."

Jules cracked a slight smile.

"My own mother would have washed my

mouth out with soap had she heard it," I added, hoping I wasn't pushing my luck.

Somewhere Debbie puked. But Schwartz acted like I'd said what he'd hoped.

"Well, I'm glad to hear that, Stan. Good luck when the convention comes to Tampa. We will be watching how you handle all that company in town. I don't have to tell you the stakes in this election. It's probably the most important election in my lifetime. Jules and I will talk further."

I took that as my cue to leave.

Schwartz's having told me this was the most significant election left no mystery as to his vote. Surely he didn't mean, "If we don't elect Bob Tobias and that wife of his the country is headed down the crapper." And something else occurred to me as I sat cramped in back of a New York City taxi. Two things actually: First, who the fuck designs these cabs? Second, how many times can people say this is the most important election of their lifetime? That was a Phil line which had permeated every level of American consciousness.

"You gotta tell them that it's the most important election of their lifetime, and repeat it every day. Always add in that their children's future hangs in the balance. And then, when the election is over, even if your guy wins, start planting the seeds as to why the next election is even more important still."

"But won't they remember that I told them that before?" I'd asked.

"That's the best part, Stan. There is no institutional memory in this business. Things said yesterday are forgotten by tomorrow."

I flew back from New York the same day just so I could have a late dinner with Debbie. I hoped we were coming out of what I would describe as the big thaw. She'd remained super pissed after the debate weekend in California, and a week had passed before she'd even take my call.

"You made an ass of yourself in California, Stan," was how she put it when we finally spoke. "I might not do divorce law, but I sure as hell know how ugly things get when couples split, and the fact that James' wife said something scurrilous about him in a deposition is totally meaningless. I see that sort of thing every day. People twist things in all sorts of ways to get what they want in court. You wrecked any chance that the one sane candidate had of winning."

She was right that there had been no corroboration of James' first wife's testimony; how could there be when she was dead? But that didn't matter in this climate. The truth was irrelevant. All that mattered was that the issue be put in play, where it served notice on a sufficient number of Californians who were anxious for their party to take the White House, that Wynne

James was damaged goods. In the case of Haskel vs. James, Haskel had won. Tobias vs. Haskel was going to be equally blistering.

With three weeks to go before the convention, the I-4 corridor was already a war zone. Both Tobias and Margaret Haskel had spent time doing retail campaigning within earshot of WRGT and they were each bombarding radio listeners and television viewers with constant commercials. One Monday morning, Haskel was my guest by phone and was effusive in her praise of me while telling my audience that those in the I-4 corridor held the next presidency in their hands.

"This convention of theirs is going to be the worst thing to hit New Orleans since Katrina," she'd actually said on air that morning. "And then it'll be our turn in Tampa. And Stan, I want your listeners to know right now, that I am looking forward to you playing a very important role when I get to the I-4 corridor!"

I had been looking into the control room when she said that. Rod must have farted. Either that or Alex was repulsed by what she'd heard.

When I cut to commercial, Alex walked into my studio and handed me a note with Jackson Hunter's name and phone number.

"Your friend the governor asked that you call him immediately," she said with more than a hint of sarcasm in her voice.

As soon as the program ended, I did what I was told.

"I figured you'd be on vacation," I joked when he answered.

"The governor has asked that I come and see you, Stan. It's important," Hunter said.

Hunter was skilled beyond his years for this kind of work. Just the sound of his voice creeped me out. There was no, "Are you free for dinner?" That would have invited a response of "Oh gee, as a matter of fact I'm not." Instead it was only a question of what time. He went on to say that he was already in town coordinating convention logistics. I suggested Bob Heilman's Beachcomber in Clearwater Beach, figuring that like some hussy, I should at least get to eat a good meal before I got fucked.

"Thanks for doing this, Stan. The governor will not forget your courage."

Courage? It took no courage whatsoever to participate in a roll call of votes and stand up and say "the land of Pluto and Goofy and Tampa Bay Ray's baseball supports Margaret Haskel." If I had any courage, I thought, I'd tell my audience that your candidate was unfit.

Instead I said, "See you then."

I knew my worst suspicions were about to be confirmed. Knowing the way they'd had me dispose of Wynne James, I figured they had something even more sinister in mind for

Tobias. Jackson Hunter didn't even wait for his appetizer or a refill of his Coke with lemon to get down to business. And he'd already taught me once not to trust a man who doesn't drink.

"I know the governor mentioned this in California, but I am here to formally invite you to offer Florida's delegates in support of Governor Haskel. You will be an honorary delegate the second night of the convention and when the roll call vote comes to Florida, you will stand and announce the Sunshine State's delegates for the governor. And Stan, Florida will not just be one of the 50 states—Florida will be *the* state. We will be monitoring the count and we will go to Florida in prime time so that it is Florida that formally puts the governor over the top. It will be the perfect time to frame the issue for the nation."

What the "issue" was, or what that framing might look like he did not immediately say.

"Have you thought about what you want me to say?" I asked.

"Well, yes we have. Nothing too lengthy. You'll only have 60 seconds. And you won't have to say too much in terms of your affection for your state because it will already have been stated."

They had the whole thing planned. There would be nothing spontaneous about my role. I sipped. He spoke.

"You need to define the fall election, Stan."

I felt my ass tighten.

"What does that mean?"

"Draw a distinction between Governor Haskel and Bob Tobias. A distinction that you are uniquely qualified to offer. You are the individual who from day one recognized that this guy is outside the mainstream of popular religious belief in America. But I don't think even you realize how far outside the mainstream he is. Now you will be the first to let the nation know that Bob Tobias is worse than a secularist. He's a man of faith, alright. Only his Holy Land is Area 51."

I took another sip from my Jack and Coke and looked around the restaurant. Even in the middle of summer, the Beachcomber was packed and given my recent notoriety and the familiarity of my face, we were already getting lots of looks and nods of recognition. Thank goodness they didn't know what we were discussing.

After we ordered and the waitstaff had moved away from the table, Hunter discreetly slipped his left hand inside his sport coat. Another fucking envelope. Only this one didn't contain a debate question. Inside was a frayed, black and white, 5 x 7 photograph of three people that I had to hold in my hands at an angle so that I had the full benefit of the dim candlelight. I studied it as my eyes brought the image he'd handed me into focus. In the foreground was a man I instantly recognized, although he looked a few years younger than today. His face was plainly visible and so too was a sign caught in the foreground, hanging from an adjacent building. There was another man at his side who looked familiar although I could not immediately place him. And there was a woman walking with the two men whose profile and light hair color I could see, but whose face was partially hidden because of the angle at which the picture had been snapped. None of the three was looking at the camera, and it was clear that none of them had posed for the photograph. It was almost like it had been taken surreptitiously or captured by paparazzi.

There was no doubt that I was looking at a younger Bob Tobias and I knew where it had been taken. Tobias looked to be exiting the Ft. Harrison Hotel in the company of a second man and a female who damned sure looked like Susan Miller. The photograph would have no meaning but for the location. The hotel depicted was no longer the place of public accommodation where reportedly Keith Richards had famously penned the words to "(I Can't Get No) Satisfaction" after dreaming up that guitar riff in one of the hotel's beds. It was the immaculate, renovated incarnation that now served as a retreat for members of the Church of Scientology, not far from where Jackson Hunter and I were now having dinner.

Two things immediately suggested to me that the photo was legit. First, photoshopping has today reached an art form, but this picture wasn't something created on a Mac. It was old school, like some of those pics of Bill Clinton at Oxford in the '60s. A frayed, yellowed, not-entirely-clear version of an image that, judging by Tobias' clothing, mop haircut, and younger facial features, had been taken at least ten years ago. Second, if you were going to fabricate an image of a politician and link them to a controversial cause, you'd make the causal connection much more clear that just three people leaving a building. On its own, it didn't prove anything. But it sure would explain a number of things.

My mind raced as I began to contemplate the possible political significance of what I held in my hands. That this was a potential tinderbox was without question. It would substantiate the audit report I'd received, for starters. Not to mention Tobias' longstanding refusal to acknowledge the usual Judeo-Christian line about our nation's founding. And it would certainly explain why Susan required no directions when I told her I wanted to meet at my off-the-beaten-path—but not far from Scientology HQ—dive bar. Finally, it would suggest that our recent reunion was a bid for my silence—and maybe with Tobias' acquiescence. Any linkage between Tobias and the teachings of L. Ron Hubbard would be too much for American voters to bear.

Our appetizers arrived. And Jackson Hunter began to tell me how he thought the photograph should be used at the convention, now just a few weeks away.

CHAPTER 16

"Please welcome, the next Vice President of the United States . . ."

No, I didn't really think "Wynne James" would be the name coming out of Margaret Haskel's mouth, but I had my fingers crossed when the governor of Texas made her pick nonetheless. She actually beat Bob Tobias to the punch to announce a VP despite the fact that the Democratic convention came first.

Just a day before Democrats were to arrive in New Orleans for the start of their convention at the Louisiana Superdome, Tobias still hadn't named his VP, but Margaret Haskel was about to pick hers. I was pretty sure that Tobias was going to select Cindy Davenport, the congress-woman from Michigan, a good female offset for the fact that Margaret Haskel led the GOP ticket. But the longer he delayed the more I wondered if there was a problem with what seemed like a logical selection. Davenport was from a critical state and had strong labor creden-tials, but as a soccer mom turned politician, she wasn't anyone's version of Jimmy Hoffa. She would keep Democrats satisfied while extending the appeal of the ticket to Independents. And she was good on her feet, which would certainly help in the one and only vice presidential debate. But Tobias didn't announce Davenport, or anyone else, before his delegates arrived. His was a risky strategy intended to add some drama to a gathering that was otherwise so staged for television that it was hard to glean any spontaneity. Of course, the downside of his delay was that he'd lost the ability to double up on fundraising and expand the reach of his campaign by having his VP pick doing separate events. That and the fact that while he waited, Margaret Haskel grabbed the spotlight from him just as the Democrats were arriving in the Big Easy. She announced her pick on Saturday morning, assuring that she'd control the week-end news cycle just as the DNC was starting to get under way.

Of course Wynne James would have been a smart pick for Haskel had I not wrecked him at the Reagan Library. He deserved it on the merits based on his credentials and for having run a good campaign where he finished as runner-up. Moreover, his non-zealot status would have helped sell her candidacy to Independents, or so I thought. Not that I made such an argument on WRGT or in the countless cable TV and print interviews I gave in the days leading up to the convention. Instead, I continued to chant Phil's "conservative, consistent and compelling" mantra to the end. Hell, on air, I said that Redfield, Lewis and Figuera were all solid VP prospects. But no matter what I said, there was no way that Margaret Haskel could offend the evangelical Christians who constituted the base of her party by taking a guy they now widely assumed had been in an orgy. The Internet had fueled no shortage of crazy rumors about my question, so tenuously based on a decades-old assertion from a now-dead woman in the midst of a divorce. James was now damaged goods, despite his decent showing in the primaries.

Besides, others on the right had a different way of doing the math. Instead of recognizing how James had fared against Haskel, they added up the Haskel, Redfield, Lewis and Figuera quotient—the conservative bloc—and argued that together, this represented the core of the party which needed to be reflected in its VP choice. There was lots of strong-arming for one of those three to be named, but in the end Margaret Haskel went in a different direction.

". . . A God-fearing, great American, Senator Finn O'Malley!" was the way she announced it.

My P1s were elated with the pick. A 95 percent approval rating from the Club for Growth while representing Ohio in the U.S. Senate, Catholic and, of course, pro-life. O'Malley had a good-looking family and was a bit of a dolt, but that was just fine as a complement to the extroverted Governor Haskel.

"Finn's a great American, Stan," I heard from more than one caller to *Morning Power*.

Finally, three days later in Louisiana, Tobias made his announcement. And it was, as predicted, Congresswoman Davenport. I thought the timing might take away from Susan's prime time speech at the convention that same night, but it only seemed to create more electricity in the cavernous stadium when she walked out onto the stage and acknowledged his selection.

"My husband's not afraid to surround himself with women who have sound opinions," she said to thunderous applause. It was a tip of the hat to Davenport, a bit self-congratulatory, and somewhat condescending toward Haskel all in one sentence.

I was at Delrios, of course, given that it was a Tuesday night. Like clockwork, I was standing at the bar with Carl and Clay as Ralph poured our kamikaze shots. It was hard to hear what exactly she was saying, but like everyone else, I was mostly interested in how she looked. Fabulous, was the answer. Beautiful skin. Tight body. Gorgeous eyes. She looked extremely poised, despite the importance of the moment. The fact that we had fucked in a nearby hotel room just weeks earlier seemed even more surreal. Then, in what had now become a convention tradition, when her speech ended, Tobias walked out on stage to congratulate her while she acted surprised to see him. And just like they were watching a movie, the delegates suspended their belief and ate it up. She looked equally radiant that Thursday night after Tobias gave his acceptance speech, when the top of the ticket and all family members gathered on stage for an extended photo op while the balloons and confetti fell.

And then, at last, all eyes shifted to Tampa.

I got my first look inside the Tampa Bay Times Forum on Saturday morning. There was now a small army of Secret Service, Homeland Security and local law enforcement protecting the arena where I'd seen many concerts and had watched the Lightning skate. It looked nothing like what I was used to. All of the decoration and set-up had been concluded, and there would be 2,286 delegates arriving this weekend and about the same number of alternates. But more important to me, there would be 15,000 members of the media, each needing a quote, or a piece of sound, or a snippet of video to feed their respective beast. Every one of their outlets was already going to have audio and video of whatever happened in prime time; the reporters on the ground wouldn't have to lift a finger to get those feeds. So in order to justify their airfare, hotel and credential cost, every one of these journalists needed to send something back to the mother ship, namely some item of local interest from the ground in Tampa. The visibility I had commanded in the past few months, capped off by the *Real Time* and Reagan Library debate appearances gave me instant recognition and sufficient street cred for supplying a sound byte.

The purpose of my Saturday visit was just to get the "lay of the land" in advance of Tuesday night's roll call vote, and to meet with Jackson Hunter who'd asked that I call him after I cleared security. I was anxious to see where the Florida delegation was positioned and make sure I got the feel of the place before it was filled with delegates. Walking onto the floor, I saw that Florida was right up front, directly next to Texas. That Texas would be in poll position was no surprise given that it was Margaret Haskel's home state. But there was Florida, right next to Ohio, Colorado and Virginia, the other critical swing states. I also had a hunch that given Tobias' selection of Davenport, the Michigan delegation might get a seat upgrade here in Tampa, so that state's delegates would be in the camera frame for the important speeches as well.

I had a badge that allowed me full access to the floor but I didn't get very far. It wasn't the cops who stopped me, it was the members of the media. I ended up giving an hour's worth of spontaneous interviews to news outlets all across the nation. Once I'd finish with one reporter, there was another waiting to take his place. It was just as Phil and I had envisioned months earlier when we mapped out our plan.

"Stan, what are your listeners looking for from this convention?"

"Does Susan Miller help or hurt Tobias in the I-4 corridor?"

"Stan, does Haskel have a shot against Tobias here in the general election?"

"Why do you think Haskel picked O'Malley?"

"Would she have taken Wynne James but for you?"

And there were a few like this:

"Why do you continue to raise questions about Tobias' faith? What is it that you think you know?"

If only they knew that was exactly what Tobias' wife kept asking me!

While I was chatting on camera with a reporter from Colorado Springs (a swing district not unlike the I-4 corridor) I looked up and saw Jackson Hunter listening to what I was saying. You'd think the press would be more interested in a young aide who was closer to the nominee than me, but he'd done a good job flying beneath the radar and doing on-camera interviews was not his role. He looked like an older choirboy in a Brooks Brothers suit, but this young guy played some serious hardball.

When I finished the interview, he motioned for me to follow him, which I did. Hunter escorted me into a super box that was serving as the Haskel command center. There were television monitors in the box that seemed to show every inch of the arena and a backstage area I had yet to navigate. As I surveyed the scene, he introduced me around and then asked that we be afforded some privacy.

"So are you ready for Tuesday? The governor is counting on you, Stan."

I said nothing.

"Look, everyone else who speaks during the roll call is limited to 60 seconds. We control the audio right from this booth. We've told the state delegations that if they exceed their allotment, we will kill the mics just like an acceptance speech at the Oscars, not because we want to be pricks but because we cannot afford to have the evening run late. I'm not old enough to remember McGovern accepting after everyone had gone to bed but I surely know the story. We figure that the threat alone will keep everybody honest and we actually won't have to do it."

I thought that was a funny expression—keeping people honest. There was absolutely nothing honest about what he was asking.

"But Stan, nobody is running a clock on you. This is where I will be on Tuesday. You take whatever time is necessary to cover your talking points. You will have the attention of the delegates and the nation for however long it takes."

He extended his hand. I shook it without acknowledging what he'd said and walked out.

That night I took Debbie out for a couple of steaks at Backwater, right across from my condo in Sand Key. Lots of heads turned when we walked in the door, which used to be on account of her good looks. We both knew things were different now. Politics was on everyone's mind. After months of planning and hype, the convention had finally arrived and I had a profile akin to one of the candidates, at least in these parts. It's the sort of attention I had dreamed about but now felt embarrassed by, at least in Debbie's presence because it confirmed so much of what she'd been saying. But that didn't stop me from trying to convince her otherwise.

"It's you they're looking at," I offered lamely.

"Please, Stan. Even at my law firm, you are all that people talk about. Everyone is speculating about what role you'll be playing this week. They're calling you 'the Hatchet's hatchet.' "

I scanned the restaurant and watched as a man who'd just entered with his wife nudged her and tried (unsuccessfully) to make a disguised gesture in our direction.

"I'm happy for you to get the notoriety. I just wish it were more authentic. And I worry about whether you will be happy when you get all you've been working for. So they roll you out all over the country and you have to keep spewing this stuff," she went on. "No matter what they pay you, and how many heads turn when you walk into a restaurant, I doubt it will be worth it."

But despite my misgivings, and those of Debbie, my callers were really stoked on Monday. Everybody was totally into the convention. This was a great moment, they said, for Tampa/St. Pete, Republicans, and conservatives everywhere. Although ratings technology is always improving, there was still no way to instantly know how many people were listening to *Morning Power*. But the program felt different and the excitement lasted the entire week. No one waited for me to say anything. By the time the bumper music ended coming out of every break, all the lines were lit and they stayed that way for every segment. Rod had a spring in his step. Alex looked less than thrilled, but she was, nevertheless, a consummate professional. She'd made certain the entire week was booked with A-list political guests, all of whom were in town and anxious to speak on *Morning Power*. In prior years, it had always been a question of who we could get to do the program. Now, it was a function of who we wanted. This was in part an added benefit of my TV work; when Alex called or emailed their staffs, there was now a level of recognition that I had previously lacked.

The pitch used to be: "I was wondering if the senator would like to appear on Stan Powers' radio program which is called *Morning Power* and is based out of Tampa, Florida?"

Those days were over.

"Stan Powers would love to have Senator Bullwinkle on as a guest," was now all it took.

After the program on Monday morning, I was due back on the convention floor for another round of interviews. As I made a dash for the door, Alex handed me a phone message from Wilma Blake. Once again, the note was produced without comment. I tried to show no emotion which I am sure only heightened Alex's suspicion.

I was surprised to hear from Susan. With all the attention on the GOP for the next week, I figured Tobias and his family would grab their final week of vacation until November.

"Shouldn't you be on a beach somewhere?" I asked her.

"Who says I'm not?"

"You looked great last week."

"Let's talk about this week, Stan. You know she plays dirty. They don't call her Molly Hatchet just because of her fiscal axe. I'd hate to see her use you."

That was an odd word choice from someone I suspected of knowing a thing or two about using people. But she was obviously wise to the fact that I'd be playing a small role in the festivities.

"It's all over the Internet, Stan. Politico says you'll actually be the one to put her nomination over the top when you cast Florida's votes. That's a great honor *only* if you don't embarrass yourself."

Since I was now fairly committed to what I would do, the only question was whether I should tell her. She was a friend, after all. Or was she? She'd used me as a fuck buddy back at Shooter's many years ago, which was fine for Stan Pawlowski. But I was now convinced she'd done the same with Stan Powers. Thinking it through, I saw no need to offer her anything. This was the last time I'd probably speak to Susan Miller.

"We could see more of each other after the convention is over," she offered. "I'll be back in Florida a lot, you know."

"I don't think that's a good idea."

Since I wasn't biting, she tried one more approach.

"We all do things when we are young that we regret. You certainly know that, Stan."

I took that as an admission. The Scientology link was real.

"Good luck, Susan," I said.
"Do the right thing, Stan."
Click.

I could hardly sleep on Monday night. It was a combination of excitement and dread. I'd worked for years to get to this position and had plotted with Phil for seven straight months as to exactly how to seize this opportunity. But it was coming at a high cost. It'd be bad enough if I just had to parrot talking points, many of which I didn't believe, but this was far worse. Because I'd shilled at the Reagan Library, I was being rewarded with the unseemly task of politically knee-capping a sitting governor one week after he'd secured his party's nod. What elevated my concern was what I detected in Phil's voice during our final call earlier that afternoon.

"You've reached the pinnacle, Stan. The circumstance doesn't really require anything more from you."

"Too late," I wanted to say, but I didn't.

Phil might have known many things, but he had not been in the advance loop about Governor James. It had been implied in my meeting with Jackson Hunter that I would never reveal the role of the Haskel campaign and I had honored that bond. Even if Phil had figured it out, best for all involved that these matters not be discussed. And it was the same with Tuesday night. Phil knew my role and he knew who put me there. But he did not ask exactly what I was going to say, nor did I tell him. And yet he did not waste either of our time mapping out remarks, which he had done so many times on the road that led to this. For as long as we'd been working together it was always Phil trying to take things up a notch. But not now. And that had me worried.

"Have you settled on what you are going to say?"

"I'm ready."

"Are they your words?"

I wasn't sure how to answer that. I said nothing.

"Try to enjoy it, Stan. I got close myself once. When it's over, you'll have to tell me how it feels."

I wasn't prepared for that dropping of his guard.

No barking. No edge in his voice. No condescension.

No "Don't be a pussy, Powers."

Not even a final "Be conservative, consistent, and compelling."

In that moment, I felt sorry for the man in Taos, sitting in front of an electronic board, programming everyone else's career but still regretful of the personal mistakes that had prevented him from fully realizing his own.

"Thank you, Phil."

I'd never thanked him for his advice, and now I was grateful for him not giving me any. Maybe that should have been a sign all along.

On Tuesday morning, I awoke early, put on my game face, and followed my usual routine despite the enormity of the day.

"Welcome back to *Morning Power*," I began, "and greetings to our Republican guests in town for the convention.

"This morning, we really do hold the power. Friends, tonight I have the distinct honor of representing the great state of Florida during the roll call. I'm sure you know the normal drill. Each state is afforded a short time to announce their delegate votes and tradition holds that you say something nice about your state when you do.

"I'm thinking that the stakes are too high in this election to let the moment pass without a serious comment about the choice the nation faces. And I'm wondering what advice you might have. What is it that you think I should say tonight when the eyes of the nation are upon me? Call me now, toll free, and give me your ideas."

Rod was festooned for the second day in a row in red, white, and blue and a big button on his lapel which said "Let Molly take a Hatchet to Washington." Alex sat screening calls in a black t-shirt that said "Keep Out of Direct Sunlight." Over her shoulder were two network affiliates from out of town shooting some B-roll for tonight's news. The call board lit up immediately.

"Why not say, Florida, the state that gave America Anita Bryant, casts all it votes for another great lady, Margaret Haskel?"

"Great suggestion. Let me think about it."

"Hello, Stan. It's an honor. Remember what the Seal said when he shot bin Laden? 'For God and country.' That's what you should say. For God and country, Margaret Haskel."

"Amen, thanks for the call."

I actually thought that could work with what I had in mind.

By the time my air shift ended, I was feeling punch drunk and knew I'd never get any sleep without a mother's little helper. All morning long my phone wouldn't stop vibrating, mostly, I was sure, with media outlets wanting a few minutes. But there was no escaping one last call with Jules before the big night arrived, so I figured I'd better get it over with before I tried to rest. Of course, he was tied up when I called, and then, back at my condo, after I had just popped two Ambien in my mouth, the phone rang. I debated whether to answer it but curiosity got the better of me. Right now I really needed to crash, but I recognized Jules' number.

"Please hold for Mr. DelGado," Philippe said.

I hated that. I made a mental note to never have my calls placed for me if I ever became a big shot. Well, a bigger shot.

"Stan, are you sitting down? I have an offer from Chuck Schwartz. The deal points are in writing and if you approve, a contract will be drafted. There are some things we need to work through, but this is going to happen, and fast. They want you syndicated immediately to take advantage of your role in this election cycle. You will be rolled out in just 30 days!"

He probably expected me to shout "Hallelujah." But I was feeling a bit numb both from the meds and from the stress about what was to unfold tonight. I tried to mask my sudden ambivalence by thanking him for his work, and asked that he email me the deal points. And then I crashed.

I awoke, showered, ate something and waited for my car. Margaret Haskel wasn't taking any chances that I wouldn't get to the church on time, so they sent a Town Car at 5 p.m. for me and a guest. But I had no guest. The only person who would've been personally appropriate was Debbie, but then again, she would have been entirely inappropriate given the professional nature of this mission. I couldn't do that to her. Frankly, there was no one—no family member, personal friend, or significant other—who I would have felt comfortable bringing with me to what was supposed to be one of the biggest nights in my life. Which should have told me something.

Every night the convention had a different headline event. Last night it had been the keynote address. Tonight was the roll call vote and formal nomination. Wednesday would be the vice presidential acceptance speech and Thursday was the finale, when Margaret Haskel would accept the nomination and the balloons would drop on her and Finn O'Malley. Of course, those were the highlights, and there was plenty of other filler. Tonight's climax would be preceded by prayer, music, speeches by elected officials and what passed for convention business but was really intended to give the events a feel of authenticity.

Upon my arrival at the arena, I was escorted into a green room where a table full of food, drink and convention nicknacks awaited me. Sadly there was no booze. But amidst the buttons, bumper stickers, a straw hat and a bottle of Molly Hatchet Salsa (labeled "Hot enough to be president") was the official party platform that was being ratified before the roll call began. I thumbed through it with one eye on the TV monitor as I sipped a Coke. Reading it made me nauseous.

There was the "human life amendment" which opposed abortion with no exceptions for rape or the health of the mother.

Marriage was defined as being between (only) a man and a woman.

The drug policy opposed the legalization of marijuana.

And the party stood for opposition to any limitations on business in the name of climate change.

I closed the pamphlet and stared at the note-card Jackson Hunter had handed to me. All alone in my room, I looked up at the TV monitor as the roll call began. The order was alphabetical so Alabama went first, and Wyoming would be the clean-up.

"Mr. Chairman, the great state of Alabama, with one of the most diverse delegations in this hall, is ready to cast the first votes for the next president of the United States, Margaret Haskel."

"Mr. Chairman, Alaska, the great battleground state, the frontier state, proudly casts all its votes for Margaret Haskel."

"Madame Chairperson, on behalf of the 600,000 American citizens who seek equal treatment as American citizens, who pay federal taxes and who have fought and died in every war including the war that established the United States, the District of Columbia proudly casts its votes for Margaret Haskel."

From what I watched, it looked like I was the only participant without a portfolio. Every other spokesman was an elected official or a party representative. Governors, senators, congressmen, and state party chairs were the norm. And just as I remembered from when I'd first watched this as a kid, mostly they offered commercials for their states. It had been years since the process was anything more than a formality; more than one roll call vote hasn't been needed by either party since the early 1950s.

The Haskel campaign had done the math and knew exactly when she would exceed the number of votes needed to formalize the nomination, and when that moment arrived, I would be center stage. Because of the alphabetical structure, Florida would be called upon before Haskel had enough votes and the plan was for the state chair, Herb Barness, to deliver his own commercial, but then to "pass" and not offer the state's delegates. When it came time to close the deal, I'd be the one with the microphone. That the order would be juggled around like this was normal. But typically, it was done so that the presidential candidate's home state could be the delegation to make the nomination official, which in this case would've been Texas. What was unprecedented was juggling the order for another state. But such was the importance of Florida in the November election, that Barness stood at the ready when the spotlight first hit Florida.

"Mr. Chairman, it is an honor for the great state

of Florida to host this convention where Governor Margaret Haskel will be nominated and eventually elected president. The Sunshine State, birthplace of Tim Tebow, home of the Super Bowl Champion Dolphins, and the world's best stone crabs elects to pass at this time."

That was my cue. Like clockwork there was a knock on my door, then it opened and an intern whose daddy had probably written a huge check told me it was time. I put the note card I'd been thumbing in my pocket and walked out onto the convention floor. The count continued. Each vote was greeted with thunderous applause.

"Maine, a state with great tourism, great people . . ."

"The free state of Maryland, home of the wonderful Chesapeake Bay and blue crab, home of the 8th wonder of the world, the Terrapins and the United States Naval Academy . . ."

"Michigan, the Great Lake State, home of the American Automobile Association, home of Gerald Ford and the Red Wings . . ."

"Minnesota, the North Star State, the state of 10,000 lakes and five million people, and the most productive agricultural lands in America . . ."

"Missouri, America's bellwether . . ."

"North Carolina, the home of Billy Graham, ACC basketball, and Nascar, and the most military-friendly state in the United States . . ."

This sort of happy horseshit was perfectly fine

with me and I'd have been thrilled if I was just following every other state's lead. That alone would've put me in prime time and reaffirm my position as a presidential power broker. Phil had always been convinced that if Haskel won Florida, I'd get credit whether I deserved it or not. I could've just used my platform like every other one of his clients and gone through the motions. But me, they were not letting off so easy.

I was greeted amidst the Florida delegation like a conquering hero. People were backslapping me and shaking hands and several wanted to snap pictures on mobile phones. At any other time, my ego would have soaked it in. But I was too preoccupied with the microphone that sat on the aisle. During the walk-through on Saturday, I'd been shown where it would be. I continued to smile for photographs and shake hands while the vote count progressed. When it got to New Jersey, the Garden State passed, lest Margaret Haskel would pass the threshold and pass the 1,144 vote mark based on a blue state that Bob Tobias was already certain to win.

"Mr. Chairman, the home of Jersey tomatoes, the country's best corn and prettiest beaches, the state that makes what America takes, the state that not even Super Storm Sandy could slow down—the great state of New Jersey passes and calls upon the great state of Florida."

The events in Tampa were now in prime time, and a nationwide—hell, worldwide—audience was streaming or tuning in. Above me, a giant scoreboard normally used to tabulate sports scores posted a delegate count that made clear that the nomination was about to become official, the end to a nearly two-year campaign. And as the hall filled with 20,000 began to get silent in anticipation of an eruption, I stepped toward the microphone. What a country. A former slacker and perpetual stoner, with no regard for either party, was nevertheless about to formalize the candidacy of a woman to run against the husband of his former, and recent, fuck buddy.

"Mr. Chairman, my name is Stan Powers."

I actually had to pause and wait for the applause to die down. While I waited, I saw that it was my image that now adorned the video monitors scattered throughout the arena. Florida delegates suddenly produced placards on sticks that read "*Morning Power* for Molly." The ego boost provided by the personal acknowledgement gave me the final bout of courage I probably no longer needed.

"It is my great honor to cast the ballots of the Florida delegation."

The members of the delegation, having encircled me in anticipation of this moment, now roared.

"But before I do, there is something that needs to be said."

I heard shouts of "quiet" and things got soft.

"This country was founded on Judeo-Christian values and we need a president who will return it to these principles."

There was another burst of applause and I needed to wait until the room got quiet.

"We need a president who fears God, not the head of a Galactic Confederation. A president whose good book was written by Matthew, Mark, Luke, and John, not a failed science fiction writer. A president whose actions are guided by his heart, not his thetan."

There was no way this crowd knew, literally, what the fuck I was talking about. But they got the message. Bob Tobias wasn't one of us. He was some kind of other. I knew that within minutes, the photograph would be posted online that would fill in the blanks. But this crowd didn't wait for any frayed picture. They roared their approval. So much so that as I finished the official part of the nomination that put Margaret Haskel over the top, the crowd was deafening. While I know the audio was heard through televisions across the country, in the arena I was being drowned out. I was screaming now and the only thing that could be heard was:

"For God and country . . . the great state of Florida casts all of its ballots for the next president of the United States, Margaret Haskel."

When I said her name, there was an explosion from up above, no doubt orchestrated from the booth where Jackson Hunter and his colleagues were choreographing everything. The sky opened and balloons and confetti fell. At a deafening level, Lee Greenwood's "God Bless the USA" blasted through the sound system, and when the sky cleared, standing on stage was Margaret Haskel. I hadn't seen a place go so batshit since I caught Lynyrd Skynyrd making a stop in Ft. Myers in support of *Street Survivors* just before the plane crash. It was bedlam. Margaret Haskel didn't speak, she just waved for about five minutes, and then exited the stage. I'm sure that at that precise moment, it was time for a TV break. All I wanted to do was go home, but I was mobbed as I looked for the intern who'd delivered me to the floor and hoped she'd find me a quick passage. After 30 more minutes of posing for pictures and signing autographs, I was finally in the back of a Town Car and headed for home.

Now, for the third time in a month, I looked at my iPhone as a form of flash returns. All the usual suspects were voting via texts.

"Balls" was Phil's text.

Not exactly congratulatory, but maybe I was reading too much into it.

"When are we signing?" from Jules.

The next text was from Steve Bernson, not someone who often communicated with me this way:

"Vernon Chinkles just called. Complaint pulled from HR file, congrats."

And then there was this:

"Pathetic. Feel sorry for u. Don't call me again."

I read it twice. Three times. Four. It could have come from one of two people. Or both. Frankly it didn't matter. I expected that reaction from both Susan and Debbie and couldn't blame them.

I was stone cold sober and in need of a fix. This being a Tuesday night, I told the driver to take a detour on the way home.

The first thing I noticed when I walked into Delrios was the television. I breathed a sigh of relief when I saw it was tuned to ESPN. I thought I'd found refuge but the feeling didn't last long. Ralph, of course, looked up from pouring shots and gave me that look that said he knew exactly where I was coming from. Maybe it was the flag pin still in my lapel. But then I spied Carl and Clay exactly where I hoped they'd be and they were three sheets to the wind.

"Hey . . . fuckin' L. Ron Hubbard is here!" said Clay slurring his words.

I immediately decided that coming had not been such a great idea. Either that, or I had a whole lot of catching up to do.

Carl told me the TVs had been tuned to the convention and that nobody paid attention until I came on. He said Ralph whistled when I started to speak and the room got quiet.

"What did he say?"

"Nothing. He just whistled. And everybody knew."

Knew what, I did not ask. I would have liked to have seen that. It sounded like a visual image of the hooker code at Delrios. I was sorry I missed it.

"So what was the reaction?"

After all, this was the same room that had gone crazy when President Summers announced he wasn't running six months ago.

"That's the funny thing," said Carl. "Nobody reacted. It was like a fart in church. You didn't know whether to laugh out loud or feel sorry for the guy who cut it."

I wasn't sure what to make of that. But I remembered that I had a designated driver—as if I needed any encouragement—and ordered another shot. When Ralph came over to pour it, our faces couldn't have been more than a foot apart. He looked at me like he was reading my face. Neither of us spoke. He poured. I drank.

When I finally stumbled out of Delrios it was midnight. I needed to get up in a few hours and bear witness to the reaction of my stink bomb.

Like I had after Maher, and the final debate at the Reagan Library, I was again leading both Drudge and now Huffpo, too. On one I was a savior. On the other I was a cocksucker. You can figure out which. I agreed with the latter. But both had the grainy picture posted outside the Fort Harrison Hotel.

Wednesday and Thursday were a blur. On both days, there were a bunch of TV cameras in studio capturing Stan Powers as he preached to his flock of I-4 followers who held in their hands the next presidency of the United States. God help us.

The Tobias family had in fact been on vacation all week in Martha's Vineyard. Presumably that was where Susan had called me from on Monday, which seemed like an eternity ago. Now, Tobias had scheduled an emergency Friday press conference from Boston where he would respond to an unrelenting media that wanted answers to the issues I had raised in my Tampa speech. In the meantime, there was a loop of the family on the beach at Chappaquiddick that had been surreptitiously recorded by boat, which made me want to throw up. Some talk hosts made a connection to Ted Kennedy and said that Tobias' presidential aspirations had also ended on the tiny island. On the right there was speculation that Tobias would even leave the race, something I am sure had been the intention of the Haskel camp. Vic Baron, having lost the primary and been passed over for the vice presidency, was presumed to be the instigator of the Dump Tobias campaign.

My audience was loving every minute of it.

"God bless you, Stan, for exposing this Martian," one guy actually said.

The calls came in one after another on the morning of Margaret Haskel's acceptance speech. I just blew through them and kept my thoughts—and embarrassment—to myself. Rod practically had a boner. Alex looked defeated.

And then, suddenly, I made up my mind.

"Don't book any guests for the final half-hour tomorrow," I told her as I walked out of the studio on Thursday.

"Okay. Don't forget that CSPAN is televising the entire program tomorrow," she reminded me.

"Right," I said.

It would be perfect. In addition to the steady parade of TV journalists from across the country who wanted to justify their trip to Tampa by recording Stan Powers as he held court, CSPAN was going to broadcast the entire final hour of *Morning Power* on Friday morning right after Margaret Haskel accepted the nomination. That reminder only made me more anxious to go home and prepare the next day's program. I knew now what I was going to do.

Steve Bernson was waiting for me in the

hallway outside the studio. So too was Don Fortini. I had messages from Jules DelGado and Phil Dean. But I hurried past them all and peeled out of the garage without giving a wave to my fishing buddy. In the rearview mirror I thought I saw him standing motionless. I stepped on the gas.

My iPhone didn't stop ringing or vibrating, but I responded to no one. I was a man on a mission. Funny, I often struggled to come up with a closing monologue about the politics of the day, but this time, the words flowed with remarkable ease. And for once, delivering them was going to feel good. I wrote through the afternoon and into the evening. The only question in my mind was whether I would have the chance to do what I wanted. I needed Alex to make it happen. That night, I didn't even watch Margaret Haskel accept her party's nod. I no longer cared what she said. I was too busy worrying about what I was going to say.

Come Friday morning, the convention was finally over. Delegates were rushing to catch flights. Journalists were filing their wrap-up pieces. The general election was on. And Tobias was scheduled to speak from his interrupted vacation that afternoon. I spent the first three hours interviewing a combination of conservative journalists and Republican officeholders who were anxious to frame the contrast for the general election. Taking their cues from me, each was sure to work in a mention of religion.

Finally, at 8:30 Friday morning, the control room was down to three people. Rod, Alex, and a cameraman from CSPAN. All morning I'd been banking on the fact that Rod's body clock would remain consistent. When he stood at the final break to go take a piss, I breathed a sigh of relief. Then I gave Alex the order.

"Lock the door," I said.

She was temporarily dumbfounded.

"Lock the door," I said again.

But a moment later, she did as she was told.

There was only one way into the studio and it was now sealed.

The guy from CSPAN didn't have a clue what was going on, but he kept his camera shot locked. If I'd been thinking clearly at the time I'd have realized that CSPAN doesn't take commercial breaks, so my instructions to Alex had just been televised nationwide—which I later learned, sent off shock-waves in the Twitterverse. Anyone who was watching had just heard my command. A whisper down the lane of "hey watch this" took over.

As far as I knew, there was no way to kill the signal. The "on air" light came on, and I was ready to roll. I had 18 minutes to get the job done until we needed to break.

CHAPTER 17

"Welcome back to *Morning Power*," I began. "You're tuned to WRGT. And my name is Stanislaw Pawlowski.

"That's a mouthful, right? Not exactly the sort of name that rolls off the tongue for morning radio. No wonder I was just 'Stan' in Pittsburgh before I came to Tampa/St. Pete. But I'm already getting ahead of myself.

"You know, I am often asked, how did you get into talk radio?

"Well, you might say it's always been my calling.

"And I don't mean because of any deep-seated love of the news and politics.

"I'm thinking about my childhood, growing up in Ft. Myers.

"I'm thinking about Saturday mornings sitting in a beanbag chair in our rec room just off the lanai, where I'd watch pro wrestling on a TV that had no clicker to change channels.

"This was before cable. We had only about six channels on our TV, split between something called VHF and something called UHF. What I remember is that UHF had worse reception and there was always snow on the TV screen, but it had something else. It had pro wrestling, or 'rasslin',' as we used to call it.

"This wasn't like the modern crap with the thumping music, chicks in thongs and pyrotechnics. And it was long before they staged big events and put them on pay-per-view.

"This was a different era, the age of the 'Living Legend,' Bruno Sammartino. Haystacks Calhoon. George 'The Animal' Steele. And my favorite, 'Chief' Jay Strongbow.

"There were good guys and bad guys and no in-between. Everything was black and white. You knew the bad guys because they often carried what were called 'foreign objects' in their trunks and they had managers. Characters like 'The Grand Wizard of Wrestling,' 'Classy' Freddie Blassie, and 'The Captain,' Lou Albano.

"I loved this stuff and always rooted for the good guys. We all did. The only time I was ever confused about who was which came one Saturday morning when two good guys—Pedro Morales and Bruno Sammartino—were in a tag team title match against 'Professor' Toru Tanaka and Mr. Fuji. During the bout, Tanaka and Fuji rubbed salt in the eyes of Sammartino and Morales. The good guys couldn't see. They got confused. And while blinded from the salt, they started to fight each other while Tanaka and Fuji just stood and watched. Sammartino and Morales then had such a bitter rivalry that they had to settle their differences in a grudge match in front of a huge crowd at Shea Stadium.

"My friends and I would take turns acting out all the parts of our favorite wrestlers. I would imitate Chief Jay Strongbow's war dance. These are some of the happiest memories of my childhood.

"And look at me now. I'm in the media equivalent of pro wrestling!

"We purport to be a news station, but this is really all about entertainment. Not just WRGT, but all of talk radio, and almost all of cable TV news. In everything we discuss, one side is virtuous, the other is evil. And the outcome of every debate has been predetermined based on the alignment of the political parties. Just like rasslin'. Only, back then, adults knew that wrestling was fake and treated it accordingly. The problem is that today, the media equivalent is treated like it's serious debate. Too many of you are mistaking this form of entertainment for reality. And worse, so do the politicians. And when politicians take their cues from the rasslin' in the modern media, we're all screwed because we get polarization, and the nation suffers.

"I'm sick of it. I'm embarrassed about the role

I have played in it. And I don't want any part in it anymore.

"We will never be able to change Washington unless we first realize what is really causing the problem.

"*We* are! When in a world with so much choice as to where we get our news and information, we take ours in the form of entertainment delivered only by the likeminded, we close our minds to real discussion and debate. And so do those we elect.

"Only when politicians stop taking their cues from a guy like me and instead start responding to their real constituents are things going to get better.

"It hasn't always been like this. When I was getting started in the radio business, spinning records at a 5,000-watt daytimer on Saturday mornings, talk was different. Ideology didn't matter. Personality did. You didn't need to pass any litmus tests to get on the air, you needed to be able to carry on a conversation. Guys like Frank Sellers used to do just that. When I was growing up, my parents listened to talk radio. There was a station in Ft. Myers that had a real hodgepodge of a lineup. There was a guy doing mornings who was a libertarian before anyone had heard of Ron Paul. There was a guy who was an acerbic liberal. There was a conservative who was better known for his command of the

English language than his politics. But the guy my parents really liked to listen to was named Bernie Herman. Bernie was on from 10 p.m. to 1 a.m. and his moniker, or what you'd today call his 'brand,' was the 'Gentleman of Broadcasting.' Imagine that. The Gentleman of Broadcasting would come on at 10 p.m. and talk until after midnight and he billed himself as a guy you could count on to act with decency and respect.

"How far do you think you'd get in this business today if you walked into a radio station and told the program director you were the Gentleman of Broadcasting? Nowhere.

"It all changed in the '90s and I know why. Before the Internet, before Fox, before Drudge, you conservatives didn't have a clubhouse. The media consisted of the *New York Times*, *Washington Post* and the big three networks, and each was run by a bunch of liberals. I get that. I don't fault the logic. Or the need for an alternative.

"So you established a beachhead in talk radio. And when, in the midst of the first Gulf War, a guy in Sacramento named Rush Limbaugh offered what you were looking for, you ate it up and you wanted more. And radio stations across the nation took note and they wanted Rush and a stable of his imitators. And it worked. And do you know why it worked? Not because Rush was a political expert. Hell, he didn't even vote. And not because he was an election sooth-sayer. It worked because the man is a gifted entertainer. His worst political critics have never given him the credit he deserves for his ability to keep an audience entertained for three hours a day working with no more than a daily newspaper!

"Then Fox did the same thing on TV.

"And together with the Internet, conservatives now had places to call home.

"Then the predictable happened. Liberals took note and decided they should do the same thing. They tried and failed on radio with Air America. There was never the need for a liberal clubhouse in radio because their audience always had NPR! On cable TV, they succeeded with MSNBC. It took them a while before they got it right, but Keith Olbermann was the first to emulate from the left what Limbaugh and Fox did from the right. Again, it was all about entertainment. Suddenly, CNN, lacking personality or perspective, faded into third place in prime time.

"Sure, people still tune into CNN for breaking news, but once they understand what's happened, they want someone with whom they are politically comfortable to explain the significance and tell them how they should feel. And that explanation, in order to be self-sustaining, is dependent on disagreement.

"Civility has gone out the window. Conflict is the order of the day.

"And look where it has gotten us.

"Nothing is easily solved in Washington. Our politicians on both sides of the aisle create more obstacles than they remove.

"Every issue becomes an ordeal.

"Compromise is the new C-word.

"And we are left with ongoing polarization. Meanwhile, we act surprised about the inability of elected officials to get anything done. And we wonder aloud, 'Where does this polarization come from?'

"Certainly not from the vast majority of voters.

"Survey after survey has shown that Americans would rather have a politician who seeks compromise than someone who sticks to their own principles. But you'd never know that listening to our conversations on radio and TV, or watching Republican and Democratic politicians.

"Perhaps that's why more and more Americans refuse to identify themselves with either of the major parties. They'd rather regard themselves as Independents than Republicans or Democrats.

"But as Americans become *less* ideological, our politicians have become *more* partisan.

"You want to know why things are so screwed up?

"You want to know where this polarization comes from?

"I can explain it to you in four steps.

"First, you have hyper-partisan districts. Nate Silver at the *New York Times* spelled it out years ago. He pointed out that in the early '90s, there were about 100 members of the House of Representatives elected out of swing districts (which he defined as districts in which the presidential vote was within five percentage points of the national tally). Today? We have just 35.

"That means that out of 435 races, 400 are virtually predetermined by party affiliation. At the same time that competitive districts have diminished, landslide districts—those in which the presidential margin diverged from the national outcome by 20 or more points—have roughly doubled.

"So, more and more members of Congress are now being elected from hyper-partisan districts, and therefore, face no backlash from their own constituents when they are unwilling to compromise.

"Second, there is the effect of closed primaries. When those hyper-partisan districts are located in states with closed primaries—that is, nominating contests open only to party members—the voters who reliably turn out in these relatively low-turnout elections are those who are ideologically driven. Who do they vote for? The most conservative or most liberal candidates, who then end up getting their party's nomination. The more centrist, middle-of-the-road candidates never stand a chance. You combine hyper-partisan districts with closed primaries and you have the backdrop for an enormous ideological divide.

"Think about this: For the last four decades, the *National Journal* has sought to categorize the ideological leanings of every member of the House and Senate. When the *Journal* recently analyzed the voting records of members of Congress, it found that we have the highest level of polarization in the 40 or so years they have been doing this research. Every Senate Democrat had a voting record more liberal than every Senate Republican. And every Republican was more conservative than every Democrat. And the House was similarly divided.

"Maybe you think that's to be expected, but it hasn't always been like this. In the early 1980s, on Ronald Reagan's watch, the *National Journal* calculated that roughly 60 percent of the Senate was comprised of moderates who regularly voted across party lines. Back then, there was a group of moderate Republicans who met on a regular basis. They called themselves the 'Wednesday Lunch Club.' They had nearly two dozen members. Names like Packwood, Heinz, Specter and Hatfield. Weicker, Kassebaum, Danforth, Percy and Chaffee. Stafford, Simpson,

Warner, Gorton, Dole and Stevens. Today, there would be no one at the meeting!

"Third, we can't overlook the effect of money. Fundraising is the next big contributor to the polarization we face. In the past, candidates elected to Congress actually moved to Washington and lived there. But today, a typical member residence is a flophouse on Capitol Hill that they share with an ideological twin and sleep in only two or three nights a week. Nobody truly lives in Washington, moves his or her family there, enrolls children in a D.C. school, or—most importantly—socializes with colleagues. Elected officials today can't afford the luxury of spending time together and building working relationships with each other, because they've got to get back home and raise money for upcoming elections in which their success is virtually assured. It becomes far easier to demonize a political opponent when your only frame of reference is that person's ideological makeup, and you don't know the members of their family, or their true character, or the localized priorities of their constituents. What we need to do is figure out how to get the money out of politics, tell elected officials if they want the job they need to stay in Washington and actually do it, and encourage them to have a cocktail with someone from across the aisle while they are there!

"But the fourth factor is the one that I know the most about. Yessir. It's the polarized media, itself a creation of the last four decades. This is where you—the ideologically driven voters who dictate the nomination process in closed primary states—go for your news and opinion, and where elected politicians do their best to stay in good stead. Gone are the days when a successful career in Washington was dependent upon longevity in office, and the corresponding seniority that brought prestigious assignments. Today, the quickest path to success is to say something incendiary, get picked up in the cable TV news or talk radio world, and then become a fundraising magnet. Because you know who loves that sort of entertainment? The ideologically driven voters who vote in primaries in hyper-partisan districts within closed-primary states!

"Notice that in the precise period when polarization progressed in Washington—that is, the last 40 years—there has been a corresponding polarization in the media. Coincidence? No way.

"I believe there is a causal connection.

"The behavior of the media and elected officials today is reminiscent of old-time wrestling. The squabbling is all for show. Bad behavior reigns.

"But there is good news.

"While the media and members of Congress

flex their polarized muscles, fueled by talk radio and cable TV news, America is headed in a different direction. Polling shows that Americans largely consider their approach to the issues as 'moderate,' not tied to one end of the spectrum or the other.

"But around here? Moderate is a dirty word. The only thing worse than moderation is to be linked to compromise. But like I said, in the real world, while the number of voters who identify themselves as Republican or Democrat dips, the number who register to vote as Independents is on the rise. In other words, as the media has become polarized and taken Washington with it, they have left a significant part of the public behind. That part wants less polarization and more cooperation.

"I believe that we have to change this. It's not going to be easy.

"The first step is for you to realize that your selections have consequences. You know, nobody ever got hurt in the pro wrestling I'd watch on Saturday mornings. It was fake. Everybody knew it. But today, the nation is suffering when we allow our debate to be dictated by men in tights!

"When I'm pumping my gas in Sand Key, or when I'm shopping for groceries in Publix, or maybe having a few toots with my buddies at a local dive on Tuesday nights, I don't meet people who see things all one way. I meet people for whom the issues are a mixed bag. They're liberal on some, usually social issues, and conservative on many, usually the economic ones. And a whole bunch, they just don't have a clue. But politicians don't take their cues from regular people. No, politicians listen to guys like me. And that's not good. We're no smarter than you are just because we give good ear, or look great on camera, and have a microphone in front of us.

"I believe that it's time for the entertainers like me who enjoy the public trust—a trust automatically conferred on those with access to the airways—to win your support through intellectual fairness and integrity, not through scare tactics and demonization. Speaking of which, there is something else I need to say.

"I want to apologize to Governor Wynne James. What a now-deceased spouse said about you in the midst of a contentious divorce is not relevant to your fitness to hold high office. I am sorry I facilitated that charge being tossed into a presidential race, where it had no place. It's about as insignificant to me as whether another candidate prays, and if so, in what church. I similarly regret ever having questioned Bob Tobias' fitness for office in a country governed by a Constitution which expressly states that no religious test shall ever be required.

"I'm sure both of those statements come as a shock to many of you. And so will this.

"You wanna know my real platform? Well, here it is.

"I think profiling was necessary in the days after 9/11.

"I think that if you have a terrorist who has information that he won't surrender after you give him a piece of quiche and a warm blanket, you should do whatever is necessary to save American lives.

"I think that if you kill a cop, you should pay with your own life.

"I think that our borders are porous and need to be controlled before we give a path to citizenship to those who are here illegally, or their cousins will just take their place.

"And I believe in the right to bear arms.

"But hold on. Before you give me a 'hell yes' and call me a 'great American' or refer to me as your 'blood brother,' there is more I want to say.

"I also believe that we should never have gone into Iraq.

"And that we stayed too long in Afghanistan.

"I believe that government spending is too damn high, but part of that spending is the money wasted by the defense department opening a new base every time somebody thinks they see a face that looks like al Qaeda.

"I believe that while the Second Amendment may protect your right to bear arms, it does not entitle you to own a weapon designed for a battlefield.

"I could not care less about same-sex couples. What they do is their business and what I do is mine.

"Mine is a live and let live mentality.

"And speaking of which, I think we need to legalize both pot and prostitution.

"My name is Stanislaw Pawlowski. And I approve this message!"

My timing was impeccable. If there was one thing I had learned in the last 20 years it was how to manage a clock. I always did have what we call in the business, good "formatics." Alex brought up the music bed. I turned off my mic. I removed my headphones. She came into the studio and gave me a hug. She may or may not have had a tear in her eye. I grabbed my legal pad with all my notes, and I walked out the door. Past Rod Chinkles who was beet red. Past Steve Bernson who was ashen. And beyond Don Fortini who seemed to be smiling. The receptionist tried to hand me a stack of telephone messages but I waved her off as I boarded the elevator. I got behind the wheel of my Lexus, figuring it would soon be handed back to the dealer who owned it, and put the roof down. Pulling out of the lot I saw him, my fisherman friend, standing in MacDill Park beneath the metal sculpture that I'd always found perplexing. Today I saw it differently, realizing that the collision of intersecting steel that the locals called "Big Red" wasn't a three-story replica of a children's game, nor the symbolism of the inertia that comes from competing forces, but rather, the oneness that can result when non-aligned interests give each other support. I looked at my buddy. So many days we'd given one another a subtle wave as I headed for home, without knowing one another's names or situations, or so I thought.

Today there was no nod, nor did he wave. Instead he took one hand and touched one of his ear buds. With the other, he gave me a thumbs up. For the first time in years, I felt the weight of the world lift from my shoulders.

As I headed up Ashley in the direction of 275 South, my iPhone rang. Instinctively I knew who it was without looking down. On the third ring I picked up and heard Phil's voice.

"Hello?"

He was bouncing off the walls of his nerve center, just like I'd anticipated, but not for the reason I'd expected.

"Absofuckinglutely brilliant, Powers."

I was dumbfounded. Unless he was being sarcastic.

"You really nailed it. You said everything the nation is clamoring for. I've been telling all the big mahoffs that people have had it with this polarization shit, and that the future is in the middle of the dial, Stan. We've killed the golden goose and it's time to reset. You are the guy. Only you can make this happen."

I just laughed and hung up the phone; the only person I wanted to speak to was Deb. Then I turned up the classic rock on my satellite radio.

And headed for home.

Center Point Large Print
600 Brooks Road / PO Box 1
Thorndike ME 04986-0001 USA

(207) 568-3717

US & Canada:
1 800 929-9108
www.centerpointlargeprint.com